MURDER IN FRIDAY STREET

Further Titles by Amy Myers from Severn House

MURDER IN THE QUEEN'S BOUDOIR
MURDER WITH MAJESTY
THE WICKENHAM MURDERS
MURDER IN FRIDAY STREET

Writing as Harriet Hudson

THE WINDY HILL
CATCHING THE SUNLIGHT
TOMORROW'S GARDEN
QUINN
TO MY OWN DESIRE
SONGS OF SPRING
THE STATIONMASTER'S DAUGHTER
WINTER ROSES

TWINSBURG LIBRARY
TWINSBURG OHIO 44087

MURDER IN FRIDAY STREET

Amy Myers

Mys
Mye

This first world edition published in Great Britain 2005 by
SEVERN HOUSE PUBLISHERS LTD of
9–15 High Street, Sutton, Surrey SM1 1DF.
This first world edition published in the USA 2006 by
SEVERN HOUSE PUBLISHERS INC of
595 Madison Avenue, New York, N.Y. 10022.

Copyright © 2005 by Amy Myers.

All rights reserved.
The moral right of the author has been asserted.

British Library Cataloguing in Publication Data

Myers, Amy, 1938-
    Murder in Friday Street
    1.   Private investigators - England - Kent - Fiction
    2.   Fathers and daughters - Fiction
    3.   Detective and mystery stories
    I.   Title
    823.9'14 [F]

    ISBN-10 : 0-7278-6301-0

Except where actual historical events and characters are being
described for the storyline of this novel, all situations in this
publication are fictitious and any resemblance to living persons
is purely coincidental.

Typeset by Palimpsest Book Production Ltd.,
Polmont, Stirlingshire, Scotland.
Printed and bound in Great Britain by
MPG Books Ltd., Bodmin, Cornwall.

Author's Note

The place name Friday Street sometimes marked a cluster of houses on the road to the gallows (see Judith Glover's *The Place Names of Sussex*). Some still survive and have now grown into villages, or have been absorbed as street names in others. I have situated my fictitious village of Friday Street on the Kentish North Downs, an area where it is still possible to imagine such remote communities might exist despite the super-highways and mega-rail lines that run nearby.

For help and guidance while I was writing this book, I would like to thank Peter Francis, Dr Martin Porter, David Johnson, John Endicott of the Kent Police Museum in The Historic Dockyard, Chatham, and court reporters Marten Walsh Cherer Ltd. That I ever managed to finish writing it I owe to my husband, Jim, my sister Marian Anderson and my friend Jane Pollard; and that it then was published is thanks to my wonderful agent, Dot Lumley of Dorian Literary Agency, and the ever helpful Severn House staff and my editor, Amanda Stewart.

The Gang and their families

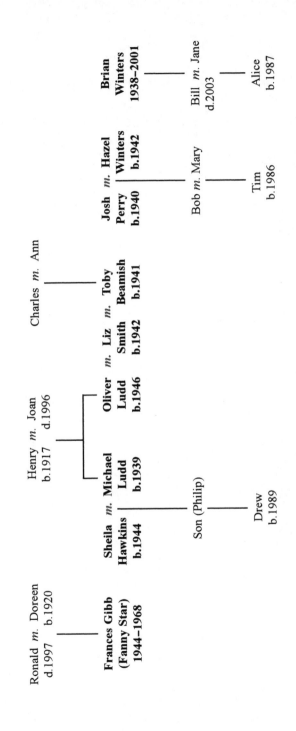

One

'Ghosts!' Peter grunted.

'What ghosts?' Georgia sighed. Her father was supposed to be checking *The Wickenham Murders*, so that she could return the proofs to its publisher on schedule. No ghost should dare to raise its head until that was done – if then, as she was deep in internet research for the next book and did not need frivolous interruptions. Even so, she had to admit that the word *ghost* held a certain attraction.

'This poor girl,' Peter waved a newspaper her. 'Murdered on Easter Saturday in the middle of a ghost tour.'

The sheer incongruity of this made it all the more horrifying to contemplate, and Georgia instinctively recoiled. Ghosts conjured up the violence of the past, the unfinished business of long ago. A present-day murder in such a context became even more starkly real. It was police territory, not directly that of Marsh & Daughter. Theirs lay in the past, though preferably without ghosts.

'What happened?' she asked.

'She was found stabbed at the place where the tour ends, apparently. Her boyfriend, Jake Baines, has already been charged.'

'She was on the tour?'

'No, I gather the tour ends with a reconstruction of the story of the murder of Lady Rosamund in a lonely tower, and Alice Winters, the murdered girl, was employed to re-enact Lady Rosamund.'

Georgia was confused. 'She was murdered during the performance?'

1

'Before, I think.' Peter scanned the article quickly.

'Where was this?'

'In deepest Kent, of course. This,' Peter waved the newspaper again, 'is the *Canterbury Express*.'

'But where?'

'Not that far away in fact, as the crow flies. About ten miles to our west, way out on the downs. A village called Friday Street. Do you know it?'

She did. They *both* did. 'That was the village we visited at Christmas,' she said flatly. They had come across it by chance. Ten miles might seem a short distance – and so it was if one travelled on the main highways. For the Kentish North Downs, however, it could be a very long way indeed. There were villages and hamlets so remote, and lanes so twisting and tortuous, that one could be within a mile or two of one's own front door and not realize it.

'Gadzooks,' Peter remarked. 'So it was.' He was as taken aback as she had been. His eyes met hers. 'That tune – remember it?'

'Of course.' She would never forget it. A weird haunting melody that caught at the heart, played on a simple flute, by a lad in his late teens. There had been nothing unusual about him. Jeans, tee shirt, shock of light brown hair; fine-featured. He'd looked vulnerable, but perhaps that was only to her, because of his association with the tune.

Altogether it had been an odd experience. A village pub, miles from anywhere, that had obviously been forced to widen its horizons by serving food. It had a small, quite smart restaurant with about ten tables, although the bar area was still very firmly local. And that's where she and Peter had sat, he in his wheelchair, she perched at the end of a bench where the local drinking fraternity had unwillingly made room for her. Georgia remembered the stillness as they sat drinking their beer. Had it been their presence or was it because of the lad playing the flute? He hadn't played the tune for very long because the big burly man behind the bar had leaned over towards him, said a few words and the tune had promptly been switched to 'Penny Lane'. That had brought a distinct sense of relaxation amongst the drinkers. Nevertheless the tune had lodged in Georgia's memory, and every so often she was reminded of its haunting sound.

Haunting? Ghosts, she remembered. According to the *Canterbury Express*, this was a village that held ghost tours.

'A sad place,' Peter commented.

Georgia considered pouncing on this subjective verdict, but honesty forbade it. It *had* been a sad village, or at least a sad pub. Their shared nose for such things was what made their partnership thrive. They both had an instinctive feel for the atmosphere lingering in buildings or villages, or even parts of towns. The past, they knew, whether it be recent or long gone, laid the fingerprints of unfinished business on the present. If this translated itself for some people into ghosts, who were Marsh & Daughter to say they were wrong? Well, Peter for one. He'd always been vehemently opposed to the idea of headless horsemen or piteous wailing damsels. Something in this newspaper article, however, had caught his interest beyond the normal human reaction to a young life brutally ended.

'We don't *know* Friday Street is sad,' Georgia argued. It was part of her job to put a stopper in the bottle when needed, to prevent Peter's enthusiastic genie from bubbling out. 'We didn't even explore the village afterwards. What we witnessed at Christmas might simply have been a bad hair day for the pub.'

'Alice Winters, the girl who was stabbed, was a farmer's daughter in her gap year. She was also part-time barmaid at the pub.'

That silenced her. Georgia fought an inner battle of logic versus instinct. One couldn't base too much on half an hour's experience, and yet the coincidence of place could not be entirely ignored. Nevertheless, logic informed her sternly, it proved nothing.

'The problem is,' Peter continued loftily when she made no comeback, 'that a positive is easier to prove than a negative.'

Georgia agreed. Marsh & Daughter's true-crime series linked past to present. If they failed to find a positive connection between today's 'fingerprints' on a location and violence or trouble in the past, that didn't necessarily prove there wasn't one. But how far did one delve back before admitting defeat?

'Back to Bronze Age burials?' she asked, half seriously.

'Why not?' Peter countered, *very* seriously. 'There's a lot in these parts.'

'Surely living memory has some part to play in fingerprints on time?'

'Don't forget living legend. Former generations handing the story down.'

'I'm not digging back to Bronze Age,' Georgia said firmly. 'Luke wouldn't approve.'

Luke was their publisher, and also her lover, thought of in that order since she was currently in the office. He was more lover than partner, since he worked and lived at South Malling on the other side of Maidstone, but he was very much present in both their business and private lives. *The Wickenham Murders* would be their sixth book for him, each centred on a case, or cases, in which unfinished business from the past had laid its shadow over the present, and in most instances Marsh & Daughter, their trading name, had found a satisfactory solution. Usually it fell to Georgia to do most of the legwork, and Peter, less mobile than she (at least in theory) after his police career had ended when he had been shot and paralysed, spent more time at the computer, in administration and doing most of the writing. Luke had his own ideas on what this should be. He liked archaeology, but not on his true-crime list. Archaeology was local history, and from that he would not budge.

'He won't have to. We've nothing on Friday Street at all, except a funny tune.'

'And the village's name,' Georgia admitted reluctantly. 'I did look up its origins at Christmas.'

'Why?' It was Peter's turn to pounce.

Georgia was trapped. 'The tune, I suppose, and the way the locals still cling together as a community.' The atmosphere in the Montash Arms (even the name had stuck in her memory) had been heavier than the usual clannishness in a village community.

'And what came out of your investigation?'

'There are, or were, a lot of small hamlets called Friday Street in England, mostly in the south; Friday used to be thought of as an unlucky day. Still is sometimes. In fishing communities—'

'Is this a lecture?' Peter interrupted.

'Yes,' Georgia replied with dignity. 'Like the one you gave me on the EU last night.'

'Point accepted,' he admitted graciously.

'Fishermen avoided going to sea on a Friday.'

'I don't imagine there are many fishermen on the North Downs.'

'And,' Georgia continued doggedly, 'some authorities think that the name might have developed because it was the road leading to the local gallows.'

Peter glowed. 'Could it be, I wonder, that—'

'The gallows atmosphere lingers?' she finished for him. 'Possibly, since our Friday Street seems to have swallowed the village next to it rather than the other way round. I remember it as a distinct community with several streets spreading out from a crossroads, but when I looked at our old maps of Kent, the village was called Pucken up to the eighteenth century, and Friday Street was an adjacent hamlet. Pucken, incidentally, means evil spirits.'

'I'm amazed we survived our half pint of bitter there.'

'But nothing I've said means Alice Winters' death has anything to do with the village's unlucky past – if it had any,' Georgia said quickly. Even as she spoke, she found herself wondering about the story of Lady Rosamund. And also why there were apparently so many ghosts in Friday Street that they deserved a tour.

'No.' Peter smiled angelically at her.

5

She left a short pause, then asked as casually as she could, 'Who runs these tours?'

'I thought you'd never ask.' Peter, now serious again, read on. 'It seems it's the local manor, still called Pucken, incidentally. The tours have helpful re-enactments throughout of the grisly deeds that have taken place over the centuries and no doubt – before you challenge me, Georgia – all this concentration on the past could well suggest why we felt it such a sad place. Anyway, in all probability this has nothing to do with Alice Winters, I agree. All the same, Georgia, it's beginning to interest me.'

'Not before you've checked those proofs.' Finishing them to schedule was essential if Luke was to speak to her again.

'She was found stabbed in a remote corner of the village.'

'How old was she?' Georgia asked abruptly.

'Eighteen.'

That was the trouble with their job, Georgia thought wryly. It wasn't like a police investigation, which had a duty to remain objective and start from the facts. Marsh & Daughter began with a choice as to whether they investigated or not. However much their investigation worked on factual evidence thereafter, its birth began as 'fingerprints'. That meant that, although their cases were usually in the past, the constant risk of upsetting present-day family or friends remained. Sometimes they would be digging up sad memories without a case emerging to justify doing so. Alice Winters' death was an exception, however.

'It's backwards, isn't it?' she continued, as though Peter could read her mind. They worked together so closely that often he seemed to, and she his. 'Usually we try to unearth the problem in the past. If we take a present-day case such as that of Alice Winters to be our starting point, we'd be working from a very dodgy hypothesis, because we'd subconsciously be looking at the past to see if it provided an answer to the present. And in any case it seems the police already have the answer. Anyway, it's a police matter. Not for us.'

Silence fell. Georgia listened to the drumming of Peter's fingers on the table until she could stand it no longer.

'Why don't you give Mike a ring?' she asked with resignation.

The drumming stopped immediately. 'I was hoping you'd say that. Even though,' he added, 'I'd have done it anyway.'

'Of course.'

DI Mike Gilroy had been Peter's sergeant in his police career days, and though Mike was steadily rising through the ranks in Kent Police, Stour area, and looked set to rise further, Peter still treated him as his personal sergeant.

'Just in case there's any doubt about this Jake Baines being guilty. Not that Mike would talk about it if he's already charged him. Still, you never know. Might pick up a few vibes from what he says.'

Haden Shaw, where they lived, was a somewhat larger village than Friday Street, but a quiet one. Georgia could see from the atlas that Friday Street was on a through road, if one could so term a succession of what were now minor lanes from the A20 leading to Ospringe and Faversham. Haden Shaw, on the other hand, was effectively a dead end, since the lane leading to it from the Canterbury road then doubled back on itself in a loop to rejoin the main road.

'It took one look at Haden Shaw, changed its mind and went back, thank heavens,' Georgia had once observed to a cross and lost motorist who complained bitterly that the road led nowhere and for no purpose. Obviously he hadn't seen their jolly pub.

Peter and Georgia's adjoining terrace houses pandered to their desire for independence and to their need to be together for work purposes, the office being on the ground floor of Peter's home. The arrangement suited Georgia splendidly after her divorce from conman Zac Taylor, and changing it for the spaciousness of Luke's home was a decision she kept delaying. Not that the house was the key factor. Her independence was.

When she let herself into Peter's home the next morning, she followed her usual practice of checking out the situation with Margaret, who was far more than just Peter's carer. She was strong enough to stand up to his moods, knowing when to walk away and when to stay; she was an amazingly good cook, and she had his interests firmly lodged in her heart, which was just as well since Peter's bad turns were unpredictable.

Margaret was in the office, clearing away his so-called breakfast, which was coffee and an apple, with the former taking precedence. Georgia lifted an eyebrow, their silent code, as Margaret came out with the tray, and was relieved when she nodded.

'Ah, Georgia.' Peter spun round in the wheelchair, beaming. 'About that Friday Street murder. I've had a word with Mike.'

'Was he pleased to hear from you?'

'Exuberant. And there is nothing about Alice Winters' death that suggests anything other than a lovers' tiff that went wrong.'

'So why are you beaming?' Only a tiff? Some tiff, to end in murder, Georgia thought.

'Just this and that.'

She was going to have to work for it, that was obvious. 'Do you mean open and shut, as Mike sees it? In other words the evidence points towards the story behind it, the story behind it points to the culprit, which in this case is Jake Baines.'

'Precisely. He was found with the body at the ruined tower where they re-enact the medieval legend of Lady Rosamund. Alice played Lady Rosamund's ghost. Jake was – well, I'll save the details.'

Georgia decided not to rise to the bait. 'Who conducts the ghost tours at the manor? The owner?'

'Yes. He's a dedicated ghost buff, or, if one is being unkind, a dedicated eccentric in the interests of maintaining an old pile of stones. That's Mike's description of the manor. This buff, Toby Beamish, takes groups of tourists around, caters for the children by giving them divining rods—'

'Stop right there. For water? Damp through the roof?'

'Divining rods,' Peter repeated patiently, 'for ghosts. And before you ask me, I don't know how or why. That's just what Mike told me.'

'Exactly how many ghosts are there?' Georgia demanded. 'I thought Pluckley claims to be the most haunted village in Kent.'

'Probably it is. Maybe the ghosts go on holiday to Pucken Manor once in a while. Anyway, the ruined tower where Alice was found is half a mile away, and known locally as Rosamund's Tower, based on an old medieval legend. Toby Beamish has some kind of theatre he's converted or built at one side, where the tourists are taken by bus from the manor for a real live ghost show.'

'Solid flesh ghosts?'

'No, Georgia, actual ghosts.'

'You don't mean,' Georgia was intrigued now, 'a fully fledged Pepper's Ghost arrangement with ghostly apparitions floating across the stage recounting their woes?'

'Precisely. What a learned daughter I have. In fact they only play out the most well known story, and that's the one of Lady Rosamund, the hero and the big bad villain.'

'All ghosts?'

'Two of them, I gather. Alice and Jake. Toby Beamish plays the villain and is solid flesh.'

Georgia became so side-tracked imagining this spectacle that she returned to the stark facts guiltily. 'Who found the body if it was discovered before the show?'

'Jake Baines. He claims she was dead when he arrived. They had to be there first to be in position, and Toby came along a little later with the punters. All he had to do was don his top hat and black cloak.'

'Somewhat out of period for this medieval legend,' Georgia commented. 'Any forensic evidence to go on?'

'Mike refused to come clean. Jake Baines claims he moved her in case she wasn't dead, and might have touched the dagger while he did so. It was still in the wound.'

'He doesn't admit to killing her then?'

'He strongly denies it. He admits they had a row the previous evening, but says she told him to come later because she had to meet someone first. He couldn't say who, and it all sounded very weak.'

'The row could have been after he got there.' Georgia stated the obvious. Always a good plan since it was all too easy to discount it. 'Where was she found? In the pit or wherever they worked the illusion from?'

'No. On the stage itself. She was already in costume; there's a cubby hole on one side where she changed clothes.'

'These ghost tours,' Georgia frowned, trying to set this in context. 'Who are they for? Just tourists?'

'I gather aficionados come from time to time. And there are the historical buffs too.'

'Can ghosts be historical?'

'The tours are packed full of historical detail as well. And what's more, Beamish runs a museum, and you can't get to see it without doing the tour.'

'A museum on ghosts? Limited, isn't it?'

'It's on deodands.' Peter paused for effect – which he achieved. What on earth were they? Georgia wondered, racking her brains in vain. Peter looked smug. 'Where's your grasp of medieval law?'

'The same place as yours, deeply buried.'

'They're something to do with death caused by violence. Again, the details will no doubt wait.'

'Will they?' Georgia asked mildly. 'Mike's invited us down, has he?'

'In fact, no. He was very firm about it.'

'Then why were you beaming as I came in?'

'Margaret had just informed me that Ted Mulworthy was born in Friday Street.'

*　　*　　*

10

Georgia was on the best of terms with Ted. It behoved everyone who was interested in eating well to be on good terms with the butcher – save for vegetarians, of course. Georgia, however, had moved a step beyond that stage, having helped Ted's daughter Pat with her university modules. The timber-framed house in which Ted and his wife lived and worked had had a red-brick slaughterhouse behind it at one time, but this was now a 'des res' for Pat and her husband. Ted's wife, Joan, played her part in the business, and Georgia had reason to be grateful for it. Her pies made wonderful instant suppers.

'Morning, Georgia, what can I do for you?' Ted was a gentle giant of a man, but nevertheless looked formidable, chopper in hand.

She embarked on an innocent discussion of topside versus fore rib versus sirloin, since Luke was coming to lunch on Sunday. Once this had been settled, she turned to other matters. 'Margaret mentioned you were from Friday Street.' Her voice ended on a suitable note of enquiry, and the chopper paused in mid-air.

'Long time since I lived there.' Chopper laid carefully on board.

'My father mentioned a barmaid had been murdered. A farmer's daughter.'

'Young Alice. I heard.' He looked at her, his clipped tones daring her to say more.

She decided to tread cautiously in this fencing match. Like most butchers in her experience, Ted usually took everything in his stride, but the Winters might be his best friends.

'Do you know the Winters?' she asked.

'Everyone knows the Winters. Been in Friday Street for hundreds of years, built the place, some reckon – those that don't claim to have built it themselves. Bill Winters died a year or two back. His wife Jane has the farm now, and Alice was their only child.'

That made it even worse. Georgia was appalled. 'What a great tragedy,' she said sincerely, 'not only for the Winters

11

but for the whole village, since it's such a small place.' There were plenty of such small communities tucked away in Kent. Highways thundered past, leaving them slumbering. When generations of the same families had remained there undisturbed, however, such slumber could bring nightmares as well as sweetly pleasant dreams.

Chopping resumed, with no comment.

She persevered. 'I gather they've arrested the young man who did it.'

'*If* he did it.' Harder chop.

'Why do you say that?'

He turned round, chopper in hand this time, and his face red. 'Nowadays you never know, do you? Take them in one day, free them the next, find them guilty, then give them a free pardon. Don't know what they're doing half the time.'

'At least there's no longer a gallows in the village. It's not too late to find someone innocent.' By the look on Ted's face, Georgia knew she had to get off this topic quickly, and began to talk about an eighteenth-century murder by a girl lodging with her aunt. She was convicted of murdering the aunt, although she had no apparent motive, and calmly denied her guilt all the way to the scaffold. There were no Ludovic Kennedys to cry 'Foul' then, no investigative journalists to plead her cause.

This didn't fool Ted. 'Why are you so interested in Alice Winters, Georgia? For one of them books of yours?'

'We aren't concerned with modern murders,' she replied truthfully. Well, almost truthfully, barring a few ifs and buts. 'That's the police's job.'

'Keep away from Friday Street, Georgia. That's my advice. Unlucky place and always has been. What's more, Friday Street likes to keep itself to itself.'

'Even if there's been a miscarriage of justice?' she asked, not knowing quite what made her persist, when even she agreed with the advisability of shutting up and scuttling away with her fore rib.

'Friday Street has its own ways of dealing with that.'

'Lynch law?' she asked, startled.

His face darkened. 'No. The music.'

'What music?' Georgia was shaken. Ted seemed to have plucked out the core of her disquiet.

'Don't you go talking about it. I haven't told you, see. It's the music, the flute. Always heard in Friday Street when there's been a miscarriage of justice. It sounded when Jake Baines was taken in, so I heard. And that's twelve pounds twenty, if you please.'

'Superstition,' Peter snorted.

'Superstition has to spring from somewhere,' she argued. Georgia knew he was as taken with the idea as she was, but someone had to argue for the other side. 'Was any music heard?'

'I doubt if it's the kind of thing Mike would count as evidence.' Peter must have caught sight of her face. 'I'll ask him, but don't blame me if we get blasted out for damn fool questions.'

Georgia doubted if Mike Gilroy had ever blasted anyone out. It wasn't his style, which verged on the dogged and phlegmatic. It was Peter who specialized in blasting.

She finished the proofs on his behalf, trying to ignore the nagging question in her mind as to what this music was. She longed to know if it was the music they'd heard at Christmas. It would explain the odd reaction in the pub. There had clearly been some special significance to it. When they'd politely asked what the tune was, they had been told it was a traditional village melody, and informed that the boy was a lazy bugger and should be giving a hand in the kitchen and not playing daft music.

Could that have been Jake? She remembered the barmaid too, a fair-haired girl, with a pert lively face. Alice Winters? That pub must employ several girls to work as barmaids or waitresses, so she decided not to let this image of Alice take hold in her mind.

When she next saw Peter, he had a very long face indeed.

'Mike laughed his head off, did he?' she asked sympathetically, somewhat guilty that she hadn't rung him herself.

'No, darling daughter, he did not. He said he had picked up a whisper of music during the investigation, but they didn't reckon the playing of an old flute would stand up in court as proof of innocence. But he might be wrong, Mike added.'

'Sarcasm will get you nowhere.'

'Nor will chatting about folklore.'

'It's unlike you to take that line. What about our fingerprints from the past?'

'There are more urgent matters to consider.'

She had overlooked the gleam in Peter's eye. He'd been holding back on her.

'What is it?' she asked sharply. 'You think Jake Baines is innocent?'

'I've no idea and it's not me who's holding back. It seems to have been your beloved butcher, Ted. Margaret was surprised Ted hadn't mentioned it. If there's a ghost in Friday Street, it would be a lot more modern than Lady Rosamund. I can't think why on earth neither of us remembered it.'

'What?' Georgia cried, agog, when he paused.

'There was another murder in Friday Street, well within living memory, and which caught more headlines than Lady Rosamund could have boasted, or even poor Alice. Perhaps because it was so famous a murder that one tends to forget where it happened in favour of whom it happened to. I'm amazed the national press hasn't picked up on this Winters murder because of it, especially the tabloids. I suppose that's the reason. They remember the names in the earlier case, but not the location, so no one thought of checking out Friday Street in the files or on the internet.'

'Who was it?' Georgia demanded again. 'Or shall I go back to my trusty computer, which can be a lot quicker than you when telling a story?'

'Speed is not my aim. Accuracy is. All right,' Peter yielded. 'It was in 1968. Ring any bells?'

14

'No – yes – *tell me.*'

'Sweet Fanny Adams. SFA or Sweet Fuck All to those who dared to speak the word in those days.'

'Of course,' Georgia breathed. How could she have forgotten? Sweet Fanny Adams was the name of a famous and controversial sixties pop group, or rather duo. Their songs were as wild as their image – 'Down among the Dead Men', 'Poison Green', 'Allan Water' – many of them based on old folk melodies with twisted new lyrics and rhythms. 'Adam Jones and Fanny – what was her name?'

'Star. Frances Gibb was her real name, in fact. Fanny was stabbed and Adam Jones found guilty of her murder.'

'And the murder was in Friday Street?' she asked incredulously.

'It was.'

She cast her mind back. 'Adam Jones served a life sentence, came out and drowned himself on release, didn't he? He stabbed her after a gig.'

'A gig at Friday Street.'

'How could a village that small afford a gig for a duo as famous as that?'

'Fanny was born there. She left for ever in 1961, but relented and came back this once, only to be murdered for her pains.'

'By Adam Jones.'

'So the court found.'

A pause, then Georgia voiced what they must both be thinking. 'I wonder if that music was heard then?'

Two

Born in Friday Street. For some reason Peter's casual words haunted Georgia. She felt she was back in the Montash Arms, facing if not hostility then protective clannishness. But over what? And what was there about life in Friday Street that had turned plain Frances Gibb into Fanny Star? She suspected Peter was thinking along much the same lines, for work on their previously planned new book slowed, and there were unexplained flurries of activity on the internet, long telephone calls, and packets of documents arriving by post. All normal, she supposed, but not all at one time. Finally she could stand it no longer. One of them had to speak and it clearly wasn't going to be Peter.

'Coincidence, do you think?' she asked cautiously, when Peter put the phone down hurriedly as she entered their office.

Peter was good at bluffing. 'Expand, if you please.'

'Coincidence that apparently brought the relationship between Fanny and Adam to such a point that it resulted in his murdering her in the village where she'd been born. Where all her relatives and erstwhile friends would still have been living.'

'Could be.' Peter was making her work for it, damn him.

'*Crime passionel*? Were Fanny and Adam more than working partners? They lived together, didn't they?'

'Convenience.'

'Come off it. She was twenty-four and he was twenty-six.' Georgia had been doing research of her own.

'Devoted to their art.'

16

'Quit stalling, Peter. You're hooked on this case, aren't you? There's not nearly enough to go on yet, and you know it.'

'Very well. I confess. I looked at *The Times* reports on the microfiche, then sent for copies of Crim One files on the case from National Archives. Just to have a look,' he added plaintively.

'What did you order?' she asked, intrigued rather than annoyed.

'Only witness statements.' He looked glum. 'I couldn't track down any complete transcript of the trial, either shorthand or recorded. If there'd been an appeal I might have been lucky. I tried all the court transcript services in the hope of finding one still tucked away, but no joy. Too far back.'

'So tell me what you do have,' she commanded. They might as well chew this over, if only as a means of dismissing the Fanny Star case once and for all as a Marsh & Daughter investigation.

Peter wasn't going to let her get away with it so easily. He sighed heavily. 'I'm stifled in here. It's too hot. Let's go somewhere where I can clear my mind.'

'Not to Friday Street,' she bargained.

Until they at least partly understood the facts of a case from printed sources of research, it was a mistake to visit the place where it had happened, where local reactions and atmosphere might sway them one way or another. She would rein Peter in (or sometimes vice versa) until they reached that point, however much she might be interested herself. Particularly when, as in this case, there might be libel issues to consider, as Fanny's contemporaries would still be reasonably hale and hearty.

'Sea air?' she suggested. 'Whitstable?'

'No point gazing out to sea when the problem lies locked in an inland village.'

'How about the Devil's Kneading Trough?'

'Perfect.'

Being a weekday, this popular spot on the Wye Downs,

north-east of Ashford, was not crowded. There were only two or three other vehicles in the car park and no one to be seen on the long stretch of grass overlooking the magnificent hillside and the view beyond it, over to the Weald of Kent. Beneath them to the right were the gently curving green folds that gave the Kneading Trough its name.

'Why the Devil's?' Georgia wondered aloud.

'Where there's a devil, you'll find a saint,' Peter replied, as he wheeled his chair into his favourite spot above it.

'In Wye church?' Georgia asked.

'No. Interesting county, Kent,' Peter said. 'For centuries different civilizations have tramped all over it – the twentieth century distinguished itself by tearing it all up for roads and railways and what have you – and yet it's still down there. Look at that view. Nature wins, okay? Devils and saints come and go, but Kent stays. And no, the saint isn't that of Wye church. There's a holy well over there somewhere,' he pointed to beyond the Kneading Trough, 'dedicated to St Eustace. It used to have healing powers, but today people prefer the surgery. And over there – ' his finger swivelled to the left – 'the surviving place names suggest a prehistoric settlement with holy ground of its own, which in turn probably made them considered devils later. Which,' he added, obviously seeing Georgia's eye upon him, 'brings us back to Friday Street.'

'I don't see how. You're looking in the wrong direction. It's behind us.'

'The *right* direction. What we sensed there at Christmas was what we're seeing here. The present as a product of the past. However much one generation tries to obliterate it, it only succeeds in adding another layer, both physically and mentally. As in Friday Street, I suspect.'

'It would be a mental archaeological dig for us, then,' Georgia said.

'Exactly. At the moment we have—'

'Sweet Fanny Adams,' Georgia supplied helpfully.

'And plenty more layers further down too. A mere thirty-odd years couldn't have produced what we ran into at Christmas.'

'So, back to Frances Gibb,' Georgia said firmly.

Peter grinned companionably. 'Have it your way. Let's talk shop. She left Friday Street in 1961 when she was seventeen to find fame and fortune, or so she claims in a magazine article.'

'The year Epstein discovered the Beatles.'

'According to the same article, our Fanny had heard the Beatles play in Hamburg before that, and was already convinced that they were the future. Amazing what hindsight can remember.'

'Not to mention sheer invention. She could only have been sixteen then, if that, and Hamburg would have been an odd choice for a school trip in those days. Perhaps she had adventurous family holidays.'

'Her background doesn't sound that adventurous. Mother Doreen Gibb, father Ronald Gibb, ex-navy turned village carpenter.'

'To want to be a pop star she must already have had some musical experience. What pushed her into leaving Friday Street for the big unknown world outside?'

'You wouldn't remember,' Peter said, to her annoyance. Georgia hadn't been born till the 1960s were over. 'The glorious sixties and the great revolution in music didn't just begin with a clap of thunder as Epstein walked into the Liverpool Cavern and heard the Beatles. By 1960, revolution was not only stirring, but erupting. Elvis might be king, but in the UK Tommy Steele was rivalling Bill Haley and the Comets on the rock and roll scene, and the fifties' ballad singers had vanished. Lonnie Donegan had reinvented skiffle and folk music with his acoustic guitar, and every young rebel in Britain was already intent on starting his own rock band. Donegan's "Rock Island Line" could well have inspired young Fanny to head for London's bright lights.'

'Is that where she went?'

'Not known. She took her time turning into the wild thing

she was by 1968, when she was killed. Her first single wasn't released until 1965. It was a single, but then she burst upon the world in partnership with Adam, initially as Fanny and Adam and then, as the revolution really exploded, as Sweet Fanny Adams.'

'So what's known about her early life?'

'Lots of stories, not many facts. Received opinion is that she must have had a hard struggle at first, then probably joined a group, got into LSD, and finally emerged as Fanny Star.'

In the two weeks since Friday Street had re-entered their lives, Georgia had found a video with a clip of Sweet Fanny Adams, and had played it several times, struck by Fanny's vitality, which came over as vividly as though she were still in the charts. A slight girl, not tall, but full of an energy that even on film seemed to radiate around her. The clip was black and white, but she'd found another shorter clip in colour, which had shown the full effect of the mop of wild ginger hair and the glittering green eyes. Adam was the calmer one, the dreamer of the two. He was not much taller than she was, and his long pleasant face contrasted strikingly with her sharp, freckled features. If either of them were to be a murderer, Georgia's money would have been on Fanny, not Adam. So what had turned him into one?

'You lived through the 1960s, Peter. You would have been . . .' Georgia calculated. 'Twenty-two when Fanny died and—' She broke off, realizing where she was heading. Dangerous ground, to be avoided at all costs.

'Courting your mother.' Peter finished her sentence for her. 'I was a little past teenage rapture over pop music, but I suppose I was affected by the general mood of freedom.'

'The spirit of the times?'

'Spirit of the times is acknowledged after the time has past, not during it. When one is living through it, it seems perfectly normal. I suppose I was aware of conventions breaking down. I remember Elena –' Peter hesitated, but then continued smoothly – 'your mother deciding, with great daring, to defy her mother and not wear gloves to the theatre.'

Elena. He never called her that now, Georgia thought. A rare slip. Her mother now lived in France with her second husband, having been unable to take the pressure of her son's disappearance and, a year later, Peter's accident. Georgia's brother, Rick, had vanished while on holiday in France and there had been no explanation then or since. No body, no voice at the end of the phone. It was the Marsh family's own unfinished business.

'Looking back now,' Peter continued, 'I can see how great the change was, especially in music. At the time it seemed like a craze that would pass, then it became an irremovable wart on the side of "real music" and only gradually passed into being part of "real music" itself. Sweet Fanny Adams was on the wilder edges. The Beatles, the Rolling Stones, Jimi Hendrix, Dusty Springfield, the Seekers – somehow SFA managed to epitomize them all, and that was due to Fanny. She was the magnet, she was life.'

Extreme words for Peter. Georgia was impressed that he felt so strongly. 'Tell me about the music,' she asked. 'I only know the famous album, the one of folk songs in rock and roll beat, "SFA's United Kay".'

'The one we all remember. I don't know the earlier ones either. Only that because "United Kay" came out sufficiently long after the Beatles' "Sergeant Pepper" and before the Rolling Stones truly hit the target. Not too much peace and harmony, but urging a positive, if wild, life force – not destruction and violence. Then two months after its release she was murdered.'

'Why though? What was Adam Jones' motive?'

'According to the prosecution, she was the leader of the two. She wanted to go solo. Adam didn't. For all his fame, it was unlikely he'd be able to go it alone.'

'Murdering her would seem to defeat his purpose then,' Georgia pointed out drily.

'True. But in the heat of the moment would he think of that?'

'She was stabbed. Was it usual in the 1960s for young men to have a knife handy in case things got heated?'

'No, Georgia, it was not. The prosecution also claimed that more was involved. Sex, in fact. According to witness statements, there was someone else in her life, their manager Jonathan Powell, and since Adam and Fanny were living together it was easy to make a case of personal jealousy as well as professional rancour. An "if I can't have her, you certainly won't" situation.'

'Possible,' Georgia granted. 'Who were the witnesses for that?'

'I've read two statements by people present on the day of her death, including our friend Toby Beamish. Jonathan Powell was at the gig. It seems to have sparked off fireworks.'

'Where exactly was it held?'

'In the grounds of Downey Hall. I don't think we saw it while we were there. A Henry and Joan Ludd owned it then. It's an eighteenth-century house marked on the ordnance survey map, as there had been two ancient houses preceding it on the site. Also rumoured to have smuggling connections, but that might be just to rival Pucken Manor's ghosts. The event on the twenty-second of June, 1968, was to celebrate the engagement of the elder son, Michael Ludd, to one Sheila Hawkins. There was a public show in the afternoon to which the whole village was invited, then a dinner in the evening which was to be followed by a private performance for invited guests only. Fanny was found dead shortly before the latter was due to begin. She was in the woodland area in the far corner of the grounds, lying on a plastic mac, the dagger lying by her side.'

'A plastic mac seems out of character,' she commented. 'Who found the body?'

'Adam Jones. Crying his eyes out, when found, and still with her body when the next arrivals came, Henry and Michael Ludd.'

That sounded pretty final. In Peter's mind anyway. She

was on the side of caution. 'What about evidence against Adam?'

'He admitted he and Fanny had a row earlier that day. Her blood was on his clothes, his fingerprints on the sharp instrument. He claimed, just as Jake Baines did, that he found it still sticking in her chest. Unlike Jake, he says he instinctively withdrew it, spattering some blood on himself and around the body. There was already some on the mac.'

'There would have been more than *some* if he'd killed her and withdrawn it straightaway.'

'Good thinking. There must have been enough not to make it a point in his favour.'

'Sharp instrument,' Georgia picked up. 'Not a kitchen knife then, or a handy Swiss army knife?'

'No. A sixteenth-century French dagger.'

That took Georgia aback, as it was probably meant to. 'Why on earth would anyone be carrying that around unless with malice aforethought? And even then there must have been plenty of easier alternatives.'

'There is cause for speculation.' Peter looked smug.

'Good.'

'It's the same dagger that killed Alice Winters last month.'

Her stomach churned. Out of the realms of the logical, back into that quagmire of the past. Then she realized that she was extremely annoyed. Peter had been holding back on her. This was vital information and he'd kept it to himself.

'How could that be?' she shot at him.

'Quite easily. It's a deodand.'

'It seems,' Peter explained over a Kentish cream tea in Wye, 'the majority of deodands are not instruments of murder, but of death by violent accident. It caused the death, so it takes the blame. "Deodamdun" means surrendered to God, but the good old English legal system made it okay to give it to his agent on earth, the English king. It wasn't even necessary for the owner of the offending cartwheel or horse – or in later days, ships and even locomotives – to be the offending party in the death. The king didn't always get the booty himself – usually the local sheriff sat on it as the king's representatives, often the local lord of the manor. Sometimes the object appears to have been passed on to the victims' family in compensation, though as a kindly act rather than through legal compulsion.'

'Did you say locomotives?' Georgia asked curiously. 'You mean if a man was killed by a railway train then the *train* was forfeit?'

'Under some circumstances, yes. Fortunately for British Rail, its predecessors and successors, deodands were abolished in the mid nineteenth century, but at least one had already been handed over.'

'And this dagger was one of the forfeited objects.'

'Yes again. It was originally a murder weapon, in fact. It's listed in the deodand museum owned by Toby Beamish at Pucken Manor.'

'The dotty ghost lover?'

'The same. The deodands are a private hobby, not as much of a money-spinner as the ghosts.'

'And the same dagger was lifted from there not once but twice to perform a murder?' Surely Peter must have this wrong, Georgia thought doubtfully.

'You sound like a particularly vicious prosecution,' Peter complained. 'In fact, no. It used to belong to the Ludd family at Downey Hall, although it was a genuine deodand. It was surrendered at the inquest of Arabella Nevers, who was killed with it by her philandering French husband in late Elizabethan times. It landed up with the Ludd family, either because Arabella was a daughter of the family then living in the house that preceded Downey Hall, or because the local lord of the manor lived there, and it remained part of the house's chattels. It was kept in a case in the entrance hall. Toby Beamish's father and grandfather, who had been at daggers drawn – if you'll excuse the phrase – with the Ludds, coveted it for many a long year. The fever for collecting deodands had been rife in the family ever since they were abolished.

After the dagger was pinched for the murder of Fanny Adams, Ludd let Toby's father have it. He didn't fancy it in the house any more, so it was from the museum that it was taken for the murder of Alice Winters.'

'An adventurous little dagger,' Georgia said. 'Was it by chance or design that Jake Baines used it to kill Alice Winters? The Adam Jones story is more understandable. Adam could have grabbed the dagger from Downey Hall and rushed out to kill Fanny.'

'As Adam admitted he had a blazing row with Fanny, he could have done just that, though I don't think the times fit.'

'What was the row about?'

'Going solo, he claimed.'

'No mention of lover boy Powell?'

'Adam denied there was anything in it.'

'Was there any doubt about the verdict at the time?'

'Nothing permanent. There was a protest, but it died down, chiefly, reading between the newspaper lines, because Adam Jones himself didn't co-operate. After all, look at the weight against him. He had access to the weapon, he had a motive, he had opportunity, there was forensic evidence. All might be explainable,' Peter added hopefully.

'Dr Crippen probably thought the same.' Georgia demolished him briskly. 'Did Adam Jones ever admit his guilt?'

'No.'

'And . . .' Was this taking things too far too quickly? 'What about his death?'

'He was found in the River Medway. Near Maidstone.'

'Any doubt that he drowned himself?'

'The verdict was clear that he did.'

'Where did he do his stretch?'

Peter grinned. 'You're on the path, Georgia. A long way from Maidstone is the answer you want. And, moreover, he was a Dorset lad by birth and upbringing.'

'So why come to Maidstone to drown himself?' she asked slowly. She wasn't sure where she was heading but it might be significant.

'The newspapers considered he wanted to die where he last saw Fanny.'

'If he murdered her, that seems strange.'

'It does indeed, daughter dear.'

Now for the big question: 'And the Friday Street music? Was that mentioned anywhere in connection with Adam's arrest?'

'Not a word about it.'

She was irrationally disappointed.

'But there wouldn't be, would there?' Peter continued. 'As Ted told you, Friday Street keeps itself to itself.'

'So there isn't a case to answer yet.' There was nothing firm to cling to, not even a tune.

'There might be,' Peter still argued. 'There are unanswered questions. What about Powell, for instance? And what – surprised you haven't yet asked, Georgia – made Fanny come back for this particular gig? It was small beer for the likes of Sweet Fanny Adams.'

She agreed. 'If something other than fame and fortune drove her from the village, it's hardly likely to have been sentiment that brought her back.' She hesitated. She didn't want to start Peter steaming off on a false scent, but it had to be placed on the table. 'The dagger links the two murders. Could there be other links?'

'What do you think?' Peter asked blandly.

'Mike says that the Alice Winters case is straightforward.'

'They often are until one looks below the surface.'

'We only have coincidence at present.'

'And our Christmas experience.'

'All villages on the downs are sad at Christmas time,' she countered. 'The skies are bleak, the fields are bleak, and it's family time, not be-jolly-to-strangers time. And,' she finished firmly, 'might I remind you that the police have the Alice Winters case in hand, and as regards Fanny and Adam, SFA is exactly what we have. We don't even have a rumour of the music being played. I submit, my lord, that there is no case to answer.'

26

Peter's eyes gleamed, as though, damn him, he realized she was only waiting to be convinced. 'Very well. I challenge you. Go back there, armed with our knowledge of Adam and Fanny, plus what little we know about Alice Winters, and then come back and tell me we shouldn't enquire further. The trouble with you, Georgia, is that you don't believe that cases on our own doorstep can be valid. They are. The nearer to home, the greater the mote in one's eye. Look at the number of people who tell the press with great excitement that mass murderers were ever such nice neighbours.'

Georgia snorted. 'Generalization.'

'Don't get off the point.'

'Very well, I accept your challenge. I'll drive over . . .' She thought for a moment. 'No, I won't. I'll go anonymously.'

'Large hat and dark glasses?'

'I'll be a bone fide rambler.'

'A conspicuous one on your own.'

Georgia laughed. 'I won't be on my own.'

'Publishers,' Luke announced loftily, 'do not traipse across fields in pursuit of their authors' research. They expect a nice word-processed synopsis to be presented to them plus a summary of sources.'

'In that case, no dinner.' Georgia smiled sweetly. 'But come with me and I'll buy you a sandwich in the Montash Arms.'

'Poisoned, no doubt,' he remarked. 'Friday Street seems to be a village of serial killings.'

'You like walking.'

'Strolling under the leafy boughs of a French forest or through Italian vineyards is hardly comparable to muddy Kent fields with footpaths untrod by human foot for generations.'

'Where's your spirit of adventure?'

'Tiptoeing away behind my duty to my desk.'

'You don't have one. It's Saturday. You don't really object, do you?'

'Of course not.' Luke smiled at her, and Georgia laughed. 'Good. I've already packed the emergency bag.'

'For the Kent downs? Not much need for hypothermia survival packs, is there?'

Georgia ignored this. 'Let's go. There are three miles to walk before lunch. That's to get us in the mood.'

He shot an amused look at her. 'Bodes well for tonight.'

'You never know your luck,' she agreed. It was at times like this that she thought how easy it would be to slip into marriage again. With Luke, at any rate. What scared her was the fear of the gates clanging behind her, leaving her alone with a man she thought she knew – only to find that she didn't. Suppose, just suppose, he was another Zac Taylor. It was an unfair thought, but insidious.

Luke often stayed with her over the weekend, and occasionally she would go with him to South Malling. In consideration for Peter, however, Haden Shaw was preferable. Not that Peter appeared to care, she often thought, even though he enjoyed Luke's company.

As Luke had predicted, the footpath to Friday Street was scarcely well used, but it was a fine day and there were only a few patches of mud. With spring apparent in the young growing crops, and the signs of green in the trees, it was hard to imagine that these windswept fields presented anything other than a normal rural scene. Nevertheless, when the outskirts of Friday Street appeared on the horizon Georgia felt her heartbeat quickening. Ridiculous. They were going to wander round a village and drop into a pub, that was all.

'I won't be prejudiced by what happened at Christmas,' Georgia told herself as they approached. Friday Street must have experienced quite a few outsiders in the weeks following the murder, even with the limited publicity surrounding Alice Winters' death. If anyone had linked the murder with Sweet Fanny Adams then the village would have been inundated with media attention. Two more curious individuals would hardly be noticed.

The main road – if that was the right word for what was little more than a lane – turned a sharp corner at the point the footpath joined it. Across the road a stile led into the churchyard and, on the grounds that the church was the centre of a medieval village, they climbed over it. True, the church looked very late medieval.

'We might be lucky and find Lady Rosamund's grave,' Georgia joked. As they walked up the path, however, it was the name Winters on several tombstones that drew her attention, a grim reminder of why she was here.

'Locked,' Luke called, rattling at the door of the church.

Another sign for outsiders to keep away? She was being paranoid, Georgia decided, most churches were locked nowadays. She studied the notices in the porch, hoping to find the name of Gibb. Fanny might have had brothers, even if her father were no longer alive. She scanned the church flower rota in vain. Sheila Ludd – she must be the former Sheila Hawkins, whose engagement to Michael Ludd was the event being celebrated on the day Fanny Star died. She appeared to alternate her Saturday afternoon duty with Hazel Perry. Not a very onerous duty, it seemed, since services were only once a fortnight. Hazel was last on duty on Easter Saturday, the day Alice Winters had died, and not on duty again until a month later, which was this coming Saturday. Church coffee mornings and afternoon teas were also once a fortnight, all these being under the stewardship of one Miss C. Broome.

'Pub?' Luke enquired plaintively at her side.

'Not yet.'

'Soon?'

She relented. 'Why don't you go to the pub while I explore? You never know, the great brotherhood of chaps together might work wonders.'

Luke considered this. 'Good idea. I might even sense this weird atmosphere of yours. Together it might not work so well. If I find a real clue of my own, do I get a mention in your acknowledgements?'

'You always do, darling,' she reminded him. 'Don't you read your own publications?'

She watched him disappear down the road. There was something about his back view that inspired confidence. It wasn't just that he was tall and broad-shouldered, but his walk displayed what she could only sum up as a purposeful amble. Whatever it was, it seemed to get him what he wanted. Except her – so far. And probably one day . . .

No, think Sweet Fanny Adams, she reminded herself, as she set off on her exploratory walk. Luke was right. Alone one could sniff a place more clearly.

The church must once have been on the Pucken Manor estate, for she passed its driveway a little further along the road. The house was set well back, however, and was shielded from view. All that faced her was a wooden signboard, bearing an obviously home-generated poster headed 'Next Ghost Tour', which she stopped to read. The tour was to be on the Saturday of the bank holiday week at the beginning of May. Tickets £10, including tea. www.puckenghosts.com. Now that was a nice present to take home to Peter. He'd be on the internet in a flash.

She strolled on through the village, taking in the mixture of houses, old cottages sandwiched in between nineteenth-century village houses. No new estates, it seemed. The going could be tough out here in winter. But perhaps Friday Street was so far off the map that the developers had never driven their elegant BMWs this far. The village had the appearance of having grown in fits and starts as need occurred, with little planning behind it. She walked past the pub, where through the window she could see Luke, pint in hand, chatting at the bar to a rather pleasant-looking dark-haired woman in her forties, at a guess. So he hadn't met a wall of silence, unless he was remarkably thick-skinned today.

The Montash Arms stood at a crossroads, or rather cross-*lanes*, one of which must have been the original Friday Street, she reasoned. Whether or not it originally led to the gallows, Lady Rosamund's tower lay down that way, according to the ordnance survey map. She, however, kept straight on for Downey Hall, which was set in spacious grounds, fortunately with a public footpath through it. Useful for taking a peek at the house, she thought, for Peter would expect a report.

The footpath led through a huge, gently sloped rough grass area. A few cows munched in the distance near a large oak tree, their calves protected amongst them. Beyond them Downey Hall was clearly visible on the crest of the incline, gleaming white, well proportioned and with an impressive columned entrance. A long white wall on both sides of the house divided this more public part of the grounds from what must be their private gardens behind, and that was probably where the gig had taken place, she imagined. What must it have been like for Frances Gibb, she wondered, coming back after years away as a famous singer? What thoughts were in her mind? Pride? 'See what I've done'? Fear, even? But fear of what? That it might not be the perfect haven she dreamed of? Or fear of what she might have to face? But if so, why come at all?

The footpath circled round back to a lane joining the road that would eventually reach the A20, but she crossed over to the fields opposite where another path would take her back to the village.

It also took her past, so she had noted on the map, the site of an old church. That made sense, since the one she had seen could only have been late medieval. If so, why not build it on the site of its predecessor, she wondered? Unfortunately a site was all it was. When she reached it, there was nothing to be seen save uneven ground that suggested geophysical surveys might well produce something of interest.

She found Luke still chatting at the bar, no longer to the dark-haired woman, but to the proverbial old man in the corner, although this man was not so old. In his early sixties, she thought, and hardly retiring. Just as she was about to join him, however, she saw a familiar face. A young man. For a moment she could not place him, but then she recognized him. It hadn't been Jake Baines playing that tune at Christmas; it was him. Before she could move towards him, however, Luke saw her, and it was too late.

'Come and meet Josh Perry.' Luke used prearranged anonymity towards her. She was impressed. He hadn't wasted any time. 'Josh used to be the landlord here, and now his son Bob has taken over.'

'Now driving from the back seat,' Josh drawled. As Luke coped with drinks and sandwiches, Georgia settled down to talk further. She remembered the name Perry from the witness statements that Peter had passed on to her, so she'd go carefully here. No hostility from him, she noted immediately, though his eyes were shrewd, even wary.

'Don't get many walkers here,' he observed.

'I'd have thought it would be a good stopping-off point for pilgrims in need of a drink,' she joked.

'Too far off the Canterbury Road for that. Most of 'em stick to the Pilgrims' Way.' That ran along the downs well south of Friday Street. 'You're local history anoraks, I gather.'

'That's right.' Luke published local history books after all.

'Not much history round here. We're a backwater, and glad of it.'

'You're on a minor through route over the downs to the A2,' Georgia pointed out as Luke returned with the drinks.

'Thanks, cheers.' Josh took a sip of his pint. 'Not so you'd notice. The Doddington route to Faversham and the Charing road to Canterbury are the trade routes, as you might say. We're just a farming community.'

'Not from what I've heard,' Luke said cheerily. 'Didn't there used to be smuggling round here?'

Did she imagine it or was Josh giving Luke a distinctly old-fashioned look? If so, why? It seemed a harmless enough topic, and served to establish good relations so that she could ask her question.

'Used to be,' he agreed. 'Stuff came over from Whitstable way. Masterminded from what's now Downey Hall with the help of the parson. The goods were stored round the village though, and some say a few cottages have tunnels or store-rooms under them. Old wives' tale, if you ask me. Anyway, those days are long gone. Bring it in free nowadays. And a fat lot of good that's done the pub trade.'

'You seem to be doing well here,' Georgia observed. 'By the way, who's that young man over there?' She pointed towards the bar. 'I saw him before, when I passed through at Christmas.'

'Did you now? Not surprising, that. He's my grandson Tim. In for his lunch, no doubt.' Josh heaved himself off his barstool and departed for the inner regions. 'Take care, both of you.' Pause. 'And don't forget to take a look at Lady Rosamund's tower. That's what you came for, isn't it?'

He spoke easily, but there was no smile on his face. Cordiality had gone.

'Shall we leave it at that?' she asked Luke when they were outside again. 'With any luck he thinks we're standard gawpers.' She felt shaken, but Luke urged her on.

'No. He was challenging us, and anyway, I want to see this tower.'

'That was the boy playing the flute music at Christmas. I thought it was Jake Baines, but it wasn't.'

'Is that important?'

'It might be.'

'Onwards then. To the tower. Don't let Friday Street beat you,' Luke told her. 'After all, if we get lost in the dark we've got your emergency bag.'

The walk took them deep into the countryside again, past some remote cottages, until at a turn in the lane the tower came into view: stark, tall, three-floored, judging by the pigeon-hole windows. She had expected more of a tumble-down pile of stones, but this looked more or less complete, at least from the outside. There were even some crenella-tions remaining at the top.

There was no way in, however. The gate was firmly padlocked, and marked 'Private Property'. Like Friday Street itself, it was saying 'Keep out'.

Georgia was irrationally annoyed. Here the Lady Rosamund of legend had met her death and now, centuries later, so had Alice Winters. At Downey Hall, Fanny the bright star had met her death. Why should they keep out? 'Never send to know for whom the bell tolls. It tolls for thee.' No man was an island. Even so, Peter might be right. Should she report to him that they should keep out of Friday Street, at least until they had inquired more deeply into these murders? Surely *someone* had to. Wasn't that just why the music had been played?

Three

'If I was a ghost,' Georgia said, drawing a deep breath as they confronted the full glory of Pucken Manor, 'I'd move in right away.'

Hollywood could have invented no better home for phantoms than Pucken Manor, which was a hotchpotch of medieval hall house, extended and patched up with Tudor brick, and with occasional later flourishes poked in all over it as later generations decided to do their bit for architecture. Ivy shrouded it in appropriate places, dark trees overshadowed it on both sides. The owners of Pucken Manor had clearly not had money to throw away, since this desirable residence for ghosts must be much less hospitable for more solid flesh, she thought. Tiles were missing from the roof, wood and paint were in sore need of attention, and there was a general air of dilapidation.

One look at the website and Peter had sent off for tickets immediately. 'It's so awful,' he pronounced with glee, 'we have to see it.'

Georgia agreed. Pictures of 'phantoms' rivalled those of the Cottingley Fairies, and where no pictures could be presented, graphic illustrations of ghastly murders provided keen competition. The grisly coachman, the dairymaid done to death in the dairy, and a panoply of noble ancestors – all, it seemed, victims of violence – regularly returned to Pucken Manor to complain of their treatment.

To do Toby Beamish justice, there did indeed seem some respectable authentication for the haunting, enough to have brought serious students of the occult here over the last hundred and fifty years, judging by the enthusiastic critiques. Nevertheless the effect of the website was to make the memory of Alice Winters, who had died during such a tour, all the more poignant. Murder past and present. If there were any conceivable link between them, Georgia decided Marsh & Daughter could do no better than begin their closer acquaintance with Friday Street here, especially since Toby Beamish had been a witness at the trial. Apart from his statement about Fanny's plans to go solo, he had seen her leaving the Hall after the dinner, and must therefore have been one of the last people to see her alive.

The tour group numbered twelve. 'The maximum our ghosts will permit,' Toby explained heartily, as he swung open the ancient wooden door to allow them to enter. It groaned on its hinges in protest. How, Georgia wondered, did he manage to get it to do that? He scored a point in her eyes, however, since he didn't even blink at Peter's wheelchair.

Toby Beamish fitted the stereotype of mad collector perfectly, even including a touch of the sinister. Like Josh from the pub, he must be in his sixties. He was rounded both in face and figure, wore large, black-rimmed glasses, and was as manic about his ghosts as the immortal Mr Toad for motor cars. Not so lovable, however, she thought. Toby was distinctly lacking on the charm front. His enthusiasm for his subject was, however, tempered with some nervousness – and no wonder, considering the terrible outcome of the previous tour. She and Peter waited until last to enter and, once inside, found not exactly an ancient retainer, but certainly an extraordinary woman.

'By the reception desk shall a house be judged,' Georgia whispered to Peter.

She was tall and angular, and, Georgia judged, in her late forties or early fifties; her hair was secured unfashionably high on her head, with strands escaping from it as fast as they could with each shake of her jangly earrings. To match Toby Beamish, her eagerness had more than a touch of Joyce

Grenfell. Hands waved ecstatically as her high-pitched voice screamed welcome at her new brood of ghost hunters.

'Welcome to the house of the Montashes. You *must* enjoy the tour. You *shall*. I said to Lord Montash only this morning, pray make your best materializations this afternoon.'

'So you're Lord Montash, are you?' a member of the group asked Toby.

Toby looked suitably reproving. 'His lordship, the fifth baronet, died three hundred years ago, poor fellow. We'll meet him soon. Cadenza, the wheelchair. Would you officiate?'

Cadenza? Could that really be her name? Georgia wondered as the lady flowed towards Peter. She was even dressed the part, in a long Indian-fabric dress that suited the ambience. Was she wife or volunteer? From the adoring look she shot at Toby, the latter seemed the more likely.

'I'm afraid that you will be confined to the ground floor,' Cadenza explained earnestly to Peter, 'but some of our best ghosts do materialize here from time to time.'

'In that case I shall stick closely by your side for protection,' Peter informed her graciously.

'Oh.' Cadenza blushed. 'I shall be gratified to keep you company. I could perhaps introduce you when I feel a presence.'

'Please do,' Peter said gravely.

If the rest of the entertainment lived up to this, Georgia thought, it was going to be an interesting afternoon, and worth it for that alone. If any of the group were nurturing macabre hopes that Alice Winters would materialize there was no hint of it. Today's crimes were a grisly reality, a world away from this plunge into fantasy land. Georgia doubted if there would be any mention made of Alice. Or of Fanny Star. Well, she could soon change that.

Toby Beamish must have been living here at the time of her murder, since a quick look around the entrance hall established that the family had lived here for generations. One fairly modern oil painting was clearly – from the dress

37

fashions – of Toby's parents, with a toddler held aloft. A younger Toby, presumably. If Toby took after his father, he must have been good looking in his youth. There were few traces of it now.

The group was a varied one, with a family, several tourists, and, she realized, the dark lady whom Luke had been talking to in the pub. He'd said she was an estate agent in Faversham. Georgia picked her out as a possible voice of reason should one be called for. Pucken Manor promised to be a relaxing diversion from the hostility of the Montash Arms, especially since Toby Beamish seemed only too eager to reveal Friday Street's secrets to the world, as least as far as the manor was concerned. Georgia bought one of the guide books to read in bed later that night. It would make up for not having Luke, who was visiting his sister for the bank holiday weekend.

The inside of the manor lived up to its exterior. Dark panelling promised hidden glories. Deathwatch beetle looked to be positively encouraged in this house. Creaking stairs and the odd cobweb completed the illusion. The ghosts, however, dated from well before the time of Sweet Fanny Adams.

Toby obviously knew his history, Georgia thought, as he flung open cupboard doors and they peered up chimneys in search of manifestations. Perhaps too much so, for she decided she wouldn't want to argue the toss with him as to how solid his ghosts were.

With Peter left on the ground floor, she was all the more aware of the strange atmosphere of this house. Like Friday Street, the house seemed claustrophobically closed in upon itself, and what had begun as a potentially enjoyable experience began to assume a much darker edge. This was not least because of Toby himself. He could almost, she thought in a moment of fantasy, be an incarnation of a particularly nasty ghost himself, a spook resurrected to introduce his ancestors one by one.

'Is that the Lady Rosamund I heard about?' demanded one of the group, in a bedroom that would have done justice to

Dickens' Miss Havisham. The bed had been provided with a dummy of a strangled woman, no doubt to attract her ghost.

'No, this is Lady Montash,' Toby explained. 'Done to death by her coachman lover.'

Georgia saw her chance. 'Ghosts always seem to date from hundreds of years ago,' she complained. 'Why don't more recent tragedies leave ghosts behind?'

'What an interesting question.' Toby cast her a displeased look. He was obviously thinking out the answer. 'Perhaps it's because ours is such a fast-moving generation that ghosts don't have time to linger. In the past they imprinted themselves on to a rarely disturbed atmosphere. It's hard to find such places now.'

'So Fanny Star wouldn't be haunting Friday Street?' Georgia asked innocently. Put the cat among the pigeons and see what it catches.

What it caught was a distinct wariness on Toby's part. 'Far too recent,' he said briefly, and hastily excused himself to summon Cadenza. 'Miss Broome, the rods, if you please,' they heard him calling.

Cadenza duly arrived clutching an armful of what appeared to be coat hangers mutilated into suitably pronged shapes. 'We shall see what power comes through today,' Toby announced, handing them out. 'Do any of us have the gift?' he enquired, as Cadenza demonstrated how the rods should be held.

It appeared one of the children had, as they all moved round the room holding their rods out solemnly. The hanger held by one of the little girls was definitely quivering, but Georgia had no such luck. She might have had suspicions of this particular child, had it not been for the fact that the dark lady of the pub also seemed to be experiencing quivers.

'I'm clearly not receptive,' Georgia whispered to her. 'Could I place my hands over yours to feel what it's like?'

The woman shot her an amused look. 'Be my guest.'

As soon as Georgia laid her hands on top of hers, she felt the sensation coming through, and so far as she could tell it wasn't faked. Impressive, and despite her attempt to apply reason to the situation, she realized she was shivering. Suppose, just suppose, Fanny Star had been summoned here by the concentration of their thoughts on her. Nonsense, she told herself sharply, watching Cadenza's hanger quivering violently. It was extended dramatically before her, Cadenza's eyes were closed, and her head held back. Georgia half expected her to launch into an 'Is anybody there?' routine, but fortunately she did not. As soon as she lowered the hanger, Georgia took the opportunity to say chattily: 'My father's always been so interested in Fanny Star. He'll be disappointed if she doesn't materialize.'

Cadenza stiffened. 'The poor girl has no need to do so. Justice was done and the murderer convicted.'

'Are you sure of that?'

Cadenza looked indignant. 'Of course. Everyone is. Now, if you'll excuse me, I must return to your father.'

That pigeon had scuttled away rather quickly, Georgia thought, as Toby concluded the tour. It had, however, flushed another one out. The dark lady approached her as they walked to the minibus, which would take them to Rosamund's tower. It would have accommodated Peter's wheelchair, too, but he and Cadenza had vanished. Obviously they had already departed in Peter's car, which suggested he must find her good value.

'So what brought you here?' enquired the dark lady.

Easy one. 'My father and I dropped into the pub here at Christmas, liked it, and thought we'd come back for the tour. And you?'

'I'm new to the village, renting a cottage till I find a place of my own.'

'The village must be deeply affected by the murder,' Georgia said. What luck – a disinterested resident. 'It's too small to be otherwise.'

'Yes. Not a good time for me to arrive.'

'It doesn't strike me as a place that would welcome outsiders even at the best of times.'

'You came back,' the woman observed. 'Anyway, I'm not making a claim on the place.'

'An interesting way of putting it.'

'Friday Street,' said the woman brightly, '*is* interesting.'

Press her now, Georgia wondered, or later? The latter, she decided. If her new acquaintance had something to say, as she suspected she had, then she'd make another overture.

Peter was already waiting outside the tower with Cadenza, who was in full throttle. Peter made a good listener for one so voluble – when it suited him, as it clearly did now. Toby explained in hushed tones that today the re-enactment of the story of Lady Rosamund would not be held, owing to recent sad events. Only the tower would be shown. The tower had a modern door and surprisingly was wheelchair-accessible. The only upper flooring that remained was the flat roof itself, though the beam marks showed where two higher floors had once lain. The roof seemed to be intact – restored, perhaps – although in one corner she could see that the stone circular staircase, which twisted out of sight, petered out in places higher up, where masonry had crumbled.

'Lady Rosamund's tower,' Cadenza began in ringing tones. 'Legend has it that that was her name, but in fact she was a miller's daughter, who caught the eye of a local nobleman. She would not submit to his foul desires as she loved another, a village lad by the name of Piers Brome. The nobleman locked the fair Rosamund in the tower until at last he forced her to submit to his dastardly will.'

No one else, thought Georgia, could possibly have got away with this, but from Cadenza even such words as dastardly sounded quite natural.

'Every day,' the story continued, 'her sweetheart would pass the tower and call out to her. Then through treachery he came to believe Rosamund had betrayed him with the nobleman. He devised a way into the tower to rescue her, or, as some versions have it, to murder her. He found her dead, and was taken up for the crime. It was, we believe, the lord himself who murdered her. On his way to the gallows, it is said that her sweetheart doffed his cap but nevertheless cursed her for her unfaithfulness. Ever since, her ghost has haunted the tower, pleading that she was faithful to him.'

'How did he kill her?' Peter's voice boomed out. 'Was she stabbed?'

Cadenza looked grave. 'It is believed so.'

'Did Piers play his flute on the way to the gallows as a sign that he was innocent?' Georgia chimed in. 'Is that how the legend of the Friday Street music began?' She had no evidence that Tim Perry's flute melody had originated with Lady Rosamund, but it was a reasonable guess.

Her question could have meant nothing to most people there, but Toby went very white, and there was an audible intake of breath from Cadenza. Knocked from his routine patter, Toby admitted reluctantly, 'Some say he played the pipes, yes.'

'I believe it to be true,' Cadenza declared loudly, her cheeks red. 'Indeed I do.'

'There's fact behind the legend.' Toby began to recover his form. 'This used to be Knights Templar country. There was a Templar preceptory not that far away, in Waltham, where they owned considerable land to raise funds for the fighting of crusades and protection of pilgrims in the Holy Land. When the Templars were overthrown early in the fourteenth century, the Knights Hospitallers, their rival order, benefited by taking over most of their lands, though not without a hell of a legal fight in many instances. I'm reasonably sure they took over this land and established a priory here.'

'Opposite the pub?' Georgia asked, raising an unintentional laugh. The priory church might easily have been the site marked on the ordnance survey map.

'This would once have been a road over the downs used by pilgrims and soldiers heading for refuge at the lodging house at Ospringe.' Toby was not to be swayed from his patter. 'The priory here was a holy order, of course, but it probably had civilian help, not only in working on their lands, but also running them. Younger sons of noblemen

42

often found themselves a living like that. And it could be that the miller's daughter was a serving maid at the priory.'

'And is Piers Brome factual?'

'Most certainly. He was a shepherd who was hung in 1335 for the murder of one Rose Smith.'

'And Rose became Rosamund in the legend, I suppose,' Georgia said chattily.

Toby swelled once more with tour-leader pride. 'Rosamund was a popular name for ladies murdered in towers, stemming from Henry II's mistress who was bumped off by Queen Eleanor, in what's known as Fair Rosamund's bower. Ours is clearly one version of it.'

'Assuming Piers Brome was innocent,' Georgia said, 'and unjustly accused, one can assume the tune that has survived is what he played.'

Now he looked distinctly hostile. 'There's no proof at all. Good gracious.' He made great play of inspecting his watch. 'Is that the time? We must be getting back for tea and the museum.'

By the time the tea was over, most of the party had drifted away, and only Georgia, Peter and the dark lady, who introduced herself as Dana Tucker, remained to see the deodands. Georgia could see that Toby was torn between eagerness to display his beloved collection and doubt as to whether the Marshes seemed worthy of the honour.

The museum collection was in a converted barn behind the house, and Toby, once she had forced herself to overcome her distaste for the man, proved an interesting guide. Each object was ticketed with the details of the deed it had apparently committed. Hardly surprisingly, the collection stopped short of including locomotives or ships.

One case was conspicuously empty, which enabled Peter to pounce. 'I presume that usually houses the dagger that killed Alice Winters? Would that be the one that Jake usually used in the drama played in the barn?' Peter was now openly declaring their mission, since to Georgia's knowledge no newspaper reports had released this detail.

'In fact, yes.' Toby scowled. 'Though wildly out of period.'

'And where is it now?'

'It's with the police.'

Poor Toby. They were rapidly turning into the tourists from hell.

Peter had no intention of letting him off the hook. 'So was I at one time,' he said casually. 'Is this museum kept locked?'

Peter's revelation roused Toby's hackles again. 'At night, but not during the day,' he replied reluctantly. 'Its value to anyone but a collector like myself is minimal.'

'Apart from the French dagger.'

'Correct.' Toby looked increasingly bullish. 'Though how could I know anyone would want to steal it? This case *is* kept locked.' He pointed it out proudly. 'The pride of my collection. The Montash Carver, forerunner of the table fork which was not introduced in this country until the seventeenth century and then not common. This carving fork dates from much earlier.'

Georgia gazed at the crude but sharp-looking double-pronged carver and its ornate carved handle. 'A deodand?' she asked. Stupid question, of course it was.

'Lady Montash killed the sixth baronet with it, and her family naturally treasured it.'

Naturally? She tried not to catch Peter's eye.

'We, the Beamishes,' Toby continued, 'are descended from the Montashes, despite the claims of *others* in Friday Street that the Montashes lived where Downey Hall now stands. Alas, the title has now vanished.'

'Owing to there being the odd murderer or two in the family,' Peter suggested jovially.

'You must have known Fanny Star quite well.' Georgia switched subject, as if to help an awkward situation. 'Since you accepted the deodand that killed her, when the Ludds offered it to you.'

'I'm a collector,' Toby retorted angrily.

'I hope I haven't upset you,' Georgia said anxiously. 'You seem so interested in the murders that have taken place in the village that I assumed you'd know all about Fanny Star.'

Toby did not reply, but Cadenza did for him, and with some dignity. 'Naturally we are interested, Miss Marsh.'

Peter had obviously introduced himself to her during their tête-à-tête. That must mean he saw her as a useful contact.

'I shall explain why, Toby. Why should I not?' Cadenza continued. 'Cadenza is a traditional family name meaning one who is musical. My father was descended from the Piers Brome who went to the gallows, though we now spell our name "Broome".' (The Miss C. Broome of the church teas, Georgia realized.) 'I am *proud* of my ancestor,' Cadenza continued, 'and I am quite certain he was innocent. Justice has not always been done in Friday Street. Our poor ghosts are evidence of that. It is for those who live to clear their names. That, Mr and Miss Marsh, is what we try to do in our small way.'

'Did that answer your question?' Dana asked casually as they left.

'We're just curious by nature,' Georgia stonewalled.

'Don't worry,' Dana said. 'I'm an incomer and my shoulders are broad. My interest in Fanny Star and Friday Street is as keen as yours.'

'You're a fan of her music?' Peter asked.

'I am. You might like to see my cottage. It's the one where she was born and brought up.'

'The Gibbs' home?' Georgia asked in excitement.

Dana laughed. 'I suspect your interest goes beyond the casual.'

Peter glanced at Georgia and she nodded. Time to come clean. Peter explained their job and their purpose in coming to Friday Street, while Dana listened intently. 'So there's a rumour that this music was played after the Alice Winters murder. How about Fanny Star's?' she asked.

'Nothing yet. The village clams up at any mention of it.'
'Why, I wonder?'

'And I wonder,' Georgia added, '*who* plays it?' Had it

45

been Tim Perry after Jake's arrest? One thing was certain: Friday Street was unlikely to tell her.

End Cottage – not the most original of names, Georgia thought – was set well back from the road along a gravel lane. 'Nineteenth-century, converted piecemeal over the years,' Dana explained, when Peter parked the car. 'When Fanny was growing up there was probably still a privy in the garden and a well for water. It still doesn't have mains drainage.'

'Is there anything left to link it with the Gibb family?'

'Not that I know of. What you see is what you get.'

What they saw was a standard nineteenth-century cottage with functional furniture, some nice prints and books, and a long cottage garden behind the house. 'I've made a start, as you can see,' Dana said. 'But I've got my work cut out. It hasn't been tended for years, not since Mrs Gibb left.' A small area had been cut back for cultivation and to provide a sitting area.

Georgia had been hoping for a sense of unfinished business in this house, but she was disappointed. 'When did Mrs Gibb die?'

'She didn't,' Dana replied. 'She's still alive and well in a home.'

'Here? In Friday Street?' Peter demanded.

'I don't know where. I can find out if you eager sleuths wish, but don't get your hopes up. I was told she has Alzheimer's and her husband died some years ago.'

Georgia's hopes plummeted again. Still, it would be worth visiting her in due course – if, she reminded herself, they went ahead with this case.

Dana paused, hands stuck in pockets staring out to the open fields beyond. 'This legend about the music,' she said. 'Does it imply that Jake Baines could be innocent?' When Georgia nodded, she added, 'So if it *was* heard when Fanny died, it implies that Adam Jones was too.'

'That's right.' Georgia looked at her curiously, wondering what was on her mind.

'In that case,' Dana rallied briskly,' you must meet the Ludds. Fortunately, this being May bank holiday weekend, the grounds of Downey Hall are open tomorrow, and from what I know of Michael, he'll be right there.'

'Is he the owner now?'

'I presume so. He's Henry Ludd's son. His father now lives in a house in the grounds, I gather. Probably to keep an eye on the place. He's frightfully keen on family and tradition, even though the Ludds have only scored a little over half a century there so far. I was told he's rising ninety, but he doesn't look it. Michael and his wife Sheila live in the main house and their grandson Drew is living with them a lot of the time. Dynasty creation, you see. He's a student at Canterbury and a mate of Tim Perry. I suppose he's sacrificed freedom for cheap lodgings. He's all right, is Drew.'

'Will you be going to the hall?'

'I wouldn't miss it for the world. I like prowling in the steps of two famous sleuths.'

'We're hardly Poirot and Marple,' Peter protested mildly.

'Even *they* might be baffled by Friday Street.'

'Are we being encouraged?' Peter asked as he drove home.

'Definitely prodded.'

'Why?'

'Newcomer's curiosity? Friend of the family? Friend of Adam Jones' family? Or just that Dana's living in Fanny Star's birthplace? Anyway, let's go. We could have lunch at the Montash Arms. We're known faces now so there's no harm to be done.' Indeed, Georgia thought, with a place like Friday Street the mud needed to be stirred a little before it would yield its secrets.

When they arrived on the Sunday, the restaurant was crowded and the garden tables too, though they managed to beat the competition to the last table. Or rather, Peter did, by driving his wheelchair up full tilt, which as usual left him the victor. It could have been any pub anywhere, for the general air of hostility they had encountered earlier was now dispersed by the holiday crowd.

As she walked through the bar to the toilets, she caught a sight of the burly man whom she had seen at Christmas and, hearing him addressed as Bob by Josh, sitting in his familiar place, confirmed that this was his son – Alice's employer. Tim resembled Josh more than Bob. At that moment Josh glanced up, and she waved at him, conscious that his eyes followed her. On her way out he beckoned her over.

'Who are you rambling with today then?' He glanced at her summer suit and sandals.

'I've brought my father. He's in a wheelchair and I thought he'd like to see Downey Hall gardens.' Brought? No one *brought* Peter anywhere, but it made a good excuse.

'Taken a fancy to our village, have you?'

'Yes.' She hesitated. 'Look, Josh, I'm very sorry. I heard about the murder of your barmaid, but didn't want to put my foot in it by mentioning it last time I came.'

Josh looked at her oddly then nodded slowly. 'Put your foot in it if you like, Georgia. Just make sure it comes out safely again. Sins of the fathers. That's the story of Friday Street.'

He called her *Georgia*. Deliberately. 'So he's known all along,' she told Peter wryly once back in the garden. 'Through Dana, do you think, or Toby?'

'Simpler than that,' Peter said. 'Ted Mulworthy. I bet you Friday Street knew we were interested in its murders before that tasty hunk of fore rib was even roasted.'

'If he knows who we are,' Georgia frowned, 'what did he mean by "the sins of the fathers"?'

'Don't put too much money on it. He's a Perry, and wouldn't be referring to his own family. It was probably a generalization to mislead outsiders. Game players all, these Friday Street folk.'

'Impressive,' Peter commented as they drove up through the grounds of Downey Hall and parked in front of the house.

At the wheel of a car her father had the dash of a mad char-
ioteer whipping his steeds onwards, which was why she
preferred to drive herself, but on occasion it was diplomatic
to bow to his wishes. Her father manoeuvred himself out of
the car, and they joined Dana who was waiting for them.

'Is the house open too?' Georgia asked her.

'Good heavens, no. From what little I know of her, Sheila
would faint at a muddy boot in her house.'

'Who plays squire in this village?' Peter asked. 'Toby
Beamish or Michael Ludd?'

'Interesting question. Toby, technically, but he seems to
leave it to the Ludds. He's not interested in the community.
Michael is a JP, and General Lord High Execut— Whoops.
Crass of me,' Dana said ruefully.

'Big Bossy Boots, then,' Georgia suggested.

'Precisely. The Ludds haven't been here long enough to
earn the gate money to admit them to full Friday Street
approval so they have to work extra hard to win brownie
points. That's why Michael and Sheila are sure to be around
today. Look, there's Drew at the gate, doing his chip-off-
the-old-block act.'

Through the iron gate in the wall to one side of the house
Georgia could see the entry desk, and Drew had the job of
directing visitors through the gate. He was a good-looking
lad with a shock of dark hair and classical features, and
Dana's comments were pertinent. Drew was almost too
welcoming.

The pathway led straight to the terrace and down to the
formal gardens, with the estate stretching out on both sides.
As they reached it, she could see a marquee to one side,
obviously the tea tent, and on the other side lay a large
natural arena of grass surrounded on one side by trees and
bushes and on the further two sides by woodland. At present
the bushes were a riot of colour with rhododendrons and
azaleas coming into flower.

'That must have been where the shows took place,' she
observed.

'Only the evening one,' Dana said. 'The afternoon one was held in the public area in front of the house for those who forked out their entrance fee.'

'They paid?' Georgia queried. 'On the Ludds' engagement day?'

'The family doesn't seem averse to the odd penny,' Dana replied. 'Not that it's short of cash.'

'How does it make its money?'

'*Used to* make it, so far as Michael's concerned. I think he's a retired businessman. Owned a thriving catering company, or something of the sort. Henry, his father, was in the RAF during the Second World War. He was stationed here and fell in love with Downey Hall, which was an RAF HQ in those days. So he popped back and bought the place a few years later. Must have come from a rich family I imagine, and then he compounded his luck by going into the family food industry and making another pile.'

'You're doing pretty well for a newcomer.' Georgia tried not to sound patronizing or sarcastic, but must have failed because Dana looked amused.

'Village gossip travels faster than Spitfires. Gossip, that is, which isn't considered a Friday Street secret. The Beamishes and the Ludds aren't, and so they're a subject of never-ending speculation. They don't speak to each other, you see. As a result, it's not done to refer to a Beamish in the presence of a Ludd or vice versa. So don't boast here about our going on the ghost tour yesterday.'

'Why the feud?' Peter demanded. 'Are the Luds fighting over the right to call the Montashes theirs?'

Dana laughed. 'Sounds good, but I don't know.'

Peter drove into the centre of the grassy area and studied it. He always liked to sit for a while, 'getting his orientation' as he put it, though quiet meditation was hardly possible today with half the village wandering around the gardens.

'If the stage was there . . . No, can't have been,' he mused aloud. 'It must have been there.' He pointed to the far side of the arena, away from the house, and behind which they could see the wooded area extending for quite a distance. 'It won't tell us much, but I'll take a look,' he declared, whirling his wheelchair round.

He was forestalled by Dana calling, 'Michael, the gardens are looking magnificent.' Georgia turned round to see Mine Host of Stately Homes of England.

'Splendid,' he announced cordially as Dana introduced them. 'I've heard of you, of course. Marsh & Daughter, the righters of wrongs.' Michael seemed genial enough, Georgia thought, well built, well dressed, well intentioned, apparently. Poured out of a middle-class mould. Despite the over-heartiness, he was at least welcoming them, which boded well. She thought back to the statement he had made to the police at the time of the murder. This was the man who, together with his father, had found Adam with the body.

'And what brings you to Friday Street?' Michael continued. 'Professional reasons? Poor little Alice Winters?'

Georgia answered. 'No, the Fanny Star murder.' No point in reticence.

'We wanted to see the scene of the crime,' Peter said, doing his own brand of genial.

Michael didn't even blink. So he knew all about them already. Hardly surprising, she supposed. 'That's natural enough,' he said. 'I'm amazed we haven't had the whole of Grub Street here this afternoon. Do you have a book in mind?' It sounded a casual question, but he looked keenly interested in the answer.

'We always do. It's the process from being "in mind" to decision-making that takes time,' Peter stonewalled. 'After all, there's never been any doubt about Adam Jones' guilt, has there?'

'Not that I'm aware of. I'll have to get back to my post, but I'll get Drew to show you round. He's fascinated by the murder on his own doorstep, so he feels possessive about it, but he might cough up a few facts for you.'

Exit Mine Host rather rapidly, Georgia thought, but he was replaced remarkably quickly by Drew, who arrived before

Peter had even had a chance to drive straight for the wooded area to sniff it out for himself. Keeping an eye on the suspects, were they?

'So you're interested in the Fanny Star murder?' she began. 'Why's that?'

Drew was immediately animated in a way his welcoming smile at the gate had failed to achieve. 'It's the music, isn't it?'

Someone at last prepared to talk about the Friday Street tune? No such luck. Perhaps, it occurred to her, she was blowing that tune up to proportions it did not warrant.

'It's lasted,' Drew was saying. 'That album of theirs was . . . well, seminal. Taking tradition, shaking it up inside out, rejecting the false and sterile, creating a platform for the future. God, when you think what they might have done if she hadn't been killed like that. I'll show you where it happened if you like.'

He led the way to the wide strip of thick bushes and trees on the far side of the arena. They followed him along a pathway, and then he disappeared into what seemed an impenetrable screen of bushes. Pushing after him, both she and Dana helped Peter steer his way through. They found themselves in a dark clearing screened by bushes and about five yards in diameter with a wooden bench in the middle. Who would want to sit in this dark place, she wondered, where it was all too easy to imagine the inert body and the weeping young man at its side?

'Here,' Drew said, almost with pride. 'Owlers' Smoke.'

'What on earth's that?' Dana asked.

Drew regarded her pityingly, to Georgia's amusement. 'Where the smugglers brought their dope and that.'

'Dope?' Peter queried with a straight face. 'They smuggled opium all the way from China when it wasn't even illegal?'

'Yeah, well. Tobacco, brandy, that stuff. This place is riddled with tunnels if you know where to look. This was one of their dumps. There's some kind of stone cellar under here.'

'And the bench is where they took their pinch of baccy?'

'Great-Grandpops had it put there.'

That seemed odd. Henry Ludd? 'Why?' Georgia asked, 'and how did Fanny come to be here? Was her body moved here?'

'No. This is where they met, didn't they?'

'Who?' Peter asked sharply. 'She and Adam?'

'No. The gang.'

'What gang?' Smugglers raced through Georgia's mind.

Drew began to look hunted. '*Her* gang. The gang they all belonged to before she left the village.'

'Who,' Georgia asked patiently, 'are *they*?'

'I don't know them all. Grandpops will know.'

'Your grandfather and great-grandfather found the body, didn't they?'

'Yeah. Then half the party came along to have a look. No crime scene managers in those days to keep the punters away.'

'It sounds as if you've made quite a study of it.'

He shrugged. 'I grew up with it, and then got interested in the music. Grandad thinks I'm weird and Grannie that I'm even weirder. Memories of nasty corpses are a stain on her beloved garden. Understandable. It was their engagement party after all.'

There proved to be more than a seat in this eerie place. Dana pointed out a memorial stone as well, and Georgia went to join her there, though the ground was too soft for Peter's wheelchair. It was not the usual engraved granite block she would have expected, but a cairn built of Kentish ragstone with an inscribed slate memorial, and etched borders of guitar and musical notes. It read: 'In memory of the bright star, Frances Gibb, 1944–1968. Rosa Mundi. Free from cold and care.'

Georgia shivered. It conjured up vivid images. 'Who erected the memorial?'

'Village subscription, I think. The body was lying here on an old mac.' Drew indicated with his arms.

'Huddled on one side,' Dana said briefly, 'at least by the time other people arrived.'

'Adam *might* have moved the body when he pulled the dagger out, except that the mac underneath her suggests that if so it couldn't have been very far,' Georgia said.

Drew began to inch away, his face slightly green. 'I'll introduce you to my great-grandfather – and Grannie too if you like. You can ask them the details.'

When they reached the tent, Dana pointed out Sheila Ludd, who was supervising the teas, and while Drew took Peter to find his great-grandfather, Georgia and Dana tackled the hostess. It wouldn't have been hard to pick her out. The ice-queen hostess: cool, calm, collected, well groomed, beautifully dressed with short fair hair with grey carefully interspersed.

'You must be Georgia Marsh,' she said, having greeted Dana. Her voice was tinkly, as befitted an ice queen. 'Michael told me about you. I understand you're interested in our grisly murder. The most recent, that is.'

'I hope you don't mind,' Georgia said frankly. 'It must be both tedious and upsetting for you constantly to be reminded of such a terrible time.'

Sheila inclined her head in acknowledgement, though little emotion crossed that calm face. 'It's a long time ago, and Adam Jones has been dead for many years too. We see it more objectively now.'

'Did you know Fanny well?' Georgia was fascinated by the lines on Sheila's face, which didn't quite fit her smile when she relaxed it. Dana was right, she decided. She wouldn't wear muddy shoes if she went calling at Downey Hall.

'Yes, I did. We were all much of an age, and I was brought up quite close to this village. Nevertheless, on that dreadful day, it was rather like meeting a stranger, for Frances had changed so much. Of course years get shorter as we grow older, don't they?' She addressed this to Peter who had just driven up.

54

'Georgia, come over and meet Henry,' Peter suggested very firmly, after exchanging courtesies, and she made her excuses to Sheila with some relief. It had felt like circling round the picket fence with Stonehenge in the middle: much to be admired, but keep your distance.

Henry Ludd was altogether different. She could see the RAF in this man, she thought as she was being introduced. Even though he was nearly ninety, he was still reasonably erect and straight-shouldered. He even had the classic RAF moustache, and his eyes were summing her up keenly, she noticed.

'You're interested in Frances Gibb, I understand,' he said.

'Yes. You must have known her quite well as she grew up in the village.'

'I did.' The calm grey eyes looked straight at her. His tone suggested that was the end of that topic, but then she decided to continue anyway.

'Did she show any signs as a child of her later wildness?'

'No. Frances was a gentle girl. And kind, yes, very kind.'

Kind, she wondered? That wild, drug-addicted whirling dervish of a singer? Had the hard edge of experience caused that much difference?

'Did she spend the whole day here, or go to see her parents and friends?'

'All day – she arrived for a buffet lunch, I recall, and was here all the time after that. Mr and Mrs Gibb came here. So far as I know, Frances did not visit her former home.'

'Were her old friends here to greet her?' Georgia continued, trying to get a picture of what had happened that day.

'The gang was here, of course.'

The 'gang' again. Georgia glanced at Drew. 'Who were they?'

'I'm afraid I don't recall all of them,' Henry said politely. 'They used to go around as a group in their early and middle teens. Michael would know; he was one of them, and that dreadful fellow at Pucken Manor. Oliver tagged along, and Josh Perry and Sheila.'

'Gran? Was she one of them?' Drew looked surprised.

'Indeed. She was Frances's best friend.'

Best friend? Georgia grappled with this image. Sheila had merely said she knew her well. True, their conversation had been brief. Nevertheless, today's elegant cash-confident Sheila bore little resemblance to the wild creature that had been Fanny Star. People changed, but did they change that much?

'Did you know Adam Jones?' she asked Henry.

'I met him for the first time that day. We all did. He seemed such a nice lad. I couldn't understand it.'

'And was the Friday Street music heard when he was arrested?' Georgia held her breath, waited for the usual dismissal.

It didn't come. He smiled at her. 'Yes,' he said gently. 'I believe it was.'

Four

'Convinced?' Peter chortled triumphantly. He had saved the dissection process until he was back in his own den, as usual. Georgia sometimes thought he drove in a make-believe world of his own, steering Dr Who's telephone box.

'By the music or by our next book being about Fanny Star?' she asked.

'Both, but number two first.'

'With reluctance, no.'

'Why not?'

'Still not a shred of evidence that Adam Jones was innocent.'

'Why else drown himself in the Medway?'

'Why drown himself if innocent? Unless . . .' She caught Peter's eye.

'Don't go there.'

'Why not? It seems logical to me. Perhaps he *didn't* drown himself.'

'I thought,' Peter gloated, 'you required evidence. There is none over Adam, only an interesting tune. Incidentally, do you recall how it went?'

'It's in my head,' Georgia admitted reluctantly.

'Would it emerge on to Elena's piano?'

For a moment she thought she'd misheard. Her mother's baby piano sat forlornly in the corner of their office serving as a base for potted plants and a dumping ground for piles of papers. It had become part of the scenery and was never, never played.

'Why?' she asked doubtfully. 'All that's important is the

fact that it exists and we're still not sure it's the same tune as that of the Friday Street legend.'

'Dearest Georgia. Play or sing it to Cadenza. She is our one possible ally, it seems to me, and it might serve to loosen the tongue, if only through shock that you know it.'

'You,' Georgia retorted, 'are a hard taskmaster.'

'So glad you're convinced about our next collaboration.'

'I'm not. Is it wise to attack the village on its sorest point?'

He looked at her reproachfully. 'Since when has that deterred you, daughter mine?'

'Never.' She gave in. 'I'll take it one stage further and tackle Cadenza. What will you be doing?'

'I thought I might educate myself on the sixties pop scene, not to mention trial reports, and also endeavour to track down this interesting gentleman Jonathan Powell.'

'Who?' For a moment Georgia had forgotten who he was.

'Supposedly Fanny's lover.'

'I thought you might like to have these.' Georgia thrust out her prepared package with what she hoped was a winning smile.

Cadenza looked completely taken aback, as well she might at an erstwhile ghost-tour customer turning up unannounced on her doorstep. Especially an awkward one.

Greeted by aghast silence, Georgia took two tentative steps back, to indicate she was no threat.

'How very kind.' Cadenza took the package and looked at it helplessly.

'They're copies of some articles I've dug out on the Fair Rosamund story and its connections to classical labyrinth legends,' Georgia explained brightly.

'Oh.' Colour began to return to Cadenza's cheeks. 'That's most thoughtful.' She hesitated, and Georgia could read her mind all too clearly. *I ought to invite her in. I don't want to, but . . .* Very well, Georgia would make the idea irresistible.

'Of course,' Georgia said, 'you must know there's a link with ancient Troy?' She pitched her voice to rise invitingly.

'No. No, I didn't.' The zest for knowledge was winning. 'Would you have time for a cup of tea?'

Georgia would. Georgia also breathed a great sigh of relief even though it would mean she would have to expound on labyrinths, mazes and Rosamund Clifford for some considerable time – subjects in which she had become an overnight expert.

'So fascinating,' Cadenza breathed, enthralled as several cups of tea and much talk ensued. It proved no great hardship, in fact. It was a delightful cottage, as Cadenza had clearly taken it over lock, stock and barrel from her parents, and seen no point in changing anything. The same nineteenth-century iron fireplace, with its colourful tiles, the willow-patterned china on the dresser, and even an old radiogram from the fifties. There was a reasonably modern television, but even that seemed to live comfortably with the world of Cadenza's youth.

'Of course, I doubt if our tower would contribute to world learning,' Cadenza added wistfully.

'Why not? You have fascinating legends here,' Georgia pointed out. 'And the main one involves your ancestor.'

'Indeed, indeed.' Cadenza clasped her hands together.

'The tale of his flute is unique,' Georgia prompted her.

Instant silence. Damn, I've fouled up, Georgia thought, furious with herself for going too far too quickly.

Eventually Cadenza replied awkwardly, 'Toby does not like me to talk of that.'

Georgia struggled for lost ground. 'Oh, but that's such a pity when your own ancestor is involved. Why is that?' She injected a note of anguish into her voice, at the same time wrestling with her conscience, which told her it was unfair to wind Cadenza up.

'He feels it would encourage imitators.' That took Georgia aback. 'If,' Cadenza continued, 'the tune were generally known, it might be used in circumstances that did not warrant it, Toby says. True villains might escape their just desserts.'

She had a point, Georgia supposed. 'Nevertheless,' she continued, equally validly, 'it is a signal to Friday Street of innocence. If the tune is not to be generally known outside the village, it becomes worthless since its value therefore depends on what happens thereafter.'

'I don't understand,' Cadenza said flatly.

'If the music is heard, does anyone investigate to discover the truth?'

'I don't know the answer, I'm afraid.' Cadenza's voice was becoming clipped. 'After all, it isn't played often. There was a case when the Winters' barn was burnt . . .'

She stopped, and Georgia realized she was again going too fast. She had to rescue the situation. 'Listen to this,' she began gently. There was a piano in the room but she didn't want to run the risk of a refusal. Instead she hummed the tune that she had heard at Christmas, hoping that sheer surprise would produce the right answer.

'Is that the tune?'

'Yes,' whispered Cadenza, obviously horrified. 'But how do you know it?'

'I heard it here last Christmas. Tim Perry was playing it in the pub.'

'But that was before . . .' Cadenza flushed at her indiscretion.

'Alice Winters' murder,' Georgia finished for her. 'Don't worry.' She comforted her. 'I think he was playing it for a joke, not realizing there were strangers in the bar. Do you think it was Tim playing it when Jake Baines was arrested?'

'I don't know.' Cadenza was very firm about this. 'No one does.'

'Tim's a friend of Jake Baines, isn't he? He could have been playing it in the hope he was innocent, rather than in the *knowledge* that he was.'

Cadenza was in command of herself now. 'He wouldn't dare. Tim works at Jane Winters' farm, as Jake did. Jane is Alice's mother and he wouldn't want to upset her. If he was the player after dear Alice's death, he would have to have *known* Jake was innocent. Friday Street is very strict about that. You see . . .'

'I won't use this information without permission,' Georgia said gently, when Cadenza once again halted. Tim Perry had as close a link to Alice as Jake? Could that be significant? 'But if Friday Street doesn't pursue an injustice itself,' she continued, 'then someone else should.'

Cadenza kept her lips firmly shut this time. The message was clear, and Georgia obeyed it.

'It's not Jake Baines I'm interested in. It's Fanny Star.'

Cadenza looked a little less obstinate. 'Adam Jones murdered her. There was no doubt about it.'

'But the music was heard then, even though it seems no one followed it up. Is it always a flute?' she added, when Cadenza made no reply. 'The same flute?'

'We do not know. Anyway,' she snapped, 'the name "flute" came in much later than Piers Brome's time. More probably his instrument was a simple three-holed pipe.'

'And what's used now?'

'Any such wind instrument, I presume.' Cadenza was clearly in agony at having inadvertently been drawn back into the subject. 'It is only the music that is handed down, and that's orally, not in written form. I was only a child when Adam Jones was arrested, but,' she admitted reluctantly, 'I heard the music during the night. It came over the amplifiers at Downey Hall. The whole village heard it.'

'So someone at Downey Hall must have played it?' Georgia knew she should not seem overeager, or she'd frighten Cadenza again. To her relief, the opposite happened. Cadenza must have realized she wasn't going to give up, and bowed before the wind.

'*Anyone* could have played it,' Cadenza said earnestly. 'It's part of the tradition that no one asks. It's anonymous, a call to the village that something is wrong, and that anyone with knowledge of the crime must reveal it. We're all on our honour. That's how it works.'

Or doesn't work, thought Georgia. Gone were the days when villagers could be so shamed before their peers.

'So no one person would have been forced to go to investigate the crime,' Cadenza continued. 'One examines one's own conscience and memory.'

Georgia could see a flaw or two in Cadenza's system. If there was no one person responsible for seeing that something *happened* after the music was played, nothing would. 'So why alert the whole village, not just the police?'

'One can have knowledge without having evidence such as the police would accept.'

Georgia accepted that. 'Was the music amplified when Jake Baines was arrested?'

'No. It was in the middle of the night. A flautist went round all the streets, piping short snatches of the tune in each one.'

'And no one caught him?'

'Why should we want to? He – or she,' Cadenza added fairly, 'is one of us.'

The Pied Piper of Friday Street, thought Georgia, only in this case the residents of the village did not flock out to follow him. They preferred to close their eyes in sleep – and perhaps their minds too. Why not, indeed? One person's 'knowledge' of guilt might not bear investigation. Time to switch subjects, she thought. She'd upset Cadenza enough.

'Just one more thing. I'd like to meet Mrs Gibb. I asked Dana Tucker where the home was, but she didn't know. She was going to ask you about it, but as I'm here . . .' She let her voice trail off invitingly.

Cadenza looked surprised. 'That's strange. I thought dear Dana visited her quite recently.'

Odd, Georgia thought. Dana had seemed willing enough to share her information with them, so why not mention that? 'Perhaps Mrs Gibb doesn't like visits from people she doesn't know.'

'She loves all visitors, for I'm afraid we're all strangers to some extent to her. She tells us all the same thing.'

'And what's that?'

'That she's the Queen of Sheba. She's in the Beeches at Charing. Now, you won't tell anyone what I've told you, will you? Toby would be very cross with me.'

'You haven't told me anything I didn't basically know already,' Georgia reassured her. 'You just enlarged it a little.'

Cadenza was easily convinced. 'You're quite right. And if there really was injustice over Fanny Star then it should be followed up. But I don't think the village discovered anything new as a result of the music or Toby would know about it. He's very clever about such things, And very kind. After all he's been through, it's quite amazing, the dear man.'

After all he's been through? Georgia pondered this as she went back to her car. She'd been hard put to it not to demand elucidation, but discretion won this time.

She found the Beeches nursing home set some way off the A20 near Charing. It was a splendid red-brick, almost gothic, nineteenth-century residence, now converted rather well, Georgia thought, as she was conducted to the public area. This was a large room with a splendid huge conservatory beyond it in which some of the more lively residents were sitting.

Doreen Gibb was not one of them. She was inside, though she looked hale and hearty. For some reason Georgia had expected a small, anxious-looking woman and was somewhat taken aback to find a plump woman in an armchair, with a mop of grey hair – once ginger, she wondered? Directly Mrs Gibb saw her she burst out laughing, more like the old fairground laughing-sailor machine than a victim of a cruel disease.

'She gets plenty of visitors,' said the nurse. 'All her old friends come over to see her. Not a lot they can talk about, but they do their best, chatting away.' Georgia had not yet decided on her own approach, but it was irrelevant. As soon as it was clear she was coming to see her, Doreen Gibb began waving wildly, still laughing.

'Hallo,' she cried. 'I wondered when you were coming, Frances.'

63

'I'm Frances's friend,' Georgia amended.

'I'll have some of that Ponds face cream when you next come, Fran.'

'I'll remember. You're Fran's mother, aren't you, Mrs Gibb?'

She shook her head vigorously. 'I'm the Queen of Sheba.'

'So you are,' Georgia replied politely.

Mrs Gibb roared with laughter. 'You'd better hang on, darling. The gang will be here in a jiff.'

Georgia misunderstood. 'The nurses?'

'No. What's his name. The Jug.'

Georgia grasped this one. 'You mean Toby?' she asked.

Mrs Gibb crowed with laughter. 'Tom, there's Tom and her and the others.'

Firm ground at last. 'Does Tom still come to see you?'

'No.' The laughter stopped. 'Good thing too.'

'And Adam? Does Fran talk about him too?'

Mrs Gibb looked puzzled. 'Don't know him, but I'm the Queen of Sheba.'

'So who's Tom?' Georgia concluded her account to Peter on her return.

'He probably doesn't exist. Nevertheless I'll make him a Burglar Bill.'

'You'll *what*?' Georgia then realized that Peter was looking highly pleased with himself.

'Our new toy. Courtesy of Charlie.'

'He's been over?' Charlie Bone was her cousin, the son of Peter's sister Gwen. He was dear to them both. His cheerful face surrounded by a mop of unruly black hair was guaranteed to liven up any day. He was a computer wizard, and their guru in times of trouble.

'More than that. He's installed Suspects Anonymous in both our machines.'

'Thanks,' Georgia said dubiously. 'Just what is it?' Charlie's ideas could either be brilliant or scatterbrained.

'Software he's invented specially for us, either as a game

or a tool. Look, I've been playing with it all day.' Peter clicked on the icon and she watched entranced as a cursor in the form of a Sherlock Holmes' magnifying glass whizzed over a succession of different coloured 'Burglar Bills and Bettys' – so named, Peter told her, because they resembled old-fashioned burglars complete with stripy tee shirts, caps, eye masks (removable, Peter explained) and a bag marked 'swag' over their shoulder.

'Evidence goes into the swag bag,' Peter said. 'Look.'

He clicked on one of them, and an evidence menu popped up. Under 'artefacts' only one item was listed: a flute.

'Very clever.' Georgia meant it. She found it charming, as Peter moved the magnifying glass so that Burglars tiptoed on and off screen. 'But what does it *do*, apart from cheer us up?'

'For one thing, we can feed data such as suspects' movements, alleged or proven, into the respective Burglar files, and then activate the game to reveal discrepancies.'

She began to see. 'Everybody present on the day of Fanny's death can be a Burglar Bill; we put in the information we have, press OK and see it as it would have played out that day. Do we have manual control as well?'

'Of course.'

'Then we can work out who's fibbing. I can't wait.'

'If they meet in a head-on collision we know someone's lying.'

'Let's go. It won't get us anywhere with Friday Street but at least we'll go down laughing.'

'If you take that attitude, we never will get anywhere.'

'You're right.'

There was no point getting ready to throw in the sponge so early on. That being so, Friday Street was the hardest nut to crack. She was beginning to realize just how close-knit the village was, and that being the case, how much closer it must have been in Fanny's day. This tradition of the music was no sweet legend; it pointed to a much darker side of Friday Street which still existed. Alice Winters' murder could be proof of that.

He grinned. 'How about a drive to the West Country?'

Peter had flummoxed her. 'Why and where?' she asked.

'To meet Jonathan Powell.'

'Really? The manager and lover himself.' Not what she'd expected, but if anyone could provide a solid reason for their continuing this investigation, he could.

'*Possible* lover,' Peter amended. 'I'm rather pleased with myself. He took some ferreting out with the help of my best persuasive techniques. In the 1980s he joined a large management group. He's now retired, not unnaturally since I gather he's about seventy. Living in Sherborne.'

'Dorset.'

'The same. Nice place. You should be grateful to me for letting you see the world.'

'I am. And you to me for obeying you so readily.'

Georgia felt rather like Mr Toad herself as she drove her Alfa Romeo 147 down to Dorset two days later. She'd chosen the A30 out of sheer sentimentality, despite its winding curves and bends, since it spoke so much of happy trips in the past. So what if some of these had been with Zac? Even more had been with her parents, and one or two with Luke. She was looking forward to discussing Friday Street with him, but not perhaps until she had made up her own mind about it. She'd thought of asking if he'd like to come today, but resisted the temptation. The request would have been for private pleasure not for work purposes, and she tried to apply the same discipline in this as the Inland Revenue did in judging her expenses, bless them. She dragged her thoughts away from Luke and on to Jonathan Powell, lover and – if it wasn't going too far – at least witness to murder.

What sort of man could she expect? She'd conjured up an image of a former pop group manager, showing signs of heavy drink and drug usage, and thus wasn't prepared for the real Jonathan Powell or for the elegant town house that greeted her when she arrived.

The house was tastefully decorated and elegant antiques

abounded. Zac would have felt at home here – except that in his case most of the latter would have been dishonestly acquired. Not stolen, he would say indignantly, but acquired by discussion. She hadn't visited Sherborne before and was impressed by the elegance of the town. Not the sort of place to entertain the pop world of Sweet Fanny Adams.

Nor did Jonathan Powell fit her image of him. He suited his cultured, almost academic voice; he was slender and white-haired, with a quiet manner and keen eye.

'Do come in, Miss Marsh. It's a splendid afternoon. Shall we repair to the garden?'

They duly did so. It was very much a town garden, small, paved, and brought to life with pots and bushes, but it was restful and secluded.

There was no mention or sign of a wife, she noticed, though the house didn't have the feel of a bachelor or gay pad. Photographs were everywhere, one of a middle-aged Jonathan with a woman. His wife? There was one of Fanny, which was outstanding, reminiscent of the famous photo of Jacqueline du Pré with her cello. It showed Fanny with a mike in her hand, mid-song, obviously transplanted into a realm of her own. There was no photo of her with Adam, but two of him alone, one in a studio, and one in a garden, looking almost shyly into the camera.

A pleasant interlude with Lady Grey tea and petits fours preceded business talk, and Georgia took her cue from Jonathan over leaving all discussion until tea was finished. She was interested by this. *He wants to size me up*, she thought. *Why? Is he wondering how gullible I am, or just whether he feels he can trust me?*

'Your father mentioned on the telephone,' he began at last, 'that you're wondering whether Adam Jones might have been innocent. You wish to discuss that possibility?'

'Yes, please, but first my father and I need to get the flavour of what happened. So far as we can discover there's never been a whole book devoted to either Sweet Fanny Adams or the murder trial. Did you ever think of writing one?'

'I did not.'

'Did you give evidence at the trial?'

She had read his statement to the police but it had told her little. At about eight forty he had walked over to the stage to check with the soundmen that everything was ready for the show. He was surprised not to see Fanny there, as he hadn't seen her in the house since she left the dining table so abruptly. He went back to the house assuming he'd see her there, and when he didn't he raised the alarm. That would have been about ten to nine. Someone suggested Fanny might be in Owlers' Smoke, and Michael and Henry went to search there while others searched the house. Henry had then come back to break the news.

'I was prepared to take the stand, but I wasn't called.'

'That's surprising,' Georgia said, 'as you were their manager.'

'Not really. The defence was reluctant to call me in case I was forced to reveal that Fanny wanted to go solo, thus confirming the prosecution's claim that Adam killed her in his fury.'

'Then why didn't the prosecution call you?'

'Because I would vehemently deny that Adam had any *personal* motive for killing her, especially any involving myself.'

'There were allegations in witness statements about that. And in magazine articles.' Several in fact. One boasted of a love affair between Fanny and Adam, two others between Fanny and manager Jonathan. Another claimed that Fanny wanted to strike out on her own.

'The witnesses who claimed to have heard Fanny and Adam arguing about my personal part in their lives were attacked by the defence in that respect, however correct they might have been over Fanny herself wishing to go solo.' Jonathan Powell began to seem more human with that out of the way. 'Am I being taped?' he asked.

'Not if you don't wish it. I can take pencil notes.'

He thought for a moment. 'Notes only at this stage,' he

replied briskly. 'If it comes to a book, you may come back to me for taped quotes.'

'Does Sweet Fanny Adams still seem close to you?'

'If Brian Epstein were still alive and had been in the same position with his group, I think he'd still find it very close. That's how I feel about Sweet Fanny Adams.'

'Were you with them from the beginning?'

'From the beginning of Fanny Star herself. I first saw her by chance in a Woolwich pub with a group that was fast going nowhere giving lacklustre imitations of Tommy Steele's "Singing the Blues". No talent, no spark. Fanny stood out head and shoulders above the rest, even though she hadn't yet found her niche. It was 1963. The pub was hardly the club centre of the world, and I thought she might develop into something, so I followed her progress for a while, then persuaded her to come off the booze and go solo. I decided it might be worth my supporting her finan-cially for a while, and, no, I didn't sleep with her. Finally she cut her first single at the end of 1964. It had a moderate success, bringing enough bookings to keep her going, but I felt she needed something more. Then I ran into Adam in the West Country, not far from here, and I had a hunch their voices might go well together. I was right. It took a year or so to work their act out, and then it went off like a firecracker. Sweet Fanny Adams was born at just the right time, sufficiently before "Sergeant Pepper" to get established and then to use it as an inspiration for their own future direction.'

'Where did Fanny's wildness come from?' Georgia thought of Henry's 'Kind child' remark. 'From Adam, or from within herself, or both? Was it born into her, or did it develop during her upbringing?'

'It came from her, but I don't know whether it was genetic or in reaction to her past. You can't just acquire that kind of fever because the music demands it. You bring the fever to the song.'

'Do you know why she left home?'

'No. She'd never talk about it. She left Friday Street in 1961, and I didn't meet her until 1963. Two years is a long time when you're seventeen.'

'What did she do in those two years?'

'Acquired a knowledge of life's hard edges, I imagine. Or *more* knowledge. I think the latter, though she wouldn't speak about it.'

'Yet she chose to return to Friday Street for the gig. Didn't she explain why she wanted to go?'

Jonathan considered this for a moment or two. 'No. She wasn't eager to go. She refused at first. In fact, she quarrelled with Adam over it. Then she changed her mind. I told her she was crazy. They were high up in the charts, and to throw themselves away on such a small event was madness.'

'Who actually invited her to Downey Hall?'

'I imagine it's in the trial reports. I think it was the owner of the place.'

'Henry Ludd?'

'Yes, that's it, and his wife, Joan. She was a sour-faced woman. I got the impression she didn't approve of the likes of Sweet Fanny Adams.'

'You were their manager. Was Sweet Fanny Adams regarded at the time as serious music or just rebellion?'

'I believe the former. Fanny was somehow fragile, as well as wild. She was like a flower out of control.' He looked at her as if to see whether she understood. 'That sounds emotional, I know, but one could get emotional over Fanny Star. If you brushed away the wildness there was the lost look underneath. That's how she touched base with Adam and the spark ignited.'

She should have felt moved by this, Georgia thought, but for some reason she didn't.

'Adam was a gentle soul,' Jonathan continued, 'so he tempered her desire to go completely over the top. They should use the wildness to create, he said, not to destroy. They took their inner compassion on to new planes by

70

demanding more from a rotten, unjust world. That developed into the wildness of SFA; it was a passion for justice for all.'

Just fine rhetoric, she wondered, or did he mean it? Hard to tell with this man.

'Do you think Adam received justice for himself?'

'I know he didn't.'

At last. A glimmer of a case. 'Do you have evidence for that?'

'The fact that he wanted to go back to Friday Street on his release from prison. He told me it was to find the truth, and he had nothing to lose now.'

'Except perhaps his life.'

He looked taken aback. 'Are you implying he might have been killed rather than committed suicide?'

'What do *you* think?'

'I think . . . I think it would explain everything.'

'Was there any suggestion of murder at the time?'

'No. There were diatoms throughout the body, so the pathologist said at the inquest, which indicates he was alive when he entered the water.'

'You seem to have gone into it fairly fully.' It was a casual remark, but Jonathan replied sharply all the same.

'He was a client of mine – and a friend.'

'And you believe he was innocent of Fanny's murder.'

'As much as one can be without hard evidence. I *knew* Adam. He wasn't capable of murder – and before you say that in some circumstances any of us might do anything, let me qualify that. He couldn't have murdered Fanny. He adored her; they were the head and tails of a penny. Two people joined at the hip.'

'But if she was threatening to go solo and leave him . . .' There was something puzzling here, but Jonathan seemed sincere.

'Even if she did go solo, he wouldn't have been driven to the point of murder. Upset, perhaps, but he didn't really *care* about his career. Anyway, luck as well as talent plays its part in this world. It could have been Adam who would have made it solo. No, he didn't kill her.'

'Even if he believed, rightly or wrongly, that she was having an affair—'

'Don't think in clichés, Georgia. She wasn't. She loved Adam, and that wasn't sexual. She lived with him, but that was solely for the sake of their music. It's hard to believe in this sex-driven age, but in the sixties people weren't so single-minded about sex. Youth wanted freedom to explore and if one chose to explore music rather than sex then that was no problem. That was what freedom meant.'

She had her doubts, but it wouldn't help to voice them. 'Can you tell me what you remember of that day? If Adam was innocent, obviously someone else there murdered her. Did you know about this row between Adam and Fanny?'

'Yes, but it wasn't serious. She was still annoyed because Adam had wanted her to come to the gig after she had initially refused, and then she found out her parents had been invited and blamed him. She was livid. To do Fanny justice she was pleasant to them and there were lots of hugs and kisses, but she let loose her feelings to Adam. She shouted she'd go solo as from that day, if he thought he could run her life. I told you I could have given evidence of motive at the trial over her going solo – and it was true that she'd talked about the possibility quite often, but never seriously. If I gave evidence for the defence, I might have been cross-examined about the row, which would have looked bad. I knew Fanny and the court didn't. She wouldn't leave Adam and he knew it perfectly well. We were a threesome.

'The row was after the public show, and they still planned to go ahead with the evening performance as though nothing had happened. They were true performers. We had dinner. Fanny's parents were there, and Henry Ludd had arranged for a lot of her friends to be there too – they called it the gang. Michael Ludd, obviously, and his fiancée, Sheila, his younger brother, Oliver, Josh Perry, his future wife and – who else – Toby Beamish. That was good of Henry, because

I gather the Ludds and the Beamishes aren't on speaking terms.'

'And Tom? Was he there?'

'Tom who? I don't remember a Tom. There were others I can't remember. Anyway, Fanny got drunk, and it didn't go down well, being a posh dinner. Sheila, who had been her best friend when Fanny lived in Friday Street, reproved Fanny, who promptly stormed out. Sheila followed her because she was throwing up by this time, and came back without Fanny after ten or fifteen minutes, just as we all moved to the drawing room for coffee. Then the party began to break up into small groups, but I saw no sign of Fanny. When it was nearly time for the show, I went over to the stage to check the sound and so on, and realized neither Fanny nor Adam was around. I remembered Adam had said he would see Fanny's parents home, so we concentrated on looking for Fanny. I alerted the party, and soon Henry came rushing back to say she was dead, that Adam had killed her, and Michael was keeping a guard on him. It all seemed completely unbelievable and it was only Henry's expression that convinced us he was serious about ringing for the police. Then people started to move, running like a flock of sheep over to where she'd been found.'

'And the dagger?'

'No one noticed it missing from the entrance hall. Michael realized what it was while we were all staring at the body, I think. I was too cut up to notice much. When the police came, it didn't take long for them to arrest Adam. He was crying, "I did it, it's my fault", over and over again. Which the police took, naturally enough, to be a confession. He was so dazed I don't think he knew what he was saying.'

'But you still think him innocent.'

'Yes. He meant he'd encouraged her to come down to Friday Street, as an opportunity for her to face whatever demons were haunting her from the past.'

'The Friday Street music supported him.'

'What's that?'

73

'It was played during the night over the amplifiers. It's a traditional village tune to indicate an injustice has been done.'

'How weird. Yes, I think I remember. We all stayed the night, so we could hardly miss it. It woke up the whole neighbourhood, and most of us couldn't sleep anyway. Are you implying the murderer played it?'

'No. But it was someone from Friday Street – and someone who had good reason to think Adam innocent.'

Georgia drove back, trying to work out why she felt dissatisfied. Powell had been co-operating, even if careful with his words. Too careful. Yes. He had given a good picture of a bygone age, of a tragic murder, and of a threesome of which he was the only survivor. A true picture? Overall, perhaps yes. Nevertheless, where better to hide a lie than to bury it within the truth? Mr Powell, she thought, as she turned off the Canterbury road towards Haden Shaw, as regards you, the jury is out.

Five

'Another slap in the face,' Georgia said ruefully, as she put the phone down.

Which was better, the witness who co-operated but possibly lied, or one who didn't and sat on the truth? In other words, it was Powell versus Friday Street. After her report to Peter about Jonathan Powell's belief in Adam's innocence, they had agreed there could be a case to investigate. Fine, steam on ahead on all fronts – except that the road to Friday Street seemed permanently blocked. On the computer Suspects Anonymous was doing splendidly at keeping track of where they were, but it too had stalled.

'Whose hand slapped this time?' Peter swung his chair round to face her desk.

'Darling Michael Ludd's. Frightfully sorry and all that, but they don't believe in raking up the past, especially—'

'At a time of village grief such as this?' Peter guessed.

'Correct. With Alice Winters' death such a painful recent memory, he feels now is not the time to enquire into Fanny Star's death. It seems to me it's *just* the time. Exactly the same line as Toby Beamish is taking. Not to mention Josh Perry on behalf of himself and his wife, Hazel.'

'How about Henry Ludd? He seemed a reasonably fair-minded chap.'

'Friendlier, but the same answer, although I did get the impression that he could be pushed a little. He still has an air of "I don't want to be involved unless I have to". There's always Drew, but I'd have to leave it a while.'

'Cadenza?'

'She put the phone down like a frightened rabbit.'

'Perhaps she is, Georgia. In which case—'

'There's something to be frightened of.' Georgia looked questioningly at her father. 'Which must imply that if Adam Jones was innocent, they think Fanny's murderer is still around.'

'Not necessarily. He could be dead or have left the village.'

'Or he could be Jonathan Powell,' she pointed out.

'You seem very taken with this theory.'

'He was lying part of the time, I'm sure of it.'

'So do a lot of people for what they perceive to be the best of reasons.'

'You remember that fork, Peter? The two-pronged carver in the deodand museum? That's this case: I'm taking one prong. The best line to pursue is Powell.'

'Mine's the other, Georgia,' Peter said firmly. 'Friday Street is where the answer lies.'

'I agree that if Alice Winters' murder has something to do with Fanny Star's murder—'

'Most athletic. That's a very long jump,' Peter said drily – and justifiably, Georgia accepted.

She subsided. 'I could jump the Medway at present,' she said bitterly. 'Just to spite Friday Street. I won't let it win. I won't. So where next? My only ally in Friday Street is Dana and she's suspect as an outsider too.'

'*Facts* are next. I've concocted a sort of timetable for the day of the murder from the trial reports and witness statements, which I've fed into Suspects Anonymous. The private show had been due to begin at nine o'clock and Adam was discovered with the body at that time, give or take a minute or two.'

'In the dark?'

'It was late June, remember, so it would still have been twilight. Adam claimed he couldn't remember how long he'd been there, but thought it was about five minutes. The police doctor said unofficially she'd been dead only a short time although no one save Toby Beamish claims to have seen her after Sheila Ludd left her at seven thirty. Sheila had escorted Fanny out of the dining room at seven fifteen and taken her to the bathroom where she was sick. The dinner had begun at six, guests repaired to the drawing room and terrace for coffee at seven thirty, and then the party split up into groups. That leaves a gap of over an hour between, say, seven forty when Toby saw her, and eight fifty, during which it would be hard to reconstruct precisely where anyone was, so even Suspects Anonymous can't help there. Adam claimed he'd left the terrace at about a quarter to eight to see Fanny's parents to their home, but Ronald Gibb testified that he had left them at the gates of the hall at about eight o'clock, leaving plenty of time for him to find Fanny and kill her.'

'It's time I did a Somebody's Son,' Georgia observed. Family trees for past members of the gang could help, if only as a reminder that family connections were vital when trying to understand a village. She'd work on it tonight.

'It's odd the guests weren't asked about each other's movements, only their own. Most of their statements imply they were merely chatting.'

'It wasn't relevant, since no one else was suspected. I've sent off to National Archives for stuff from the Crim 2 series, by the way, including the autopsy report on Fanny. Not that it would tell us much we don't know already. I'd dearly love to know if any of the investigating team are still around, but it's a long shot. They'd all have retired by probably 1998 at the latest, if they put in their full thirty years.'

'You could ask.'

'I have,' Peter said gloomily. 'Mike won't budge on any help unless we can come up with something solid. Hearsay and guesswork – his words, the nerve of the man – are not enough. And something solid means—'

'Don't tell me. Back to Friday Street, and the Great Wall of Hatred.'

'There has to be a way in, Georgia,' Peter pointed out. '*Find* it.'

*   *   *

'It's all very well saying "find it",' Georgia grumbled, watching Luke remove an exquisite *tarte tatin* from her oven and wondering why her own powers of cuisine seemed to halt at strawberries and cream nowadays. 'But a few ideas might help.' She shouldn't be talking shop at the weekend, but she felt frustrated enough to break the rules.

'There's Dana,' Luke suggested. 'Even if she doesn't have the gift of instant "open sesame", she must know the village better than you do by now.'

'Dana?' she picked up crossly, wondering how Luke knew her name. Then she recalled he'd met her in the pub during their visit in April. 'What did you talk about when you met her? Anything helpful?'

'This and that.' Luke marched triumphantly into her living room bearing the *tarte* on one hand like a trophy.

'So the "this and that" wasn't helpful as regards Fanny Star?' she persisted. She trotted in his wake feeling obscurely annoyed but unable to define why.

'I asked her if she'd heard of the case, since she can't be that much older than you.'

'Eight or nine years, I'd say,' Georgia muttered, instantly feeling bitchy. She would blame Friday Street for that too.

Luke ignored that. 'Yes, she had. Wasn't their music the greatest? Hadn't it lasted well? Which of their tracks was my favourite? She liked "Allan Water". She hoped the cottage would inspire her quest.'

Georgia reluctantly laughed at herself. 'Quest? Sounds very exotic. She's only a keen fan.'

Luke glanced at her. 'Sure?'

'That's what she told me.'

'You're the detective; I hope you're right.'

That was a thought. Georgia had assumed Dana's interest in what they were doing was no more than general curiosity. 'You mean she might be following up the murder case too?'

'No idea. Where's the cream? Try the vicar.'

Now that *was* a good idea.

* * *

Friday Street shared its vicar with several other parishes, and the Reverend Angela Tanner lived in neighbouring Cookslea, which was all to the good, Georgia thought. It meant she might be able to get an objective opinion on Friday Street.

Angela Tanner was in her thirties, and at first sight Georgia doubted whether this jolly, straightforward-looking woman would do other than stonewall her. In fact she listened with obvious and deep interest to Georgia's story.

'I'd already heard that Friday Street has closed ranks against you,' she commented.

'Cadenza Broome?' Georgia said with resignation.

'News travels fast on the downs.'

'What do you think of the moral issues behind this? Cadenza explained that if the music is heard it's a summons to reveal anything relevant that one knows. But so far as I can gather, no one has revealed anything either over Adam Jones or Jake Baines, so the call of the music has failed. It's time to let someone else look into it. Like me,' she added practically.

Angela thought this through. 'I agree, provided you're not doing the right thing for the wrong reasons, to quote T.S. Eliot.'

'You mean so that we can make a pile out of our books?' Georgia asked frankly.

'Precisely. What's your answer to that?'

'No one says the police shouldn't investigate injustice just because they're taking salaries.'

'It's their job.'

'And it's mine and my father's. He was in the police force, after all, and investigated many mistaken verdicts from the past and no one said he was wrong to do it.'

'I accept that.' Angela smiled, and Georgia knew she was home and dry. 'That's the good news,' the vicar continued. 'The bad news is that I can't see any way of helping you.'

Georgia was ready for this. 'Friday Street is a small village, but even so not everyone in it can be so closely bound up with the Fanny Star case that they would refuse to talk to me.'

79

'That's true, but there are two factors you aren't taking into consideration. I suspect that the people who have metaphorically slammed the door on you are what one might call the leaders of the village. Not leaders by political or legal definition, but in every village there tends to be a circle whose members "rule" by default. They're unchallenged because they are here, there and everywhere, and willing to be so. Most people aren't nowadays and are only too grateful for those who are. You've run into that circle.'

Which was probably also the circle that had known Fanny Star. 'And the other factor?'

'Even tougher to fight. The wheels within wheels.'

'Defined as?'

Angela considered this. 'Ever tried to do a family tree for the Greek gods, especially Zeus?'

Georgia laughed. 'No, but I can see there might be a problem.'

'Unfortunately,' Angela said drily, 'one *can't* see it in Friday Street. But it's there, believe me. Who married who, and when. And who didn't restrict their sex lives to the marital bed. And,' she added hastily, 'don't look at me so hopefully. I don't know. Even if I did, I couldn't tell you, of course, but I really don't. I just have the feeling that Friday Street might be, or more relevantly, *has been* even more closely knit than it appears on the surface.'

And that, Georgia thought, as she left, limited her humble Somebody's Son for the gang. It was a skeleton framework only. The noughts and crosses remained unknown.

She drove carefully through Friday Street to Dana's cottage later that day, conscious of her tense hands on the wheel. Quite what she expected, she didn't know. A brick through the windscreen? Rather too obvious. Closed doors and mouths were more effective. Even so, she wouldn't be staying long at End Cottage because she didn't fancy driving back through this village in the dark. She'd debated whether to tackle Dana when she was at work but that wasn't fair, nor was it conducive to chatting. Georgia was aware that after her talk with Luke her hackles were raised over Dana, probably unfairly so, and she needed time to overcome this. Was Dana an ally or unknown territory?

'How's it going?' Dana asked, pouring Georgia what she described as her own personal non-alcoholic cocktail.

'It isn't. It's stationary until I can get a visa for entering Friday Street. Otherwise we're stuck with the trial reports, witnesses' statements and Jonathan Powell's support.'

'So you've tracked him down, have you?'

Georgia glanced at her. So she knew him. Perhaps Luke was right, and there was more to this story. 'He seemed quite happy to talk.'

'Um.'

Keep those prickles down, Georgia, she told herself. Judge for yourself. 'I felt "um" about him too,' she said cheerfully.

'I met him too,' Dana continued. 'He was helpful, but only so far.'

'Are you considering writing about it?' She was going to pin this down once and for all.

'Articles for magazines.' Dana laughed, as though reading Georgia's mind very clearly. 'I won't be rivalling Marsh & Daughter.'

Why not mention this earlier, Georgia wondered, and why had her few words with Luke put a barrier where none had existed before? 'So that's what brought you to Kent?' she asked casually.

'No, that was coincidence. I came here for the job, through a contact of my parents, and realized my private hobby might fit in rather well, especially if I lodged in Friday Street. So, about this visa you want,' she said, switching direction. 'I'm afraid you're right. The word has gone out. No chatting to the Marshes.'

'Doesn't the cold shoulder apply to you too?'

'No, because I don't ask specific questions about the murder, or about the music. I'm interested in Fanny's early life, because of how her music developed. As you probably know, I saw Mrs Gibb. Sorry I didn't tell you I knew where she was. I wasn't sure about you,' Dana said frankly, making Georgia feel warmer towards her. 'Now I know you a little better, I can apologize for that.'

'No problem. I'd have done the same myself. Did you get anything out of Mrs Gibb except the Queen of Sheba?'

'A little, but it's a cryptic crossword puzzle, as I'm sure you found. It's all there inside her, but it's jumbled. The Queen of Sheba must mean something, but who knows what?'

'A link to Solomon's Temple or the Knights Templar, and from them the Knights Hospitallers, who bunged Rose Smith inside the tower. Friday Street's Fair Rosamund.'

Dana frowned. 'I don't see Doreen Gibb getting involved in medieval history. She was quite a looker, though. She gave me a photograph of herself taken during the war. A real pin-up. Want to see it?'

'Yes, please.' From the Doreen Gibb she had met, Georgia couldn't imagine what a younger version would be like, and gazed in astonishment at the black and white photo Dana produced. Here was a Hollywood-style, Hollywood-standard woman, whose beauty shone out despite the heavily lipsticked lips and forties hairstyle. She was a Rita Hayworth, and a decade or so later would have rivalled Marilyn Monroe in her liquid-eyed beauty. Georgia stared at it for some time. 'When was it taken, do you think? There's nothing on the back to indicate a date. So,' it occurred to her, 'it might not even be her.'

'It is. I showed it to Josh Perry to be sure. Although he was a small child during the war, he remembered her looking fairly much like this as he grew up.'

'Was she born in Friday Street?'

'Yes. She worked on Winters' Farm, and married Ronald Gibb just before the war broke out. He was in the Navy, so she lived with her family until after the war. Fanny was born in 1944.'

'Did Fanny inherit the ginger hair from her?' If only, Georgia thought, one could get deep inside the soul of a photograph, instead of bringing one's own less than objective baggage to it.

'I wouldn't know.' Dana studied the photo. 'Doreen's could be light red, I suppose. Or perhaps Fanny Star dyed her hair or had a wig. As the sixties wore on, colours and wigs were the fashion. "Anything goes" and all that.'

'Henry Ludd said Fanny was a kind child, and that doesn't seem to fit with her being a wild teenager.'

'That's the odd thing. From the other photo I saw she looks almost demure.'

'Other photo?' Georgia pricked up her ears.

'Jane Winters showed it to me. She's taken Alice's death very badly, and we've struck up an acquaintanceship. It was a photo of Fanny with her parents. Rather sweet. Brian Winters, Jane's father-in-law, was a member of the gang, of course.'

So Dana knew about the gang. And that Brian Winters was a member of it. It brought the name of Winters one step closer to Fanny.

'For this visa,' Dana continued, 'I suggest you try gently pushing Josh Perry. But don't blame me if you get nowhere.'

'Give me one good reason why we should talk to you,' Josh challenged her.

'Because neither you nor the village will stop me by not doing so, and I want to get my facts right, not wrong. Can I buy you a drink?'

It hadn't been easy to get this far. Georgia had chosen her time carefully, immediately the pub opened in the morning. Josh's wife, Hazel, had served her coffee, and obviously knew exactly who she was. Hazel was a small woman with a sharp face, which discouraged Georgia from tackling her as an alternative to Josh, and she found it hard to imagine her as a member of the gang. She was the other witness to Fanny and Adam's row. Georgia chose a table by the window, and summoned up her resolve to remain until they could ignore her no more. If she sat here long enough, she might win the battle of nerves. Now the battle had at least begun.

It had taken forty minutes, with Hazel coming back and forth several times, before Josh himself had emerged from the inner sanctum and come over to her. No 'good morning', or any other preamble. And 'no' to the offer of a drink.

Instead: 'You can follow me to somewhere where I can put you right about a few things.'

It didn't sound promising for a cordial chat. She followed him across the yard at the back of the pub to the cottage where Josh and Hazel obviously lived. It made a good battle-ground, if there had to be one, even if it meant she was playing on foreign turf. There was no further sign of Hazel. At least Josh was going to fight fair, one against one, and her questions for Hazel could wait.

She promptly fired the first shot. She had to take command of the situation, and this wouldn't be easy with Josh Perry. 'You can't stop this investigation, you know,' she said quietly, 'unless you can prove there's nothing to investigate. Even if your tactics did succeed in getting Marsh & Daughter to abandon the Fanny Star case, sooner or later it will open up again.'

'Why should it, Georgia? Hasn't done in nearly forty years.'

'What about in 1987 when Adam Jones came here after he was released from prison?'

'First I've heard of it.'

He was avoiding eye contact, she noticed. 'Probably on the day he died.'

Josh was even more cautious now, as though Georgia were trying to trip him up – and perhaps she was. 'He was found up Maidstone way,' he said.

'Having been here first, perhaps even silenced for his pains.' No harm in exaggerating a little, even if that scenario seemed unlikely now.

'What the blazes are you talking about?' he asked angrily. 'What bees are buzzing in your bonnet now?'

'Adam Jones maintained he was innocent; he told his manager he was coming here to find out the truth, and the next thing is that his body is found in the Medway.'

Josh glared at her. 'Suicide.'

'Probably.'

'You don't know what you're getting into here.'

The classic bluster. He'd lost his cool, which meant she'd hit a nerve at last. 'Then *tell* me.'

More bluster. 'What bloody business is it of yours?'

'This is my business, and it *is* bloody. There's blood on someone's hands. Friday Street hasn't done too good a job of tracking down the truth, despite this fancy music of yours.'

'I'm not going to discuss that with you.'

'You prefer to let one murderer, perhaps two, get away with it, do you?' She had meant Fanny and Adam, but Josh took it differently.

'Out!' he yelled at her. 'Haven't you any respect? Jane Winters has enough to put up with in losing Alice, without you poking your nose in.'

So be it. The Alice Winters case was on the table too. 'Why was the Friday Street tune played? I heard Tim play it at Christmas—'

'Are you saying our Tim's involved?' Josh interrupted furiously.

'No,' she said steadily, 'I'm not, but more recently someone played the music after Alice's death. Someone thought they knew who the real murderer was. Couldn't that someone have been Tim on behalf of his friend?' Seeing him about to explode again, she continued quickly: 'Don't you think you carry some responsibility for tracking down whom he thought it was, if so? Friday Street doesn't seem to be making much of a job of policing itself. Nothing happened after the music was played on Adam Jones' arrest, and if by any chance Fanny Star's murder was a factor in Alice Winters' death—'

'How could that be?' Josh was visibly shocked.

'I don't know, Josh. But the same dagger was used, and even if that's coincidence there could well be a link, especially if Jake Baines is innocent.' She paused, wondering if she'd been unfair in using Alice's death as a lever to get his attention. 'This is a small village and the gang that you and Fanny belonged to still lives in Friday Street. Except for Tom.'

Josh was curiously still. 'Get out,' he said quietly. 'Get out and don't come back.'

'Certainly.' She rose to her feet. 'Provided you remember that the Alice Winters case is still open if Jake *is* innocent. You can't shut yourself off from that.'

'I did rather well, I think,' Georgia said complacently, 'even if I do still think Jonathan Powell is the right prong of the carving fork to concentrate on.'

'That remains to be seen.' Peter seemed oddly uninterested, to her surprise. 'Still, you've thrown down a gauntlet. It's possible someone might pick it up.'

'And if by a miracle someone does, we'll ask Luke for the contract.'

'I have faith in you, Georgia. I rang him this morning. He wasn't there, in fact, but I left the message.'

'At lunch?'

'No, gallivanting in Faversham.'

Having lunch with Dana, was the unwelcome thought that popped into her mind. It was promptly pushed out again. 'How's Suspects Anonymous?'

'I set up a new programme. Alice Winters.'

'Peter,' she said warningly, 'that's not officially in our remit.'

Margaret put her head round the door. 'Someone hammering at your door, Georgia. Says Ted sent him down here.'

Curious, Georgia went to investigate. The miracle had arrived. Josh Perry was on her doorstep. She had difficulty in holding back a grin.

'We operate from here,' she called. 'Come in.'

He did so, looking grim rather than bearing olive branches. 'I've come to meet you halfway, Georgia.'

'Excellent.' She led him in and glanced at Peter, who nodded. The garden on a June day was better than their office, with its reminders that all cases might end in books, even in films, and that the spoken word could be retracted but not forgotten.

'Halfway,' she repeated invitingly, when they were established in the garden. 'Can you define that?'

'The past is one thing, the present something different. We leave Alice Winters out of it.'

'For the moment,' Peter stepped in.

'I'll be the judge of that,' Josh said quietly. So he could fight on foreign turf too, she thought. 'You were talking about the gang, and I can tell you about that. Ask away.'

'How did it form? Were you all at the village school?'

'Up to a point. Michael went away to prep school, so did Oliver – he's his younger brother, who tagged along after him. Toby was at the village school though. No public school for him. No money in the family. Sheila wasn't at the school, but she spent a lot of time at her aunt's house in Friday Street. We were of different ages, of course, but despite that and despite being separated by schools we stuck together. Owlers' Smoke, where . . .' he cleared his throat '. . . where it happened, was where we'd meet. Never afterwards, of course.'

'Why were you all so close? You came from different backgrounds.'

'Goodness knows – it just happens, doesn't it, when you're kids. Michael wasn't the oldest of us, but he tended to be the leader – in a way.'

'In which way?'

'He made the running. What he said, we did. We were an assorted bunch. People came and went, as they do in such gangs, but there was a steady core of us who stuck together. Michael, Toby, me, Oliver, Sheila and Frances, Hazel Winters,

87

now my wife, Liz Smith, Johnnie and Brian Winters – Johnnie Winters was Brian's older brother, killed in Korea. Brian's son was Bill, who married Jane.'

'What happened to Oliver Ludd?' And what about Tom? Georgia thought. She wasn't going to be the first to mention him though. She'd see what Josh volunteered.

'He went away to university. Lives in the States now.'

'And Liz Smith?'

'Left the village,' Josh said a shade too quickly. 'As I said, Michael was the leader but Frances was the one who had the ideas and created the fun. She didn't get on with her father and didn't have brothers or sisters, so she needed us around her. Her mother was all right, but she always took Ron's side, so there were constant rows.'

'Was Fanny still at school when she left the village or did she leave at sixteen?'

'Left school. Came to work in the pub,' Josh said briefly.

'You must have known her well then. Did your father run the pub at that time?'

'Yes.' His tone didn't invite further questions on that tack.

'Was Fanny musical then?'

'Not so you'd notice. We had a local group used to play in the pub. Oliver played with it from time to time, so did Brian. Hazel was the singer though. Odd, isn't it? Frances used to sing along with them but never stood out. I remember her telling us one day when she was in a temper that she was going to be a famous singer or musician. We made fun of her for it. We'd never seen so much as a penny whistle in her hand, but it turned out after she'd left that she was in the school choir, played the piano, and was even more deeply into listening to music than we were. She wasn't fussy. She'd listen to everything from Lonnie Donegan, Elvis and Bill Haley, to Ruby Murray or Rogers and Hammerstein, and end up with Wagner.'

'Folk songs too? Did she learn those at school with you?'

'Reckon she must have done. I remember her singing "Banks of Allan Water" once, and "Greensleeves". We sneered at her for liking them, and she said, no, they were okay songs, just needed a kick up the backside. That's what she and Adam gave them, all right.'

Georgia wondered how this gang worked. 'If the gang continued for such a long time, there must have been emotional entanglements between you.'

'Michael fancied Frances, so did Toby,' Josh said woodenly.

'And you?' The words were out before she could think twice. She waited for the blast, but oddly it didn't come.

Josh shrugged. 'I loved the girl. They all used to laugh at me. "Josh, poor old Josh" they'd say, "following her around like a pet spaniel. She'll never look at you." And they were right. I married Hazel the year after Frances left and, though it's none of your business, it's worked out. I couldn't have handled Frances, no way.'

'What made Fanny leave the village?' Peter asked. 'Too much pressure from you? Or the gang? Or her parents?'

Josh gave him a cool look. 'She left to be a singer.'

Okay, they deserved that. 'That's not the answer,' Peter said softly.

'She'd had rows with her parents for years and I reckon she decided it was time to go,' Josh said obstinately.

'Why do you say "reckon"?' Peter asked. 'If you were all so close, surely she'd have said goodbye, and told you at least why she was going, especially if she had no intention of coming back.'

'She didn't. She just went. She was in the bar one night . . .' Josh stopped, as though it were too painful to continue.

'Tell us, Josh. It's important,' Georgia said gently. She won no brownie points for her consideration.

'Can't see how. She finished washing up and was putting on her raincoat – it was pouring with rain that night – and just said, "I'm going, Josh. Won't be here tomorrow or ever again." I thought she meant she was throwing in the job so I didn't take it too seriously. Except when she kissed me. On the lips, as if she meant it, you know. I knew it then, but it was too late; she'd gone by morning. She'd disappeared up to London, her mother said. Took nothing, except every bit of cash she could lay her hands on. She'd saved up all her wages.'

'Didn't her parents try to find her?'

'Once they realized she wasn't returning, her mother did. But the police never found any trace at all, and after a while her mother just said nothing if any of us asked. "Where do you start looking?" she'd say. Her dad didn't care. Pretended he was worried, but he wasn't.'

'Had she had a row with anyone in the gang?'

'Not that I know of. You can ask Sheila about that – if she'll talk to you.'

'Ah,' Peter said reflectively, 'Fanny's great friend.'

'That's right. At that time they had a lot in common.'

'In what way?'

'You'll remember,' Josh said to Peter, 'things could be a lot simpler in those days. Some of us were village, some the other side of the posh fence. Sheila, me, Frances, Hazel were all one side, even though when the gang was together it didn't seem to matter. Odd, really.'

'Sheila and Michael say they don't want to resurrect the past,' Georgia pointed out. 'Is there anything you can do about that?'

'I might. Try Toby first.' Josh hesitated. 'Go careful though.'

'Someone told me he's had a hard life,' Georgia said, not relishing the thought of a tête-à-tête in Pucken Manor.

'Meaning that Cadenza says so. She would. Toby's Number Two to Michael in this village, just as he was in the gang.'

'Did he ever marry?' Georgia asked bluntly.

'Yes. His wife ran off with another man. That satisfy you, does it? And for all Cadenza's hopes, Toby's not likely to try marriage again.'

'Was he always as fixed on ghosts as he is now?' Georgia quickly moved to a safer subject.

'Much the same. Always some crazy passion. Trains as we grew up, then it was girls, now it's ghosts. So, now I've told you all I can . . .'

'Not quite,' Georgia said firmly. 'What about the day of the murder? You can tell us about that without going over your halfway mark. Was all the gang there?'

'Most of us. We were flattered to be asked – by 1968 the gang had more or less broken up. They were inviting Fanny back, Henry told us, and so we should all be there to make it a reunion as well as a celebration. I don't know whose idea it was, Michael's or Henry's, but there we all were, together with relatives and other friends and so forth, not to mention Fanny's entourage.'

'What did you think of Fanny? Did you find her changed?'

'She wasn't the girl I'd known. She might have been deep down, but she was brittle and wild that day. The entertainer, local girl made good. She'd crept away in '61 but she came back with a huge bang all right. Poor girl.'

'Do you think, looking back, that there was any doubt that Adam killed her – leaving the Friday Street music out of it?'

'There was no one else.'

Co-operation or not, this was still Friday Street and she'd get nowhere without pushing. 'Forgive me, but no old scores in the gang?'

'If there were,' Josh said steadily, 'it would have been difficult to settle them that day, whether by murder or anything else. We were all hanging around on the terrace waiting for the concert. Think of the risk.'

'Not so great,' Georgia said. 'If someone used the side entrance to the house, past the kitchens, and then kept to the far wall of the garden, there are enough bushes and trees to hide one very securely.'

Josh flushed. 'It would have taken time for one of us to rush to Owlers' Smoke and stab someone. It would mean planning it, grabbing that dagger and pursuing the poor girl. What about the blood, for one thing?'

'There might not have been much blood with the dagger

91

left in the wound, and, if Adam was telling the truth, that's what happened.'

Josh blenched. 'A risk, even so.'

'Were you aware of *anyone* not being in the main group after dinner?'

'Michael swept Henry off for a chat at one point. Adam left with Ron and Doreen Gibb. Nothing else. I'd help if I could, but I just don't remember. Any more questions?' He was clearly getting narked now, Georgia thought. Or was the word rattled? 'If you ask me, you're barking up the wrong tree. It's that fellow Powell who has the key to what's going on.'

'You may be right,' Georgia answered, surprised, 'but why do you think so?'

'None of us had seen Frances Gibb for seven years. Why on earth would any of us take it in our heads to murder her? The ones with the main reason had to be closest.'

'Jonathan and Adam,' Georgia said.

There was a slight pause before Josh answered, 'Yes.'

'I'd like to know who Toby Beamish married,' Peter said out of the blue.

'Nothing to do with Frances Gibb's murder,' Josh said flatly.

'The answer could be checked on the internet with patience,' Peter pointed out.

Josh glared at him. 'He married Liz Smith, if you must know.'

'She who left the village?'

'She left with Oliver Ludd nine or ten years or so after marrying Toby. She married Toby a couple of years after Fanny left. She and Oliver were both at the gig in 1968, and that's probably where she met Oliver again. She's still with him so far as I know and they live in the States. Satisfied?'

'Yes, thanks,' Peter said mildly.

That explained a lot, Georgia thought, especially about Toby. She was beginning to see the point of Angela Tanner's comment on the private life of Friday Street. 'Is that why the Ludds and Beamishes don't speak?'

'One reason.' Josh, it was clear, wasn't going to volunteer anything further. She'd still play her best shot though.

'There's one person you still haven't mentioned in the gang. Tom. Was he at the party?'

Somewhat surprisingly, this time he gave a sour grin. 'You wouldn't believe me if I told you.'

'Try us,' Peter invited.

'Tom isn't a he, it's a *they*. There was no such person as Tom. It was Frances's joke. We had plenty of them. "You, Josh," she'd say. "It's you and me against the rest." And the rest for her were Toby, Oliver and Michael. See? Tom. Michael always had it in for her, as well as fancying her, because he was jealous of her popularity. Oliver just followed his elder brother's suit. He was quite a bit younger, six or seven years. Toby . . . well, Toby really fancied her. Pawed her whenever he got the chance.' Josh looked Peter full in the eye. 'Just a joke, was Tom.'

Peter said nothing, and Georgia held her breath. Peter would win this one.

'Okay,' Josh said at last. 'It wasn't a joke, all right? She'd *try* to joke about it, but she was scared of them. Or, rather, not of any one of them in particular, but there was something about the three of them as a whole, *that* was Tom.'

'My prong of the carving fork, Georgia,' Peter said soberly. 'Wouldn't you agree?'

His cordless phone was ringing on the table at his side. Yes, she would agree, she thought as she watched him answer the call. Even sitting a yard or two away she could hear it was Mike Gilroy. Peter listened, said a few non-committal words, and put the phone down again.

'There's been a development in the Alice Winters case.' He looked first at Georgia and then at Josh. 'They've released Jake Baines. The CPS is offering no evidence.'

Six

Georgia drove into Friday Street, looking at the village with a fresh eye. Josh's support, albeit partial, would make a difference. In fact, it had already. The news about Jake's release had clearly shaken him, and he had asked whether it meant the police would be opening the case again. Peter had no idea. Marsh & Daughter were meeting Mike next Tuesday, 24th May, he said, and until then they would not know. Nevertheless, Josh had made his mind up quickly.

'Whether they do or don't,' he'd said grimly, 'there'll be trouble in the village. You've spread some half-baked idea that Frances's murder could have something to do with Alice's. I don't hold with that, but the sooner you get what you need about Frances, the sooner you'll leave us in peace to lick our wounds over Alice and Jake. To my mind, it's that Powell fellow you want, not Tom. So let's get it over with, shall we?'

It was another bargain – of sorts.

'He'll give just what he thinks is necessary and not a word more,' was Peter's opinion after Josh had left.

'That's something at least.'

'Is it? If you saw a signpost saying London, you might follow it. But suppose someone had broken off the bit that read "via Edinburgh"?'

'I'd feed it into Suspects Anonymous and see what it could make of it,' she retorted.

'Talking of which, I'll activate the Alice Winters file. And,' he added happily, 'take Tom out as a Burglar Bill.'

'I haven't finished with Tom yet.'

Thankfully she'd now been handed the necessary tools by Josh. With luck she'd at least be tolerated in Friday Street, if not welcome.

At Peter's urging, Josh had agreed to organize a reconstruction in Downey Hall of the events on the day of Fanny's murder. He had been reluctant at first, muttering that it could achieve nothing, but had obviously thought of it as a chance to see the end of Marsh & Daughter's presence. That would be tomorrow, Saturday, but today she had her sights on the man she saw as Master Tom himself: Toby.

She decided to leave her car in the pub car park, rather than the public one tucked away down a side lane opposite the entrance to Pucken Manor. She had too much respect for her Alfa Romeo to tempt fate. She walked briskly along towards the entrance gates, contemplating the delights of the manor. Would Toby still be enthusing about ghosts in his role of Mine Host, or would a more natural side emerge?

If Fanny was scared of anyone, it would be him. Even though the sun was out, it was chilly, and in the dark driveway, shielded by huge bushes, she wondered how many unseen ghosts might be striding along beside her. One of them might even be Fanny, and at her side Adam Jones, bewailing a false conviction like Piers Brome. In this gloomy garden it was not hard to imagine that they still laid their fingerprints on the present.

Toby opened the door himself, and her heart sank. He was still Host of the Manor. Perhaps that *was* his natural self. Now there was a depressing thought. The only difference was that the Mine Host suit of the ghost tour had been replaced by cords and sweater. A strand of his still-dark (or dyed?) hair fell over his forehead, meeting the thick rims of his spectacles, and his ruddy complexion spoke more of a nightly drink or two than of good health. Certainly the garden did not suggest that he bounded out at dawn to chop down a tree or two. It had more the air of being tended by a man desperately trying to keep nature at bay. Or perhaps the garden was purpose-grown to inspire ghosts.

'Come in, come in, Georgia. I may call you Georgia, I trust? Or isn't that appropriate for the Miss Marples of this world?'

She managed to smile politely. 'I don't normally turn into Miss Marple until after twelve o'clock. You're quite safe.'

'Splendid, splendid.' He led the way into what he termed his sanctum, which again looked purpose-designed, this time as a Victorian gentleman's library, complete with leather chairs, occasional tables, and wall to wall books – the latter chiefly about ghosts, interspersed with bound copies of *Punch* and Surtees' sporting novels. What did the real Toby Beamish read in bed, she wondered? Pornography? A light romance or two? Or Captain Hornblower? From what this man was prepared to display of his private life, she doubted she'd ever know the answer.

'You want to talk to me about poor dear Frances, of course. There's not much—'

She had to interrupt, before she was caught up in the familiar patter. 'No. I'd like to begin with Adam Jones.'

Sheer surprise stopped the flow and his answer took a moment or two to come. 'I'd be delighted to do so, but what could I tell you about him?'

'He visited Friday Street on the day he died.' There was no proof he did, but unless she sounded confident she'd get nowhere.

The affable host vanished. 'I saw no sign of him myself, and indeed why should he have come back to Friday Street?'

'He always claimed he was innocent. Perhaps he came to see the person he thought was guilty.'

'A vivid imagination, Georgia.'

'Reasonable deduction,' she retorted. 'When his body was found, were there any rumours that he had come back here?'

Toby folded his hands carefully and unattractively across his stomach. 'It was nearly twenty years ago now, but if there had been any such gossip, I would have heard it. Poor Frances's death was still vivid in our memories.'

Thank you, Toby, Georgia thought, for the opening. 'In

the statement you made to the police and from the trial reports in the press I gather you were present at the quarrel between Fanny and Adam that afternoon.'

'Not present,' he said, looking injured. 'I was with Hazel Perry near the walled rose garden when we heard them quarrelling on the other side of the wall. Quite unmistakable. They were talking about their future: Fanny was saying that she would be much better on her own with Jonathan, and Adam crying that she was out of her mind. Most distressing.'

'With the implication that Jonathan was her lover?' She remembered the wording of Toby's statement, and it varied slightly from Hazel's.

'I thought so at the time.'

'And now?'

'Those were the sixties. There was love and love, and I have always thought it strange . . .' He grinned. 'But my lips are sealed.'

'You couldn't unseal them?' she suggested politely. 'We don't want dirt, only the truth.'

'Then I should not spread rumours.' Another smirk.

Be blowed if she'd let him get away with that. She'd attack his weak point.

'The Friday Street music was heard the evening Fanny died. Somebody believed Adam innocent. Who else here would have wanted Fanny dead?'

Toby looked vague. 'Who can tell? Practically the whole village came to Downey Hall that day. The grounds were not locked, and who knows who might have lingered to wreak revenge?'

Revenge for what? 'It's true anyone might have lingered,' she allowed tartness to enter her voice, 'but not just anyone could have marched into the house to pick up that dagger.' She was imagining Toby as young man, pawing Fanny, thick-lipped and lascivious. He'd have been the kind to hover on the outskirts of a group, awaiting an opportunity. Had he found it with Fanny?

'Ah, now.' He wagged a finger at her. 'Miss Marple showed her true colours.'

He was beginning to get to her like a knife squeaking across a plate. 'If only I were,' she rallied, and took a way-out step into the dark. 'The music,' she said. 'Is there perhaps a tradition that the player of the music might be the true guilty party? Is it an admission to his peers?'

Toby's eyes flickered. 'Ingenious, Georgia, but unlikely, given human nature. Your theory might almost make a deodand out of the flute.' He rose to his feet, beckoning her to follow. 'Come with me. I'd like to show you my collection again.'

Somewhat puzzled, she followed him to the museum – still unlocked, she noted – and he switched on the lights. 'Gloomy, isn't it?' he said gaily. 'It's a place of death, you see. Easy to forget that, when one's looking in a museum. Everyone thinks my passion is weird, but if I had letters after my name, and a professional lab out here called Beamish Laboratories, no one would think it at all strange. Where do all the objects that cause death now land up, eh? With the police, in labs, in storage, so that they can have fingerprints lifted, glove prints, DNA, bloodstains, and goodness knows what else. They're the path to the murderers. Not so very different to deodands, or indeed to your quaint idea about the flute. What do you think about it, eh?' He was looking at her expectantly.

'You mean all these objects that caused death in the past are evidence in the same way, but we didn't have the means to extract it then?'

'Precisely. Let's say they're all here waiting to tell their tales. They were present at the crime. Take that carver fork that intrigued you on your last visit or this knife. It was used by a butler to kill a housekeeper in the eighteenth century. One wonders what illicit passions had been at stake there. Dear me, a pun of sorts. I do apologize.'

He beamed at her. 'Or take this axe,' he continued. 'It killed a girl in Chatham in the early nineteenth century. The villain was never caught. In the case of Frances, he was, although you now doubt that.'

She began to understand. 'Is that what intrigues you about the deodands? That the evidence remains here waiting?'

He gave her a strange smile. 'That's right. What a clever girl you are. And poor dear Frances's story is waiting for you to record it.'

She wanted out. She wanted to be in the fresh air, away from the claustrophobia induced by this man. She struggled to define what she found objectionable about him, but the only word that came to mind was glutinous – unwieldy, sticky – and one might never be rid of him. Cadenza loved him, Georgia told herself, but could not, in her heart, understand that. She fought for calm, as though there were nothing unusual about this place. And indeed perhaps there was not. But just for a moment, faced with Toby Beamish, she had sensed an abyss that would engulf her – as had happened to Rick, her brother, who had disappeared into a black hole of life, never to reappear. It was usually her father who suffered these strange turns, but for some reason one had now hit her. She breathed deeply as they walked back into the house, and realized she was strong again.

'One thing,' her voice still sounded strange, however, 'seems odd to me. I've been told – forgive me – that the Ludds and the Beamishes have never got on, and so it seems peculiar that you, Michael and Oliver were all in the same gang, and were even invited to his engagement party.' *Tom*, she thought, these three who together had scared Frances. No wonder. Toby alone was beginning to scare *her*.

'Perhaps you don't understand how villages work.' Toby bestowed a patronizing smile on her. 'You are quite correct that our two families are not on good terms, but at some events it is necessary to show a united social front. I was indeed a member of the gang – children fortunately are above such pettiness – ' Were they? thought Georgia. Not in her experience ' – and Henry Ludd invited both me and my parents. He was then reasonably well established in the village, and my parents thought it only polite to accept. I recall my mother commenting, "Of course, they're *trade*." Neither Joan nor Henry could, in her eyes, be considered gentry, and such things were then still important. Joan was born a farmer's daughter in the Darenth Valley, I believe, and Henry came from a prosperous flour-milling company that had diversified into what were then called fancy cakes. The cake-maker was my dear father's humorous name for him – he had met Henry and Joan during the war. My father used to say the RAF offered opportunities to smooth out infelicities of birth. The gang had the same effect.'

Georgia looked at a photograph of the Beamish wedding, which was standing on the window ledge at her side. Judging by the bride's dress the wedding was in the middle to late thirties. Charles Beamish was a handsome young man in RAF uniform (obviously a regular, not hostilities-only) and his bride a pretty, rather insipid dark-haired girl. Poor man, to produce the Toby of today, she thought, but told herself she should be impartial.

'When did the estrangement start between your two families?'

'Do you know, I'm not sure. Such a long time ago. There was always dislike, and as I am sure dear Josh has told you, my wife saw fit to prefer a Ludd to me after many years of marriage. This certainly put an end to any pretence of liking between the Ludds and Beamishes.'

'Even though Michael was your best friend in the gang?'

'Was he?' Toby's eyes flickered. 'I'm not sure I would express it that way. Did *he*? There was a bond between all gang members, still is. I'm not sure friendship enters into it. Loyalty expresses it more correctly.'

Interesting. Did it glue them together even where murder was concerned? It was time to try surprise tactics again. 'Was there sexual rivalry between you over Frances?'

A creepy smile came to his lips. No smile in his eyes though, she noticed. 'Why should there be? My former wife was a member of the gang, as was Sheila Ludd. Michael and I had our own sweethearts. Dear Josh was Frances's swain.'

He was challenging her, that was clear. She took a sip of the coffee that had arrived courtesy of Cadenza who had wafted in and out with a forgiving smile in a whirl of unsuitably girlish Indian cottons.

'Nevertheless, Fanny was an attractive girl and so over the years there must have been tensions.'

'If so, they had all vanished by 1968,' Toby said smoothly, 'the year in which you are interested. I was long married and Michael engaged to Sheila.'

'Someone, possibly in the gang, must have disliked Fanny enough to murder her.'

'The fact that nothing transpired after that proves the player was mistaken.'

'And who decides that?'

The mousetrap snapped shut at last. Toby looked distinctly thrown. 'The question was naturally much discussed in the village,' he said sharply. Then, obviously realizing she would not be satisfied with that, added, 'Perhaps I shouldn't be telling you this, but on the *slight* possibility there was a miscarriage of justice – and we in Friday Street are not omnipotent – I should confess that poor Frances was indeed a sexual creature, and there had formerly been tensions in the gang because of it. I recognized her attractiveness myself, though I quickly realized she was not my sort of woman. Liz was, unfortunately.'

'And Michael?'

A pause. 'He too liked Frances. He was older. Twenty-two when she left the village, and his brother Oliver fifteen. He too liked Frances.' Another pause. 'I should remind you there were many outsiders present that afternoon in 1968, one – ' a waggle of the finger ' – very close to Fanny.'

For a moment, deep in thought about Tom, she did not understand. Then realization came: Jonathan Powell. So it wasn't only Josh who was anxious to point out the likelihood of Jonathan's involvement.

'And,' Toby continued reflectively, 'there is poor Josh himself.'

'He told me he was fond of her.'

'Rather more than fond, my dear. No, I shouldn't so address you, should I? Most politically incorrect.' Toby giggled. 'Josh was so protective that the rest of us hardly dared address her. It's my belief, though I hate to say this, that that is why she left the village. Certainly she wished fame and fortune in the music world, but she was only seventeen when she left. I have always thought she felt squashed between her parents and Josh's devotion. Frances sought freedom, not suffocation. Josh was always *there*, her . . .'

'Her pet spaniel?' Georgia suggested when he paused.

Toby laughed. 'Her rottweiler.'

There were unexpected prickles at the back of Georgia's neck as she drove up to Downey Hall the following day. She had an odd feeling that she was covering a route already mapped out for her. As, indeed, she supposed it was. Josh had arranged for Henry, Michael and Sheila Ludd, and for Toby and Josh himself to be present. All members of the gang, in fact, including Hazel Perry. Or perhaps, as reason re-established itself, it was the thought of what might depend on this afternoon that was causing these prickles.

Peter had preferred to come separately and she could see his car parked in front of the house. The interior of Downey Hall was not as she had expected. Neat and tidy, yes, but not a bow to modern, gracious living. Instead, as Sheila ushered her through, she saw a treasure trove about the history of the house and the Kentish downs.

'When my father-in-law first moved here,' Sheila explained when Georgia commented on this, 'he scoured every antique and second-hand shop he could find for prints of Downey in earlier years, both this building and its predecessors on the site. Henry even dug out an old oil painting, which he swears is the last of the Montashes and painted in Downey, for all the Beamishes claim them for the Manor. I think he's still hoping there's a family link between them and the Ludds. A great sense of dynasty, has my father-in-law.'

The Ludds, too, were well represented, Georgia noticed, stopping before an oil painting of a woman in a 1950s strapless evening dress with billowing skirts. 'Who's this?' she asked.

'My late mother-in-law, Joan. She was a beauty . . .'

Georgia agreed, but she looked a cold one. She remembered Jonathan's description of a sour-faced woman and could easily see how it could be so. The pout of provocativeness in the painting could have become permanent with the passing of the years and ceased to be so attractive.

'I gather she was born in the north of Kent.'

'Yes. She met Henry when he was stationed at Biggin Hill in 1938. With war looming, it was a whirlwind romance and marriage. Result: Michael. Then there was a gap of nearly seven years before Oliver, thanks to the war. Still, the Ludd family history isn't what you came for, is it? There's plenty of it to be seen here, though. We were living in the cottage until about 1990. We call it that as a joke, but it's a house. You've probably seen it, a white one next to this estate with an entrance in Green Lane. Henry and Joan lived in the Hall up until then, and he still likes things kept as they were here.'

She ushered Georgia into the drawing room where the rest of the party was already gathered around Peter in his wheelchair, almost as if they were posing for a family portrait. No, that wasn't it, Georgia realized. It was as if they'd been called in to face the headmaster. In their faces, she could see the young men and women of 1968, as conflicting emotions fought in them. Hazel was belligerent, ready to be on the offensive at any slight, Michael was the head boy hurt at being unjustly accused, but nevertheless distinctly flustered. Sheila was, well, Sheila, confident that no blame attached to her. Toby (this must be the first time he had set foot in this house in a long while) was sweating, looking the picture of guilt; Josh was the good lad, determined not to grass on his chums. And Henry? Henry was the outsider, and surely must always have been, the English gentleman who was automatically above suspicion.

'Shall we begin?' Peter suggested lightly. Let battle commence would be more like it, Georgia thought.

Peter let the following silence run for just the right amount of time before breaking it. 'Where was lunch held?'

There was instant relaxation at this innocuous beginning. 'I believe,' Henry answered, 'that Fanny, Adam and their entourage arrived shortly before it began at about one o'clock. I seem to recall that a buffet lunch was laid out in the dining room and people came and went. There was equipment and testing and so on to deal with. Our party gathered for the concert in front of the house shortly before it began at three p.m.'

'Shall we see the scene of the lunch?' Peter suggested. 'We might as well follow the entire route.'

'By all means.' Michael sounded heartier than he looked as he led the way to the dining room.

'How were Fanny and Adam when they arrived?' Georgia asked. 'Was there any animosity between them then? The witness statements – yours and Toby's, Hazel – placed their quarrel after the first concert.'

'If I said so, that was it,' Hazel snapped back. 'How do you expect us to remember now? It was over thirty years ago.'

'Because of what happened, there's a chance we might remember,' Josh said quietly, taking her arm. He was right, Georgia thought; extremes of tragedy or happiness could fix surrounding details for ever in the mind. Not necessarily accurately, she had to consider; it was scary how different her and Peter's recollections of the past could sometimes be. Of Rick, of Elena – stop right there, she told herself. Why had they popped up now of all times? Was it by communal thought transference, because everyone here was thinking of the traumatic events of that June day in 1968 – or trying *not* to think about them?

'Waste of time, all this is. I'm due at the church.' Hazel looked at the rest of the party, as if inviting support, but no one spoke.

'Did Fanny's parents attend the lunch?' Peter took over again. 'Or did they arrive afterwards for the concert?'

There was some discussion on this. 'The latter, we believe,' Henry answered, sliding open the doors to the terrace. 'This is the way I left that day; I can't speak for the others. Frances and Adam had already left to prepare for the concert, as had the rest of their party. I found myself with Mr and Mrs Beamish. I remember that as – forgive me, Toby – I could not recall inviting the family to lunch. They were to join us later, as did Fanny's parents.'

'That's all right, Henry.' Toby beamed. 'We realized it was an oversight on your part, Henry. No offence taken.'

What was that all about? Georgia wondered. Clever of Toby, but the glance he gave Henry didn't suggest a warm, forgiving heart. It was the first time Georgia had seen steel in Henry. Not so much the outsider, perhaps. His face remained impassive, but the tension in the room had increased.

Michael hastily led them out of the house – he or Sheila had thoughtfully provided ramps for Peter, and Georgia's opinion of them shot up. She let Peter do the talking as they followed the path round the house to the side gate, passing the side entrance to the house, through the gate and into the front grounds, where the cows replaced the crowds that must have been here that day. Walking over the grass, she tried to imagine it packed with people, eagerly awaiting a pop concert, loudspeakers blaring out SFA music.

'Did you have chairs set out here?' she asked Michael.

'No, we all sat on the grass. Chairs would have been out of place, don't you think? In any case, we couldn't run to that many chairs.'

Georgia found it hard to see even a younger, slimmer Michael Ludd flopping casually on the grass, let alone the elegant Sheila.

'Did you know Fanny's parents well?' she asked Henry.

'I didn't care for Ronald Gibb.'

'Frances must have hated it. She loathed Ron Gibb,' Sheila

said decidedly. 'We were all sitting in a group in front of the stage, while she and Adam were preparing to sing. I saw the look on her face when Doreen and Ron came to join us. Her feelings hadn't changed.'

'She did a good job in hiding it,' Josh said defensively. 'She came right down to greet them, had quite a chat, so far as I remember.'

'Even if her dislike of her father made her leave the village,' Peter said, 'there was probably some one incident that sparked off her decision to go when she did. Any ideas, Josh?'

He didn't reply. Instead he addressed the group, almost as if he were asking permission to speak. And that, she realized, was just what he *was* doing. 'Well?' he said. Nothing. And there wasn't going to be unless she took a hand, Georgia realized. No problem. She'd had enough.

'Don't any of you even care what happened?' she stormed. 'One after another of you assures us that the gang stuck together, that loyalty was so important. How about showing some loyalty for Frances Gibb?'

Another silence, but a shocked one this time.

'We need answers,' Peter said, supporting her. 'Not half truths and dances round the merry maypole.'

It could go one way or the other. Georgia held her breath.

Josh eventually took the lead – of course. 'I'm prepared. Are you, Toby?'

'As you like, dear boy.'

'Hazel?'

'Tell them and get it over with. For heaven's sake, it's time.'

'Michael?'

Michael hesitated. 'Yes. You're right, I suppose.'

'I don't agree,' Sheila said sharply. 'It would be a betrayal of her. Henry? What do you think?'

Henry nodded. 'Tell them, Josh.'

He looked uncomfortable, forced into a limelight he wouldn't have chosen. 'Frances left Friday Street because she was pregnant.'

So that was it. So obvious, Georgia thought. Why on earth hadn't it occurred to her earlier?

Peter took it in his stride. 'Did you all know that in 1961, when she left?'

Sheila gave a short laugh. 'I knew; I was close to Frances. And *he* did.' She looked at Josh. 'Only too well.'

'Just what do you mean by that?' Hazel yelled at her.

'Quiet, love,' Josh said sharply. 'We know what she means. That Frances confided in me. It's no secret that I loved her then. She told me she was leaving, she was pregnant and going to get an abortion. I tried to stop her – she appeared to believe me when I said I'd help – but by morning she was gone. I never heard from or saw her again until I saw her on the telly as Fanny Star. That's what you meant, isn't it, Sheila?'

She shrugged, and Peter stepped in for her. 'Were you the father of the child, Josh?'

He flushed in anger. 'No, I bloody wasn't. I loved her. You think I'd let her go away to get rid of my kid? No way. I'd have chained her down if I had to, to stop her leaving.'

Peter wasn't deterred. 'Then who was?'

Silence. It was still the silence of secrets, not of ignorance, Georgia thought. The group in the headmaster's study was sticking together to protect the guilty, whether present or not.

'She wouldn't tell me,' Josh said. 'She just went.'

'But she came back,' Georgia intervened. 'Was that to see the father?'

Sheila's ice-cold voice answered her. 'Why do you think she didn't get on with Ron Gibb?'

Dear heaven. Georgia felt sick. The image of the famous pop star had been a cover for the scummy reality of her earlier life. 'Her father had been abusing her? Is that true, Josh?' Whatever Sheila said, she wasn't going to believe this without his word too.

'She never told me, but I reckoned so then,' he said stilt-edly. 'He whacked her around, she had odd bruises a lot of the time. I could believe it of him.'

107

'She told me it was him,' Sheila confirmed. 'I helped find the abortionist. Not easy in those days.'

'And you kept in touch with her?'

'I wanted to.' Her cool voice broke a little. 'When I didn't hear from her, I followed it up with the abortionist, but she hadn't used that one after all. I never heard from her again. When she hit the charts, I tried to contact her, via her manager, but she didn't reply. "No more Friday Street" was the obvious message.'

No wonder. Georgia could understand that all too well. And yet Fanny *had* returned. Why? To see her mother, even if it meant seeing her abuser too? Nothing had been said to suggest that that was the case; there'd been no mention of any tête-à-têtes between the two.

'What happened after the concert?' Peter had clearly decided it was time to move on. He must have seen the impasse too.

The head boy took over the reconstruction as he led them back through the gate into the rear gardens. 'The village audience gradually dispersed,' Michael explained, 'and the rest of us came back here or into the house. Tea was served from four o'clock but not many of us dropped in to have any. We were too busy chatting. Dinner was an early one, with drinks at six, and the meal half an hour later. Some of us needed to change. So for a couple of hours we were all wandering around drinking tea or alcohol and talking.'

'And Fanny and Adam?' Peter asked. 'Mr Beamish, and you, Mrs Perry, overheard them quarrelling. Where was that?'

'I'll show you.' Toby took obvious pleasure in having a role to play. Almost as good as his ghost tours, Georgia thought wryly. As indeed this was, in a sense. He led the way to the formal gardens on the right of the house. 'We were sitting here.' Toby halted by an old Tudor brick wall in which there was a stone bench set back with bushes on either side, and a rather nice stone fountain. 'The rose garden is the other side of this wall – if,' he said with heavy irony to Henry, 'I remember correctly.' In other words, because he wasn't welcome at Downey Hall.

It slid smoothly off Henry's back. 'You do, Toby. It is still a rose garden.'

'Did the quarrel begin after you arrived?' Peter asked. Georgia could see he was envisaging a profitable session with Suspects Anonymous as soon as he returned home.

'No.' Hazel was keeping her oar in too. 'It was in full swing as we arrived. That must have been about an hour after the concert ended, and so getting on for five o'clock. Toby thought we should stay and listen.' This was said apparently innocently, but the sting was there.

'You know what we heard. We said it all to the police at the time. We stayed,' Hazel continued belligerently, 'until that Mr Powell arrived. I recognized his voice from earlier. When he arrived, Frances said something that sounded like "I'm off", and then she was. She shot through the rose garden entrance, saw us, glared, and told us to get the hell out of it.'

'And did you?' Peter asked politely.

'We did.'

Why should Fanny walk away if she and Jonathan were lovers? Georgia wondered. She didn't seem the type to leave it to two men to sort out a quarrel in which she was involved. She was a fighter.

'Anyone know where she went then?' Peter asked. 'She was very drunk and abusive at the dinner.'

'She was all right when it began,' Josh said. 'I remember being relieved, because Doreen and Ron were there. She seemed under control. She was even saying it was wonderful to be back with her family.'

'She certainly changed,' Sheila said wryly.

But why? Georgia wondered. Or was she making too much of this?

'Let's go back into the dining room,' Peter suggested. The room took on a different aspect now, as Georgia imagined the long table set here. It was a large room, but it must have been a squash all the same. Had Fanny felt claustrophobic, shut in with the gang, and with her abusive father?

'She had too much to drink,' Sheila began.

'There wasn't much time,' Peter objected. 'She was only at the table about three quarters of an hour, before you took her out.'

'She must have been on the hard stuff beforehand, is all I can think,' Sheila replied, frowning. 'She certainly started shouting everyone down – does everyone agree? You were sitting next to her, weren't you, Josh?'

'Yes.'

Not tactful placing if by then Josh was married to Hazel, Georgia thought. 'Any ideas on why she changed?'

'It happened gradually. She was opposite Ron Gibb, remember. That must have brought back a few unwelcome memories,' he said. 'She—'

'Began to shout about Friday Street,' Toby interrupted with relish. 'Apparently we didn't know we were born. So caught up in pretty family flowers we couldn't see the shit underneath. It was all cant and c—'

'Poor Frances,' Henry's gentle voice cut over Toby's.

'It was at that point,' Sheila said coldly, 'that I thought it best to remove Fanny from the table. Do you wish to see the bathroom? It's on the first floor.'

Georgia glanced at Peter, who nodded. He wouldn't be able to get up there, but he was indicating that it would be worth seeing from the point of view of location. The group all followed – perhaps, she thought, aware that the drama of that day was approaching its end, and it was all too willing to delay it.

The bathroom – or at least the one Fanny had used, since there must surely be another in a house of this size – was approached by the back staircase, and not far from it. The lavatory was in the bathroom itself, and conjured up a vivid picture of the scene, despite its modern trappings.

'In the ten or fifteen minutes I was with her,' Sheila said, 'she was ranting on in much the same way as she had at the table about how much she hated the village and that at least now she had a chance to breathe fresh air in London. All nonsense. She'd had a raw deal over Ron, but blaming the village for that was a bit much. She told me to get out and leave her, so I did. I went back to the party to tell Michael what was happening, and then, when she didn't appear for coffee in the drawing room, went back to check she was all right. She'd vanished – she must have gone out through the side entrance – and I presumed she was all right. She'd been sick after all, and needed air to recover.'

'So there's a blank period between Mrs Perry seeing her just before five, and drinks at six o'clock, and then again between seven forty and the time of her death. Any advance on that?' Peter asked.

'As I mentioned in my statement,' Toby said righteously, 'I saw her leaving the house as the party was breaking up, about twenty to eight. I was wandering about enjoying my first *real* look at Downey Hall,' he didn't even look at the Ludds, 'and there was Frances, looking very white and in a furious temper still. She told me she was off for a quiet think. When we began to hunt for Frances, I suggested she might have been making for Owlers' Smoke, as it was the first place anyone in the gang would make for if seeking a quiet retreat. That, alas, is where Henry and Michael found her.'

'Is it possible to reconstruct where you all were during that hour and a half?'

'I doubt it,' Sheila said. 'We were here, and then – I'm sure I speak for everyone in this – suddenly we were there, looking at Frances's dead body and Adam Jones.'

'Was he standing or kneeling?'

'The latter when Dad and I arrived,' Michael said. 'Rocking to and fro.'

'Where was Jonathan Powell?' Georgia asked, determined not to lose sight of her 'prong' of the investigation.

'That's the first thing I remember in the hunt for Fanny,' Michael said. 'I'd been having a talk with Father about business matters, and then we rejoined the guests about twenty

111

past eight. We were just thinking we'd walk over for the concert when Powell came rushing in – that would have been about ten to nine – and said that he couldn't find Fanny. Father and I shot off to Owlers' Smoke immediately.'

'And the rest of you?'

'It was pointless our all running to the Smoke,' Sheila answered, 'so I searched the bedroom she'd been using in case she was lying down – and the bathrooms, of course. Another party set off to look in the grounds in front of the house in case she was collecting stuff from the afternoon stage.'

'I rushed to the stage in the rear gardens,' Toby murmured. 'Such a noise while they sound-checked. No doubt that drowned out any screams poor dear Fanny gave.'

It was an unpleasant image, and how like Toby to point it out, Georgia thought.

'No one thought the situation serious then,' he continued, 'but when I returned to the house, I saw Henry running across the lawn to ring the police. That would have been about nine o'clock. Then we all made for Owlers' Smoke. Foolish, perhaps, but that's what happened. We needed to see for ourselves.'

'Shall we go?' Peter asked gently. It was the moment that some here at least must have been dreading. Facing Owlers' Smoke and recalling what had taken place there.

'There's somewhere else we should go first,' Georgia suggested. 'The entrance hall, from where Adam is supposed to have taken the dagger.' With the display case no longer there, she had not been able to get a mental picture of how easy it would have been for Adam or anyone else to remove it.

'The display case was here.' Michael sounded belligerent, having marched them all through, as if he expected to be challenged on the point. 'It's no longer here, and nor, of course, is the dagger.'

Georgia glimpsed Toby's face. Was he thinking of the gap in his collection or of where the dagger was now, still with the police as evidence in the Alice Winters case? The same thought must have occurred to others there, bringing past and present uncomfortably close.

'Adam could have easily taken it,' Michael said.

'Even though he was on his way to escort the Gibbs home?'

'Certainly. He would have come this way and out by the front entrance,' Michael said firmly. 'He must have planned it, and it was all too easy for him to put his plan into action.'

'And how did he know that Fanny would conveniently be in Owlers' Smoke when he returned?' Georgia asked. No one answered her.A significant point to be noted.

There was silence as they walked out through the side entrance of the house across to the woodland where Owlers' Smoke lay. Crowded into the glade with the bench and memorial stone, the group stood awkwardly, as if longing to escape rather than face the past.

'The body,' Peter began matter-of-factly – the only way to do it, 'was lying on a mac. Why? Was she wearing or carrying it when you saw her, Toby?'

'I don't recall, I'm afraid. Not wearing it, certainly.'

'She could have picked it up for warmth, either on the stage or in the house,' Michael suggested.

'Did either you or Henry recognize it?' Peter continued.

Michael picked up the gauntlet. 'No. It could have been in the house though. She came from the side entrance, and there were a number of coats and boots kept there for garden purposes. It could well have been one of ours.'

'But why take it? She only had a skimpy dress and it was late evening, but a plastic mac wouldn't have given her much warmth.'

'It was overcast that evening. It looked as though it might rain,' Henry offered.

'If Fanny was distraught I doubt if she'd have cared about that,' Georgia said. Another loose end. But there was an even more important one that still defied them.

'The music was played over the amplifiers that night,' she

continued. 'Had you discussed Adam's guilt amongst your-selves?'

Alice must have been in their minds, for no one answered. They had all heard that music again all too recently. At last Sheila said, 'I can't remember doing so. Can you?' She appealed to Michael. 'But Adam's guilt seemed obvious, and we were so shocked and horrified that there was little point discussing it.'

'This music,' Georgia said, exasperated. 'It's so important to you all that you keep it quiet and refuse to talk about it. And yet it *achieves* nothing. Not with Fanny, nor with Alice. Don't you think there's something odd about that?'

Josh flushed. 'We can't change the world, Georgia. We're not Superman here. We can't roll back the curtains and *know* whether someone's guilty or not.'

Peter took up the cudgels. 'No discussion in the village? Nothing, even though you all knew Ron, for example, would have had a motive? I find that hard to believe. Just as I find it hard to believe you're ignoring Alice Winters' death in the same way.'

They were clamming up again. Head boy Michael was obviously deputed by telepathy to answer. 'Alice Winters' death is in police hands. Over Fanny, only Sheila and I, and perhaps Josh, knew about Ron. Not even her mother. We were stuck. We couldn't even raise the possibility.'

'Even though an innocent man was charged with murder?'

'We didn't *know* he was innocent,' Sheila pointed out firmly. 'We thought Adam guilty.'

'We did our best,' Josh admitted, with obvious reluctance. 'After hearing the music, Hazel and I visited Doreen on her own, just to chat we said. She told us Adam had left them at the Hall gates and she and Ron had been together after that. They heard police cars and sirens, and went to see what was going on. That satisfied us that Ron had an alibi. Besides, he's dead. He's not here to answer for himself.'

Nor, Georgia thought, was Adam. 'If Adam returned to the village in 1987, as we believe he did, he could have had two missions; firstly to see the place where it all happened, and secondly to see her parents. Was Ron Gibb alive then?'

'Yes,' Josh said. 'He died only five, maybe seven years ago.'

'He didn't come to see Owlers' Smoke, or the Gibbs,' Henry said.

It was the first time he had spoken for some time, and his words had all the more effect. 'How can you know?' Georgia asked.

'Because he came to see me.'

'I seem to be popular today,' Henry said drily as he opened the door of his home. Having refused to explain his statement before the assembled gathering he had quietly suggested to Peter and Georgia that they return on the morrow, Sunday. Peter had despatched her alone, on the basis that one might achieve more than two, particularly in this case. Besides, he explained, there was a lot of work to be done on Suspects Anonymous.

As Sheila had said, it was a substantial house, though hardly on the scale of Downey Hall. As Georgia was led through into Henry's 'den', which proved to be a comfortable sitting room that served as library, musical room and one for general relaxation, she found the reason for his comment. Dana Tucker was already installed.

'I've been pumping Henry like crazy,' she said brightly, as soon as she saw Georgia, 'about Fanny and Adam's last concert. I didn't know he came to the village on the day he died. Don't mind me, though. Just pretend I'm not here.'

Difficult, Georgia thought crossly, but if Henry didn't mind then she was in no position to object.

'I want to explain to you about Adam Jones,' Henry began. 'I didn't recognize him at first. He had changed from the young man I recalled. He was in his late forties, and had had a hard life in prison. Once he told me his name, however, I could see the younger man in his face.'

'He came to the Hall intending to see Michael?'

'No. To see me. It was – and still is, in fact – my house.

115

I believe in continuity, not in avoiding inheritance tax, though naturally I am willing to do so within limits. I was still living in the Hall when Adam Jones called, and Michael and Sheila lived here.'

'Why did he want to see you? How did he seem?' The questions tumbled out. 'Was it the same day as he killed himself?'

'It was. A Friday, the unlucky day. Tenth April, 1987. He assured me he was innocent of Frances's death.'

'Did he ask for help in tracking down Fanny's murderer, or did he want to tackle the man responsible for her pregnancy?' Georgia asked.

'No.' Henry looked tired. 'He didn't mention the latter, and didn't want the former.'

'Then,' Georgia was bewildered, 'why come to *you*?'

'He came,' Henry paused for a moment, 'to play me a song. One of their hits, I gathered, "Allan Water". It was what Frances would have wanted, he said. He'd brought his guitar specially, and asked me to walk to Owlers' Smoke with him. Once there, he played the song to me. We sat quietly for a while and then he said he must leave. I didn't ask where.'

Puzzling. 'Did you understand why Fanny should have wanted that?'

'I imagine, as he committed suicide later, that he wanted to play their music once more in the place where she died.'

Josh Perry listened to Georgia in silence. The pub was already beginning to hum, ready for the evening. He thought for a moment, got up from his chair and went to the door.

'Hazel,' he called, 'have you got a minute?'

Hazel, swathed in kitchen cap and apron, arrived looking somewhat harried, which was natural enough with evening food to prepare.

'Georgia's barking up the Ron Gibb tree now. Even if he was the father of her child, she doesn't see how he could have killed Frances, unless he left End Cottage earlier than

Adam did that night – and Adam would have told the police that. So Georgia's hunting for someone else. She's sorry to have to ask me again, but she begs me to tell her if I made Frances pregnant. What's your opinion on that, love?'

To her relief, Hazel didn't look in the least bit vexed. Instead she snorted, 'Josh and me were wed a year after Fanny left. And I can tell you, if Josh had been having it off with anyone at all, he put up a bloody good show of not knowing a bird from a bee.'

Josh cleared his throat. 'Now that we're clear about that . . . Anything else you'd like to know?'

'Yes, please.' Georgia was grateful for the opportunity. 'I'd like to ask you, Hazel, about the row between Adam and Fanny.'

'*Again*? What about it?'

'Is it at all possible that since you and Toby weren't there from the beginning you could have been mistaken about what you heard?'

'How?' Hazel looked mulish.

'For instance,' Georgia said, 'you and Toby varied slightly in what you said you heard.'

Hazel sighed. 'How?'

'You heard, "Don't forget I can always go solo. We'd be better off on our own", whereas Toby heard, "This triangle's bloody impossible. We'd be much better off together".'

Hazel frowned. 'What of it? Same thing. She and Powell were a fixture whether he was only her manager or her fancy man too.'

'Isn't it possible that the "together" meant her and Adam, not her and Powell, and that what you heard was a threat followed by a plea?'

A long pause while Hazel considered this. 'It's possible,' she agreed reluctantly. 'I can't say for sure after all this time. My mind wasn't entirely on it at the time, to be honest. That Toby was only interested in pinching my bottom, and when he pulled me down on the bench, he had a go higher up. And him married to Liz.'

'And you to me,' Josh said grimly.

Hazel ignored this, with only a friendly punch. 'I can tell you there was a row going on between us too – that's why Frances saw us as she came by.'

'I still don't see what difference it makes,' Josh said.

'It means that Fanny could have been insisting to Adam that they sack Powell as their manager.' And if so, Powell was back in the frame, and even Peter couldn't ignore it.

'That would give him a reason to kill her,' Josh said immediately.

'Yes. It's one angle. Peter still thinks the answer lies in Friday Street, though, so you won't be getting rid of me yet.'

Josh took this semi-joke seriously. 'You take care, Georgia. My shoulders are broad, but there are others that aren't. I'm warning you for your own safety. Accidents happen in these lanes. You turn nasty bends and you can't work out where you are – that's you with this case at present, I reckon. Suddenly you'll find there's a bloody great tree in front of you, and it's too late to stop.'

Seven

'Why?' Georgia asked, for the umpteenth time, when they met for work on the Monday morning. Tomorrow they would be meeting Mike and still she had no answer as to why there was suddenly a lack of evidence against Jake Baines.

'I can only think it's because the evidence was so inconclusive. Not of a lot of blood, which would fit either Jake's story that Alice was already dead when he arrived and found the dagger still in the wound, *or* his being guilty.'

'What else was there?'

'The crime scene, thanks to the arrival of Toby and his ghost tour troops, resembled a battlefield. Jake's dabs on the knife were useless since the defence would naturally say it was there because of his role in the ghost play. He'd been waving it around for the last year or two. Any DNA left on Alice's body could be put down to his touching her to see if she was still alive. Dear Toby had his prints on the knife too, and he was the one person in Friday Street who couldn't have killed Alice, since she'd gone straight from the pub to the tower at three o'clock and he was in full ghost tour mode. When he arrived to find Toby and a dozen tourists milling around, the crime scene manager nearly tore his hair out – only refrained in case it added to the scientific confusion.'

'So where does that leave us?'

'With a chance, dear Georgia.'

She could read his mind like a book in large print. 'Of finding a link between the murders? Peter, they're separated by over thirty-five years. You're theorizing too quickly again.'

'Only until I find it, then I'll have proof.' A quick glance at her. 'Or if I don't, we'll drop the case, I promise. My hunch is that we won't get any further with Fanny Star *until* we find that link. Anything your end look hopeful?'

'Far from it. We agreed with Josh to keep off Alice Winters in return for his co-operation over Fanny Star, but so far there's been no reason not to do so.'

'Until now.' A great sigh of satisfaction. 'Let us see what tomorrow morning brings forth, since Mike has so nobly offered' (which Georgia translated as 'been forcibly persuaded') 'to show us the crime scene. He did so in case, he admitted a little grudgingly, anything we've turned up on Fanny Star brought in a Winters connection. Apart, of course, from the obvious: the use of the same dagger.'

'And Toby Beamish,' Georgia added. Somehow it would be very satisfying to put him in the frame, even if, she had to admit, the Tobys of this world were seldom the sort to fit it.

'Of course, in both cases the ghost of Lady Rosamund appeared in the guise of the flute music. It looks as if whoever played it after Jake's arrest was right to do so.'

Georgia did not have sweet dreams that night. Toby, dressed as Lady Rosamund, was singing on a makeshift stage in the garden, while Hazel Perry emerged from the pub kitchens with a large knife and set off vengefully towards him. Or was he chasing her? In the midst of this maelstrom she opened her eyes with one surprisingly rational thought: how and when did Dana hear about Adam visiting Friday Street? From Henry before she arrived, or from Luke?

The morning dismissed this annoying detail for what it was. On a late spring day, with the wild flowers covering the banks that flanked the lanes, and even a short burst of sunshine to herald summer, it was hard to associate the tower with death.

As Georgia parked by the gate and Peter swung himself out into his wheelchair, the sight of Mike Gilroy marching towards them quickly brought it home that this was indeed a murder scene. Solid, tall, and his expression impassive, Mike always looked the same on such occasions, whether it was a stabbing outside a seedy back-street pub or a suspicious death in a rose garden. Georgia enjoyed seeing Peter unconsciously slipping back into police mode himself as they talked. She had no doubt the whole village was aware of their presence. How was it reacting to Jake Baines' release? An unwelcome spotlight would once again be thrown on to Friday Street.

'We've the pleasure of Mr Toby Beamish's company this morning, Peter,' Mike said grimly. 'Says he has to unlock it personally. Only one key. Nose twitcher, that's what he is.'

'Tell him he's a suspect.' Peter didn't bother to lower his voice.

'He'd vanish like a ghost at dawn,' Georgia told him. '*Are* you looking for anyone else for this one, Mike?'

'Usually with a CPS decision like this, no. In this case, perhaps.'

'So you do have a few butterflies to chase?' Georgia said. Where and who? she wondered, reluctantly aware that even she was in search of that missing link.

'Come off it, Georgia,' Mike chided her. 'You find a burglar in your house with your grannie's best silver in his hands, and we don't go looking for anyone else. That was the case with Baines; he was there with the dagger, which Toby usually brought. He had motive to kill her, and he was found with the recently killed body. Enough DNA on the body to set up a forensic lab on its own. What more could you want?'

'To know why you're prepared to open the investigation again.' Peter began to wheel his chair purposefully through the gate.

'We're not.' Mike stopped him, obviously needing more time without Toby Beamish's flapping ears. 'That's where you two *might* come in. Alice Winters was a tease with half the village running after her. Bright girl, doing her gap year, and off to university in the autumn. With the good life ahead, she wasn't going to tie herself down to Jake Baines. That's what the row was about between them the night before, he says. There was a witness to that, though, who says it wasn't serious. Josh Perry.'

'Him again?' Georgia said. Josh seemed to be the uncrowned King of Friday Street.

'Seems a reasonable chap,' Mike said, 'and the story is likely enough. Baines was afraid of losing her while he stayed on the farm, and she was off to greener fields. He wanted to put a ring on her finger, but she wasn't having any. If I can't have you, no one will. Bingo, dead body. I gather there were a couple of other swains in the picture that could have woken up the little green monster, too. Tim Perry was one. Met him, have you? And—'

'Don't tell me,' Georgia interrupted. 'Drew Ludd. Tim's best mate.'

'Right. Or perhaps not-so-best friend where Alice was concerned,' Mike said. 'Okay, let's go. Old Beamish will be busting his last button off. Thinks he's a real English gentleman, he does. Like I'm a Frenchie.'

'How do you see our Toby, Mike?' Peter asked, his chair speed nearing Olympic standard.

'Pompous ass.'

'How about pompous snake?' Georgia said. 'Don't go walking in any long grass with him.'

'Bit of a lech, is he?' Mike asked amiably.

'Used to be. May still be. I wouldn't care to find out.'

'Mr Marsh.' Toby stomped gushingly forward. 'So here we all are again. His parents are much relieved that Jake is home with them. Good souls, both of them. Do I gather my humble theatre barn is to provide the setting for another case for Marsh & Daughter?'

'It is not,' Georgia said firmly. 'We're only involved because Alice Winters' murder crosses a few boundaries with Fanny Star's.'

'Ah. My deodand dagger again. I had been looking forward to its return, but I see now, in view of Inspector Gilroy's presence, that I might have to wait a while.'

'Yes.' Mike offered no other comment.

'Of course,' Toby continued, twirling his key ring round his forefinger, 'practically anyone in the village could have taken it. My museum is not locked during the day, since I am in and out all the time. The guns are safely locked up, of course,' he said hastily. 'I hate to think that anyone in Friday Street might have crept in behind my back to take the dagger, but I'm afraid that seems to be the case. The routine, as I once explained to you, inspector, was that I collected the dagger on my way to the tower in the bus, or rather Cadenza collected it, and handed it to me. On the day of Alice's death, she was most concerned to find that it wasn't there. I was perturbed, but there was nothing I could do about it at the time, so Cadenza brought her cake knife as a substitute. It had been ready to do duty when the visitors returned from the tower.' He seemed rather pleased with himself for having such an efficient assistant.

'Jake claimed he found Alice already dead, with the dagger still in the wound. How did you think Jake got the dagger if he planned this?'

Mike hesitated, obviously because Toby was eagerly awaiting snippets of inside knowledge too. Should he go ahead? After all, it was history now. Peter put him out of his misery by giving the answer. 'Simple. No one would question seeing Jake at Pucken Manor. Even if he'd been seen with the dagger, it wouldn't have been hard to think up a reason.'

Toby nodded. 'He usually came to the barn about three thirty, the punters arrived at four o'clock and the show began about ten or fifteen minutes later, when they'd all finished their loo visits. I understand Baines says he wasn't there until five to four on the day of the murder.'

For Mike's sake, Georgia tactfully steered the conversation away from delicate territory. How did Toby 'understand' that? 'Despite what you say, wouldn't it have been a risk, Toby, for anyone not closely associated with the museum or

Pucken Manor to be seen in the grounds?' Georgia asked. He was hardly going to agree, she knew, but his answer might be interesting.

'I don't see why.' Toby looked distinctly huffy. 'People are always coming to the Manor, about this, that or the other. I am a parish councillor, after all, so even the Ludds have to call on official business every so often. Moreover, Cadenza has her duties as churchwarden and as the church is normally locked, people have to gain access somehow. We don't ask every caller whether they have one of my deodands tucked under their mackintoshes.'

'Is there usually somebody about in the grounds? A gardener?'

'One day a week. Harry Baines, in fact, dear Jake's uncle.'

Mystery explained? Georgia wondered.

'And I take it he saw nothing out of the ordinary?' Peter asked Toby. Mike was clearly torn between strict observance of protocol and interest in what might emerge.

'It was not his day for the garden. He comes on tour afternoons, however. He is Pepper's Ghost.' Toby laughed uncertainly. 'That is to say, not the ghost of Professor Pepper himself, but the effects man for the show. He comes on the bus with us, together with his assistant, Ted Hammond.'

The converted barn was more spacious than George had imagined from its outside appearance, holding about a hundred seats on a slightly raked floor. There was a roomy pit, where she could see the Pepper's Ghost apparatus propped up, a compact stage with steps down to the auditorium, a backdrop of the inside of the tower across the rear of the stage, and curtained wings. A quick exploration revealed a small changing room and toilet on one side, and a fire exit at the rear. This, Toby explained, was unlocked on tour days, and it was the duty of the first person to arrive to unlock it.

'Who was?' Georgia asked.

'Always Alice herself. She was a responsible girl, and

some time ago offered for a small fee to put out chairs and make everything ready, including the stage. She was anxious to earn money to help towards her university costs. She needed to be at the barn quite early anyway because of changing into her costume. Jake always came later than her, so Alice had the key.'

'So there is a spare one,' Peter pointed out mildly.

Toby flushed. 'Alice's key is with the police. Naturally I had the master. For the tower I alone have the key.'

Mike cleared his throat. 'I wonder if you'd do me a favour, Mr Beamish?'

'By all means.' Toby was the gracious upholder of justice.

'I need to know exactly how long it takes to drive to Winters' Farm and back at thirty miles an hour. Barring stop signs, of course.'

Toby looked put out and highly suspicious, but at least he meekly disappeared.

Mike heaved a sigh of relief. 'Now, let's get started. Baines claimed Alice herself had asked him to come later that day. There was someone she had to meet. Seemed unlikely to me.'

'Where did he come from?'

'The farm. And that takes six minutes and thirty-five seconds with a fair wind and a Honda motorbike like he's got.'

'Evidence as to what time he left?'

'Inexact.'

'Twenty minutes to the hour, fifteen, or twenty-five, according to various witnesses who heard or saw him. Alice was last seen in the pub just before three, but no sightings of her after that, so we don't know whether she went straight to the tower or not.'

'How big was the crime scene, Mike?' Peter asked.

'Biggest in a long time,' Mike said. 'We had to rope off the whole field, from where you parked beyond the gate over to the far side of the stile. And a tough job it was; being grass, there's no respect for footpaths.'

'Why the stile?'

'One or two of the tour visitors used the footpath from the church rather than the bus. More atmospheric, our Toby claims.'

Georgia had a vision of ghostly cows stolidly pursuing intrepid tourists and littering up Mike's crime scene.

'Pick up any trace evidence by the fire exit?' Peter asked.

Mike shook his head. 'Tarmac path all the way round the building. Nothing but a few cans and tissues from late-night revellers. The scientists crawled over the fields, but we can't take the shoeprints of everyone in Friday Street.'

'Any other way the killer could escape if Jake isn't guilty?'

'Plenty. He could dash across the lane and the fields opposite, or go further down the lane and pick up a track back to Winters' Farm.'

'Did the local residents hear anything?'

'Heard a few cars going up and down the road, but there always are. There's a farm entrance further along the lane, which has a fair amount of traffic, so it's not unusual to hear cars here. Not all tourists stick to the motorways, either. A couple heard Jake Baines' motorbike coming down, but couldn't be precise enough to pin it down to the time he says he got there.'

'The main trace evidence was in here, of course.' Mike led the way back to the stage and Georgia followed him, while Peter nosed around the hall.

The chalk marks that had indicated the body's position were still visible, though there were no other signs of police presence that Georgia could see. That would no longer be needed even if the case was ongoing. Everything of interest would have been bagged and removed, every detail of the scene photographed, and recordings made on the spot by pathologists and scientists. For Marsh & Daughter's purpose, however, it was valuable to be here. Here they could concentrate their minds on visualizing the scene without the distancing factors of film, printed word or sound. Evidence could only take one so far; the items had to be chained together to connect the story – and those, for Marsh & Daughter, were best considered at the crime scene itself.

Mike pointed to the main entrance. 'Baines states he came in the door, couldn't see or hear Alice, checked the audience toilets to his left at the back, then came up on to the stage to see if she was in the changing room. He found her lying here, half concealed from view by the curtains. She was turned away from him, so thinking she was ill he knelt down and leaned over her. He saw the dagger and blood, though there wasn't much of the latter with it still in the wound. He half rolled the body back towards him, thought she might be alive, caught hold of the dagger but didn't pull it out. He only had a little blood on him, and she could only have been dead a short while, even if he's telling the truth. Said he didn't know what he was doing in grabbing the dagger, and he might be right, of course. Nasty experience if he's innocent.'

'Six and a half minutes each way, Mr Gilroy.' Toby had burst in through the door like an Olympic sprinter at the finishing post.

'Five seconds out,' Mike said blandly, not a smile on his face.

'Well done, Toby,' Peter said genially. 'While you've been away we've been talking about any possible links there might be between Alice's murder and Fanny Star's. Any ideas? From all you say, there would be a degree of risk in seizing the dagger from your museum, unless it was Miss Cadenza Broome or yourself, Toby. So I ask myself why someone should bother to take the dagger?'

Toby stared at him aghast, then picked on the salient point for him. 'Me?'

'It seems so,' Peter murmured regretfully.

'It seems,' Toby whipped back with some dignity, 'someone was trying to put the blame on *me*. If I did for some unknown reason decide to kill poor Alice, I would hardly choose such an obvious weapon as one of my own deodands.'

He had a point, Georgia conceded. Or was he as good a games player as Josh Perry?

'What's the matter with you, Georgia?' Luke said finally. 'I thought you and Peter would be pleased at the way things are going. There's obviously a book in it now, and it's shaping up nicely. Normally Peter's like a dog slavering at the thought of a particularly juicy bone if he can find a link between past and present. I'd have thought even you would be pleased. Today you're more like a growly dog deprived of bones for the last month. This is a weekend, and we have an agreement over this. Remember?'

She did. No business at weekends, especially bank holidays. It was hard enough that she and Peter shared their working lives, but with Luke vitally involved in it as their publisher, the guidelines had to be straight, or work would begin to turn into pillow talk as well. She'd broken the rules, she knew, but she didn't know why. Or did she? If she was honest, it was because the opening of the Alice Winters murder had given the Fanny Star case limitless boundaries. Until the missing link – if there was one or even the sniff of one – had been found, she felt she was clutching at insubstantial ghosts. And ghosts might please Toby Beamish and Cadenza Broome, but not Georgia Marsh. Usually it was the atmosphere of unfinished business that drew her to a case, as it was with Peter, but never before had the unsubstantial shadows of the past they grappled with so obstinately refused to come forward and turn themselves into fact.

'I am not breaking it.' It was a weak answer and she knew it.

'Fancy a day at the seaside tomorrow?'

Would she? She'd be with Luke, but she'd be taking herself with her, and Luke, normally the most patient of souls, did not deserve this. Instead Georgia realized she had a sudden and irrational desire to be with her mother. That hadn't happened in fifteen years. She needed to reveal her frailties without reproach to someone who would understand, since biologically she shared half of them. Then Georgia realized how stupid she was being. Elena leaned on *her*, she wasn't in the business of being around for other folks' frailties. Her mother walked away.

'Forget Jake Baines for a while, and concentrate on Fanny Star, is my advice.' Luke returned to drying the dinner dishes. 'That's how you began this case. The fact that it's widened to include Alice Winters doesn't change the basic need to get to grips with Fanny Star's murder. I'll come with you to Friday Street if you like, and see—'

'Dana Tucker?' The words were out before she thought, and she kicked herself. She must be losing her marbles, if all she could pick on was that insignificant trifle. Or was it so trifling?

Luke looked at her – reproachfully? 'I was going to say Jake Baines or Josh Perry, but Dana if you wish.'

Georgia's foot was well and truly in the mud now. 'You seem to get on with her pretty well.'

He flushed. He *did*. So there was something to it. She couldn't stop now. 'Dana seems to know an awful lot about the case that I haven't told her.'

Luke threw down the tea towel. 'I ran into her the other day in Faversham. Okay? I didn't think there was anything secret about discussing it, if that's what you're on about. Anyone can speculate.'

'What . . .' Georgia forced herself to stop. It was no business of hers what he was doing in Faversham, and she could not, *would* not, ask. It was too demeaning. Anyone could run into anyone, she told herself. Luke was quite right. It wasn't as if she was married to him. And any resemblance to Zac Taylor was entirely coincidental. 'Zac, was that you I saw in . . .', 'Zac, how did you get . . .', 'Zac, I thought you said you were in . . .'

Oh, damn men. Damn them all.

*   *   *

'Luke's right,' Peter said, after listening to her tale of woe the next morning. Luke had departed for South Malling the previous evening and the solitude of her double bed had been painful. Not that she had told Peter that. Her woes were all business ones – well, almost all. 'We should think of Fanny Star and work outwards and then a link might emerge. Suspects Anonymous last night had insufficient data. In the Fanny Star case, most Burglar Bills and Bettys refused to come out and play for the crucial period. Though Adam Jones' Burglar did crash into Jonathan Powell as he came back up to the house.'

'I told you Powell was mixed up in it!' Georgia was triumphant.

'Don't gloat yet. Both depend on route and, in Adam's case, when he left the Gibbs.'

'Damn.'

'Don't despair,' Peter said agreeably. 'Let us have carrot cake to make us see in the dark.'

'What on earth are you talking about?'

'My parents brought me up on the quaint wartime notion that eating carrots could make you see better in the dark, because it worked for night-time fighter pilots. Cover, of course, for secret intelligence, but my poor parents believed in carrots to the day they died.'

'I don't even feel like a daytime fighter at present,' Georgia said bitterly.

'Are you going to let those Daleks win? I'm not going to play Doctor Who all by myself.'

She managed a laugh of sorts. 'No.'

'Very well then. It's back to wattle and daub time.'

The fallback situation that even Suspects Anonymous couldn't replace. When they first moved here, before Elena left, they had converted this house from four rooms on the ground floor to one through room on either side of the hallway. They had beavered away at an inner wall, stripping off the plaster to reveal medieval wattle and daub. Fortunately it wasn't a sustaining wall, since by the time

Elena had finished the daub itself had crumbled and she had found herself staring into the house next door – now Georgia's.

'At least,' Elena had remarked happily amid the ruins of their joint inner wall, 'we know where we are.'

It was a good way to think every now and then. 'Very well, Master Builder,' Georgia began. 'Wattle it is. Fanny Star was murdered. Granted?'

'Yes. One wound, not several tries, no fingerprints, she was wearing gloves, can't have been suicide, so the killer must have worn gloves too. No way to lift glove prints then.'

'They were evening gloves, I suppose. Very dainty.' As Fanny had been clad in a skimpy, mini-skirted lace dress with heavy black boots, evening gloves were a nice touch.

'Adam Jones. Guilty or not guilty?'

'Not proven.'

'Motive?'

'Possible jealousy. Going solo. Trial evidence.'

'Contradictory.' Peter thought for a moment. 'If Jones was innocent, who had reason to kill her?'

'The father of her child.'

'Qualification. Only if that wasn't Ronald Gibb, whose alibi is *probably* valid. For what reason?'

That threw her for a moment. 'Didn't want the story to come out.'

'Why not? Seven years had passed by 1968. Unlikely to be a motive for murder, unless the father *was* Ronald Gibb.'

'Accepted.'

'Who else then?'

'Jonathan Powell, of course.'

'Motive?'

'Like Adam, he might have lost his temper over her going solo.'

'Try harder.'

'My other theory is that Hazel and Toby got the wrong end of the stick. That Fanny wasn't threatening Adam that

131

she would go solo. When she talked of being together, not in a threesome, she meant herself and Adam. In short, she wanted to sack Jonathan as their manager.'

'Better, but killing her seems a funny way of keeping the golden goose laying.'

'He had the opportunity,' Georgia said obstinately. 'He says he didn't go over to the stage until eight forty. No one's confirmed that.'

'Hum. Same applies to many of them. Who else?'

'Josh Perry.'

'Motive?'

'None known, unless he was the father of Fanny's baby.'

'Weak. Opportunity?'

'As with Powell, other dinner guests, Sheila, Henry, Oliver, and rest of the gang. It's too late to establish precise movements during the last hour of Fanny's life.'

'Okay. Who else?'

'Tom,' Georgia said reluctantly.

'Which of the threesome, T, O, or M?'

'Toby.'

'Just because he's a creep, he's not necessarily a murderer.'

'She could well have spurned him.'

Peter chortled. 'How very sweet. Are we back to Lady Rosamund and her dastardly knight? How about Michael?'

'This was his engagement party. If she held something over him, he could have wanted her out of the way.'

'He could have been the father of her child.'

'He fancied her, no evidence of anything more – and Sheila wouldn't be matey with her if she was her rival.'

'Oliver?'

'Unlikely. Only fifteen at the time of Fanny's departure from the village.'

'Are you telling me fifteen-year-old boys have no interest in sex?'

'No. But unless he's a psycho, he's unlikely to be a deliberate murderer at twenty-two because of it.'

'Agreed, unlikely. End of the list.'

'Jonathan Powell's still at the end of my prong of the carving fork,' she said obstinately.

'My prong is still stuck in Friday Street.'

She ignored this. 'He was being ousted as their manager, I'm sure of it.'

'You can't be,' Peter gently pointed out.

'As a thesis, then. The row between Fanny and Adam wasn't about her going solo. He was lying.'

'Perhaps, Georgia, he's a Cretan man.'

'Eh?'

'A proposition in logic I learned at school. Empedocles, the Cretan, claimed all Cretan men were liars. Ignoring the impossibility of the conundrum, why believe anything Powell told you? He told you, for instance, that the accusations that he was Fanny's lover were false. Suppose they were true?'

'I find it hard to believe, having met him. He doesn't seem the passionate type, gay or heterosexual.'

'Or perhaps the "we" that Fanny referred to was not herself and Jonathan, or herself and Adam, but herself and a lover – as yet without a name.'

She thought about this. 'Powell would have known. Why not tell me?'

'I have no answer for that.' Peter paused. 'But that doesn't mean there isn't one – did I hear you mention lunch?'

'No, but you can share mine. Luke's disappeared.'

'You should keep a more careful eye on our partner. By the way, I have the autopsy report on Adam Jones. I pleaded with Mike to fix it for me with the Coroner's Office. I'm still waiting for Fanny Star's.'

'What did Adam's say?'

'No doubt about the verdict of suicide. Diatoms everywhere. Your Mr Powell was quite right about that.'

'The pub will be making its fortune out of you,' Josh joked as she walked in at Tuesday lunchtime.

133

'I bet the old pilgrims along this road got a warmer welcome from the priory. And free nosh into the bargain,' she retorted in kind.

Josh laughed. 'Look,' he said, 'it's no business of mine, but why don't you stay in Friday Street for a day or two? There's more to do around here now.' He was polishing glasses and squinting at one carefully.

'Stay in the pub?' Georgia thought about it. It seemed a good idea, and yet she didn't fancy it. Wouldn't she and her mission here stand out like sore thumbs rather than allow her to blend into the landscape? Josh's warning about trees came back to her with full force.

'No. That Miss Tucker said yesterday she thought it was daft you driving to and fro all the time. There's no reason you couldn't move in with her for a day or two.'

Dana Tucker? Georgia saw a mountainous obstacle there. Why on earth should Dana be interested in her welfare? Ah well, she was a good climber of obstacles. At least her worst suspicions over Luke couldn't be true if Dana was actually inviting her to stay with her. Then a sudden thought made a dive-bomb attack on her heart. Perhaps she was doing so in order to get closer to Luke?

'Where better than Frances's birthplace? Maybe her ghost will give you a few ideas,' Josh said, straight-faced.

Josh was pushing this plan. She didn't like that aspect of it, but on the other hand if she went out on a limb she might get to places she didn't even know existed. 'I heard you are involved over Alice Winters now,' Josh continued. 'You were up at the tower, with the police.'

'And Toby Beamish,' she added politely. 'Your informant missed him out.'

'He does own the place. Got to make a penny or two for the upkeep. Maybe he fancies being paid in return for help over your book, thought of that?' Josh was looking at her almost expectantly.

Josh Perry was not going to be master builder of this case. 'There isn't a book yet,' she reminded him. 'It would be nice to think so, but we're not in the business of making bricks out of straw.'

'What do you count as a brick?'

Could this be an overture? 'I told you we were looking for a link between Alice's murder and Fanny's. That would make a first-class brick.'

Josh snorted. 'Made without straw, your bricks would be. There's nothing to it.'

'Maybe. I admit the name Winters hasn't cropped up at all in connection with Fanny's murder, although Alice's grandfather Brian was a member of the gang. Not a very active one, obviously, since no one mentions him much.'

'Right,' Josh said noncommittally.

'Even Adam Jones' death is contributing to the general conviction that Fanny's death was an open and shut case.'

'You mean you think he was guilty?' Caught unawares, Josh looked genuinely surprised.

'No.' She was interested in his reaction though. 'I thought, stupidly, that if he came back here on the day of the murder, it might indicate he came back to tackle the real murderer if he was innocent.'

'And?' Josh was listening closely now.

'He *did* come back here. He saw Henry Ludd; he might also have seen Ronald and Doreen Gibb. I don't know. What we do know for sure is that he committed suicide, so there's no point wondering whether he was given a lift back home by a murderer.'

'What's that about?' Josh looked worried.

She was taken aback. 'Even in 1987 there can't have been much of a bus service, and being just out of prison he's unlikely to have owned a car or motorbike. Taxis would be beyond his reach. Yet he had to get here from a local railway station or coach stop and he had to return to the river to drown himself. He must have got lifts both ways. I wondered who from – someone he knew, or casual passers-by?'

Josh gave up the pretence of polishing glasses and planted

his hands on the bar. 'I can tell you who drove him here. And back.'

'Who?' Georgia asked sharply, shaken at scoring an unplanned bull's-eye.

'Brian Winters.'

Eight

Josh could obviously guess what Georgia was thinking, because he half smiled.

Excitement conquered her irritation at having to beg for help. 'You don't believe in volunteering information,' she said lightly.

'Need-to-know basis, Georgia. A question of trust.'

'Not of truth?'

'I don't recall telling you anything that wasn't true. Might not have been the whole truth, but who's to know what that is? As soon as Bob takes over, you can come over to the house. Hazel's at her sister's, so we can talk in peace. Likes to put in her ha'p'orth, does Hazel.'

And Josh, she suspected, preferred being sole monarch of Friday Street's affairs. The lock-keeper who controlled the flow both in and out. The problem was that she was dependent on it, a situation she didn't much relish. She was reasonably sure that although Josh was cautious he was on the right side of justice, but in Friday Street it didn't pay to rely on anything.

Half an hour later, after minding her Ps and Qs in the pub with a toasted sandwich, she was ensconced with Josh in his living room where he produced exceptionally good coffee. 'We buy it in France,' he told her. 'Bob won't let us bring back any liquor – killing his trade, he says – but he doesn't object to coffee. Or a cheese or two. He's partial to them himself.'

Georgia mentioned a disagreement she and Luke had had with a particularly smelly cheese they'd brought home from

Lille last year, and waited patiently for him to return to the subject of Brian Winters.

Eventually Josh cleared his throat. 'Now then,' he began promisingly, 'Brian was a good mate of mine. I still miss him. Died too young, he did, like his son Bill. Bill was only just forty when he went. Car accident. Tragic it was. And now Jane has the farm to run and not even her daughter to share it with.'

Perhaps he was thinking this went too near the heart to tell an outsider, for he quickly cracked a joke. 'And before you're thinking that someone here bumped him off, let me tell you it *was* an accident. You might think we've got nothing else to do up here on the downs but go around murdering each other, but we're a village. It's rare, but it does happen.'

'It doesn't always leave scars the way it seems to have done in Friday Street.'

'Murder always scars someone. So does any death. It's bloody unfair the way God made the world, but everyone has to die. For all the Reverend says we can, we can't change that.'

'Natural death makes wounds that heal,' Georgia said firmly. 'Violent or inexplicable death, or . . .' She forced herself to say it. 'Or when there's no body, only a missing question mark, then the wound doesn't heal.'

Josh looked at her curiously. 'Personal experience?'

'Yes.'

She felt more kindly towards him when he did not enquire further. The shadow of Rick hovered, then gradually vanished as Josh said, 'Suppose I said that's how the Friday Street music treats it? Open wounds.'

'Then why don't you make more effort to heal them?'

She'd clearly stung him, for his face reddened. 'We do. *I* do. But when you're standing in the middle of a situation, that's not easy. You folks can come walking in from outside, which isn't easy, either, but at least you can walk away again. We can't, except by uprooting and moving away.'

'Like Oliver Ludd?' She took a stab in the dark.

'He didn't go alone,' Josh said steadily. 'Liz Beamish went with him.'

'Were they running away from Friday Street, or from their respective spouses? Was Oliver married?'

'No. He was a likeable chap, gentle like Henry, and close to his father. Michael takes after Joan, the manager of the family.'

'You speak of him in the past tense. Aren't they in touch?'

'Henry plays his cards close to his chest. Oliver and Liz don't keep up with anyone else in the village, so far as I know, but Henry's another matter. Up to a year or two ago he used to go over to the States and, though we never asked, it must have been to see Oliver.'

'When did they leave?'

'Late 1970s.' A pause. 'Too late for you to snap the handcuffs on them for Frances's murder.'

'Damn. My little grey cells will have to think of another villain,' she replied in kind. 'Did you like Oliver?'

'Yes. He was the peacemaker in the gang, even though he was the youngest. He had a way of making you laugh that made you see how daft you were being.'

Was that a shot at her? she wondered, then decided she was getting oversensitive. 'And Brian?' she asked. 'What was his role?'

'Elder statesman. He was a few years older than most of us, and a year or so older than Michael. He had an air of gravitas that everyone respected, even the mighty Michael. Slow but sure, was Brian. And now you want me to tell you about how he came to give Adam Jones a lift, eh?'

'Anything you can. It would save me bothering Jane Winters. Unless you think . . .'

Josh looked at her quizzically. 'Not like you to beat round bushes, Georgia.'

'Do you think she'd talk to me now Jake has been released?'

'I've already suggested it to her.'

Georgia was staggered. Josh going out of his way to help? 'That's very good—'

Josh held up his hand to stop her in mid-flow. 'Not good of me at all. It's for her benefit, not yours. What do you think she feels like? She only just got used to the idea that her farmhand murdered her daughter, and lo and behold he's released for lack of evidence. What does the poor woman do? Welcome him back to work with open arms? But is it fair to deprive him of his job if he's innocent? She's still working that one out. My guess is that the police are scratching their heads over whether to pursue this case or not. I reckon that's why you and your dad were at the tower with the Old Bill the other day. You're in the business of healing wounds – here's one you might be able to help with. Jane Winters. If there's a link between these two murders – and that still sounds a load of cobblers to me – then you can persuade the police to get going again over Alice. If they drop the case, Jane will never know the answer. She needs closure and all that, and quick. If there isn't a link, well, at least she'll think something's being done, and you might – you *might*, Georgia – stumble across something that the police haven't thought of. And if so, it's my belief it will lead right back to Jonathan Powell.'

Georgia saw her opportunity. 'I'll try. But you can play your part, Josh. I need to be in the picture about the Friday Street flute music. Someone thought Jake wasn't guilty. Did the village have any kind of investigation or not?'

'I told you we followed up on Frances.'

'A bone to keep me quiet. Either this legend of the music trying to put right an injustice is true, or it's a joke or try-on. Which is it?'

'It means something to someone, Georgia,' Josh threw back at her. 'There's no rule that says everyone has to report in to the Montash Arms if they've something to tell. I imagine that's what you're thinking.'

'I'm asking you what actually happens. Cadenza told me that in effect you examined your own consciences. The playing of the tune is a plea, presumably to tell the police of any evidence, or to give yourself up if guilty. But I'm not convinced it ends there. At the very least there'd be a lot of tongues wagging the next day if the whole village has been woken up by the music.'

Josh did not comment. That didn't mean, she was beginning to realize, that he wasn't going to, merely that he'd speak in his own time, not hers. At last he said, 'You've heard of the old hue and cry system, Georgia? Used before there was a police force.'

'Yes. The local manor court or village jury or whatever decided who was guilty, but if the culprit had skipped the village they had no way of enforcing their verdicts, so a hue and cry was set up. The villagers sent out couriers to neighbouring villages, who had a duty to bung the culprit back to face the music . . . Oh!' It was an unintentional play on words and Georgia pulled a face.

Josh grinned. 'Exactly. Face the music. That's how we think this legend got going. Not that that phrase went back as far as our legend, but that was the intention behind playing it. It was our internal hue and cry. Will the real villain stand forth? If the village disagreed with the court verdict on someone, it was up to anyone in the village to come out and play the tune to express dissent and produce more evidence. Those with any fresh evidence or a guilty conscience could gather—'

'In the local pub,' she suggested innocently.

'Or church. That was usually the main local gathering place. Then they'd decide what to do about it.'

'And now?'

'It isn't played often, Georgia. There's no set routine. But on the odd occasion people have gone to the vicar.'

Of course, Georgia thought. 'Who was the vicar at the time of Fanny's death?'

Josh thought back. 'Reverend Carter, but he would have been about sixty then, so he'd be safe from you now.'

She wasn't going to be put off by jolly jests. 'So there wasn't a rush to the pub or church to talk it over in 1968?'

Josh sighed. 'We were all shell-shocked, Georgia. Think of it. Frances had been the live wire in our gang, then world-famous, and now she'd been murdered on our patch. There was no talk then of whether Adam Jones was guilty or not.'

'Even after the music was heard?'

Josh reddened again. 'No. Only what I told you earlier.'

'Don't you think that's strange?'

'Put like that, yes,' Josh said steadily. 'But we're dealing with real life here. We remember Frances Gibb here, Georgia. Having her die right here amongst us made a finger of blame point at us, even though Adam Jones was arrested. Of course we talked about it, but it was like we didn't really want to know, especially the gang. We went through the motions, all of us. We even met in Owlers' Smoke just the once.'

He caught her look of surprise. 'Our way of forcing ourselves to discuss the issue. The more we went over it, we concluded there was no other explanation than that Adam Jones was guilty. Nevertheless we didn't *want* to find another explanation, because that would have brought her death home to us with a vengeance and we couldn't face it.'

That had the ring of truth, Georgia thought. 'It's a memorable tune. Haunting.' She could hear it in her mind. 'You have no idea who played it when Adam was arrested?'

'Who plays it is not the point. The tune isn't written down; it's passed on by ear from one generation to the next. Incomers aren't taught it.'

'Or its meaning?'

'They know that. They have to.'

'Then how do they recognize the tune?'

He laughed. 'They complain about it next day.'

'Don't tell me. To the publican of the Montash Arms.'

'Who else? No resident vicar, no policeman, no doctor. That's modern civilization for you.'

'Did Brian Winters have reservations about her death? Did *he* play the music?'

'Could be. I don't know. After Frances's death, he looked after Doreen Gibb. Ron Gibb wouldn't put himself out to

help his wife with the formalities, and as Frances wasn't
married they were her official next of kin. Brian stepped
in and together with Powell cleared out the flat she had
shared with Adam, and did other odd jobs for the Gibbs.
He also went to see Adam Jones a couple of times while
he was inside. He must have taken a liking to him, because
when he knew Adam was due to be released he tried to
help him.'

'He thought him innocent?'

'Hold your horses, I'm coming to that. Adam told him he
wanted to visit Friday Street when he was released, and Brian
offered to pick him up at Maidstone and take him back. He
assumed he wanted to see the Gibbs – remember, only Sheila
and I knew about her pregnancy – but Adam only wanted
to visit Downey Hall.'

'Why?' Simply to play a song to Henry didn't seem enough.

'Who's telling this story? He duly picked Adam up about
two thirty, dropped him by the Green Lane side entrance to
Downey to avoid notice, not that anyone would have recognized Adam Jones straight off, but Brian didn't fancy being
lynched. He said he'd be waiting at the same entrance at five
p.m. to give Adam plenty of time to do whatever he wanted.
And that's what happened. Adam got out of the Land Rover
at Maidstone, thanked him and left. When Brian got home
he discovered Adam had left his guitar behind – and purposely
too, for he'd shoved a note on it addressed to Brian, saying
he'd no more use for it. By the time Brian found it, it was
too late.'

'Did Brian have any idea why Adam killed himself? Was
it because he wasn't guilty or because he was?'

'Adam Jones always told Brian that he wasn't. Brian
believed him.'

'On what grounds?'

'We'd have to ask Brian that and that's not possible.' Josh
looked awkward. 'Here's where I held back on you, Georgia.
Poor old Doreen had been lying to Hazel and me when we
went to see her after hearing the music. Scared stiff of Ron,

she was, so she kept mum during the trial about Adam coming home with her and Ron. Adam confirmed to Brian that Gibb had lied at the trial when he said Adam had left them at the gate to Downey Hall. He confirmed he'd gone right back to End Cottage. Doreen had whispered to him as they left the Hall after the dinner that she'd decided to give him something to hand to Frances, so be sure to come home with them.'

'What was that?' And what else might Josh be holding back on? Georgia wondered with frustration.

'No idea.'

'Did Adam tell him why he wanted to go to the Hall?'

'No. Or if so, Brian didn't tell me.'

'If he was innocent, he can only have come to proclaim the fact. But why to Henry Ludd?'

'If it's relevant, Brian was convinced not only that Adam really loved Frances, but that he knew who killed her.'

Georgia drew a slow breath. 'You do believe in dropping bombshells, don't you? Did he,' she added hopefully, 'name someone?' Not that Josh was likely to cough up the name. His style was to whet the appetite and leave her to munch through the meal.

'Brian wasn't too happy when Adam told him that on the way to Friday Street, because he was afraid he might be driving him on a revenge mission. Adam reassured him and said no. He did know who'd killed Fanny, but he didn't live in Friday Street.'

Jonathan Powell. Who else?

Josh was still reluctant to be drawn on Alice Winters, but he did go so far as to take Georgia back to the pub, where Tim was busy having a late lunch. She needed an introduction to Jake Baines, and who better than Tim?

'Cheers,' Tim grunted. 'I'll take you there on the way back to work. Not that I'm Number One at the moment. Jake still reckons I killed Alice.'

If this was meant to draw a reaction either from her or his

grandfather, he would be disappointed. Josh remained impassive, and all she said was: 'And did you?'

He gave her a scathing look. 'I wanted to give her one, not murder her.'

'Lucky girl,' Georgia murmured.

Tim shrugged. 'Look, that's not disrespectful. That was *Alice*. Everyone was after her and she liked that. We had a sort of race, Drew, me and Jake. She'd, like, toss a coin between us. First it was one. Then another. I reckon she enjoyed the game, 'specially between me and Drew. Thought it fun to watch the cockfight. She was a nice kid, don't get me wrong, but Drew's already at uni, and I'm off in September. We're too young to get serious. Jake was different. He did. He was the one she fancied in the sack,' he told her candidly. 'Me and Drew were her bit on the side.'

'But you don't think Jake murdered her?'

'I know he bloody didn't. He was telling me about his row with her while we were fencing Long Field that day. He was hurting, you could tell, but he could see her point. She told him she wanted freedom, so she could *choose* to come back to him. Load of bollocks. She wanted out, but he didn't see it. He was anxious to make things okay with her when he got to the tower.'

'His mood could have changed when he got there, or she might have provoked him.'

'Look, I saw him leave on his bike. I told the Bill he didn't leave here till after a quarter to four. By the time we got that fence fixed, he barely had time to get to the tower, let alone go up to the ghostie house to pinch that knife. Even if he'd pinched it earlier, and planned to murder her, he wouldn't have had time. Why would he? He wanted her alive, not dead. Anyway, who'd leave a murder till five minutes before a busload of witnesses arrived? No, Jake's okay, Georgia.'

Tim walked her to Jake's parents' home, where he was living. It was a 1960s council house, one of the few in Friday Street. Jake was working in the garden behind the house, and Tim hailed him from the rear gate.

'Hi, Jake. Lady wants to talk to you. She's not the pigs.'

As an introduction, it could have been bettered, but it would have to do. Jake Baines' photo in the paper sprang to life for her as he stuck his fork in the ground and sullenly walked over to her. 'What d'yer want? Nice chatty interview for *Hello*?'

'I wanted to talk about Sweet Fanny Adams.'

'Hey. The Sweet album?' He looked more interested.

'No. The sixties singing duo, Fanny Star and Adam Jones.'

'Oh, yeah. What's it to do with me?'

Behind his belligerence Georgia could see a scared, wary lad, which was hardly surprising given what he'd been through. Indeed, she had to remember, perhaps deservedly.

'Not much. She was murdered in this village, and the same dagger was used to kill Alice, the one used in the ghost tour show. I understand Toby usually brought the dagger down with him in the visitors' bus. That means that whoever killed Alice actually planned to use that dagger, because he or she must have stolen it. Alice wouldn't have brought it herself for any reason?'

'I've bin through this a million times. I didn't have nothing to do with the dagger. Old Beamish would have had a fit if I'd brought it down myself. Or Alice, come to that. Why would she? All I had to do was bike down there, climb into me poncy tights and remember my pipe.'

'Pipe?'

'I had to play the sodding ghost of Piers Brome, and prance along piping at the end.'

'You played the Friday Street tune?'

'Nah. I'd get shot if I played that. It's some old rubbish Toby knew. "The Banks of Allan Water".'

That rang a bell. 'Allan Water' was the song Adam had played to Henry.

'I loved Alice. No one thinks of me. Getting there, finding her there like that,' Jake continued, aggrieved. 'I thought she was messing about; she did that sometimes. "Oh, Jake," she'd say, clutching her boobs, "I could kill myself for love of you," sort of thing, and then collapsing to give me a fright. So that's what I thought, even when I saw the dagger in her.' He gulped. 'She was dead though.' The frightened boy was all too visible now.

'You told the police Alice had said she was meeting someone in the barn, and asked you to come later.'

'Yeah. First I thought she meant someone from Spookie Manor – one of the visitors or maybe Harry, my uncle. Or even Ted. They're the gardeners there. Ted fancied her too. Or maybe it was Drew or Tim. It would be like her to have a quick one with one of them while I was biking over and could arrive any minute. Liked living dangerously, did Alice.' He gulped.

'But you didn't see any sign of anyone?' she asked gently. He looked near to tears.

'Nah. She told me not to get there till about five to four,' he repeated obstinately. 'No problem. After the row we'd had the night before, I didn't want her shouting at me all over again. *Or* to walk in and find Tim on the job. So I got there later, like she wanted. And that's what I found. So,' he glanced suspiciously at Georgia, 'now you know all about me, what's this about Fanny Star?'

She tried to make this sound casual. 'Did Alice ever talk about Fanny Star?'

'Bloody right she did. Never stopped.'

At last. Georgia could hardly believe it. There could, just could, be a way forward here. 'Did she think Adam Jones was innocent?'

'Dunno. She'd often hint she knew things. Then she'd laugh and say it was a wind-up. Not that I cared. It was the murder itself that got Alice going though. Blow Lady Rosamund. She was always trying to get Toby to let her play the ghost of Fanny Star. That would really pull in the punters, she told him.'

'What did Toby think?' Georgia asked.

'Said he didn't want to entertain no ghosts who belonged to Downey Hall, and nothing in Fanny Star's story pinned her to Spookie Manor. Alice said she'd make up something about that in a jiff. But he wasn't interested. Told Alice to forget her. Very sharp he was, she said.'

Georgia walked up the drive of Winters' Farm, through a well-kept garden, to the large farmhouse. There seemed to be an untold wealth of such farmhouses in Kent. Forget the stately homes. There were Old Wealden, Tudor-brick, eighteenth- and early-nineteenth-century houses, all serving in the role. Some were mansions in themselves, and Winters' Farm was no exception. Early-nineteenth-century brick, she thought, roomy and comfortable. She'd decided to telephone straightaway, now she felt she was on a winning streak, and Jane had told her to come right up.

The driveway led to the farmyard rather than the house itself, which was reached, she could see, by a path at one side. Ahead, she could see Tim Perry working on a tractor inside a barn, and a woman – presumably Jane herself – hosing down the yard. She put the hose down when she saw Georgia, smiled and came to meet her. She was of medium height, sturdy, with short, blonde curly hair, and a sensitive, weary-looking face. Not, Georgia decided, the sort of farmer's wife who ran after mice with a carving knife.

'Come inside,' she greeted Georgia, who followed her to the covered porch of the main house. 'Josh had already told me you'd be on your way up here,' she said, struggling out of her wellingtons.

Georgia laughed. Trust Josh. 'I'm taking you away from work,' she said, conscience-stricken.

'That's a pleasure, I can tell you. I'm short-handed at present, alas. So it's tough going.'

She looked a tolerant woman, so perhaps Jake might get his job back, Georgia thought. Even so, putting herself in Jane's position, his presence here would be a constant reminder even if he were innocent. Would this woman be able to face that? Georgia thought perhaps she might. Nevertheless, Jake might not want to return. He would have his own terrors to cope with. In the horrors of his arrest, he would have had no time to grieve for the loss of his sweetheart, and now that he had would receive little sympathy for it while the cloud of suspicion remained over him.

There were no photos of Alice in this comfortable large kitchen, and only one she could see of Bill – a photo that tore at the heartstrings. Just a good-looking face, laughing into the camera, dark hair and open-necked shirt. A holiday picture. How cruel to have lost him so early, so suddenly, and then to lose her daughter, but there was no safe way of saying so to Jane.

'Just tell me to stop if I stray into bad areas.' Georgia did her best. 'I can't even begin to imagine how many there are for you.'

Jane looked at her keenly as Georgia sat down at the table, and nodded. 'I'm coping – just. Coping with the farm, that is. As for everything else . . .' She shrugged. Georgia looked at the drawn look on her face and the tautness around the eyes. 'Jake's release was the last straw. Is that unfair of me?'

'No.' Georgia knew she would have felt just the same. 'Did you ever doubt his guilt?'

'No, not even when the music was played. That's what's so awful. I feel I should have done if he is innocent. But if he's not . . .' Her voice wobbled slightly. 'If I offer him his job back, it's tantamount to saying he's innocent, and I don't *know* if he is, except legally. Is that wrong?'

'Not at this stage,' Georgia said gently. 'It will come. Don't worry, though. That's not what I want to talk about.'

'So Josh said. Fanny Star again, I gather.'

'Again?' Georgia picked up.

'Again *and* again.' The words came out in a rush now. Perhaps speaking of something other than Alice helped her. 'Bill and I were married seventeen years, and his father died four years ago, two years before Bill himself. Bill's mother had died quite early, and so he and his dad were very close. I got very used to the name of Fanny Star. Brian had a thing about it; he was a fan of her music, collected it all, played it endlessly – luckily he didn't live in the farmhouse with us – and he was always talking to people about her. I gather he was in the same gang as she was, which made it under-standable, I suppose, though the others never seemed to mention her. When Brian died, Bill got engrossed too, because his father had talked so much about it and left some stuff behind. Bill didn't have anyone to share his passion with, since I wasn't interested, and so Alice got involved.'

Did she indeed? The link seemed to be tightening, and certainly tied in with what Jake had said.

'Somehow,' Jane continued, 'Brian had got hold of Adam Jones' guitar and Alice learned to play it. She was fright-fully proud of having the guitar. Said it would pay her top-up fees at uni if she sold it. But she didn't want to sell it, even though she was desperate for any cash she could get. Too valuable to sell, she said. I thought when Bill died, she'd forget all about this Fanny Star nonsense, but she didn't. She went on playing her records and CDs and going through Bill's collection. She even became pally with the Ludds, so that she could be near the scene of the . . .' Jane broke off.

'Is the collection still here?' Georgia asked hastily. If Alice hadn't been winding Jake up, the answer could well be in it. She thought she'd gone too far when Jane shrugged wearily.

'I don't know; I haven't looked.'

For a moment Georgia thought Jane would break down, but she didn't. She risked one more small push. 'Perhaps if you do . . .'

'If I get time.' Jane glanced at her. 'No. I'm being stupid, aren't I? If it's going to help you I'll try to find it. It didn't seem to be with her other papers.'

Obviously Josh hadn't mentioned to Jane that there might be a link between the two deaths, and Georgia was grateful. There'd be too much hanging on it. The collection might be a treasure trove, or it could be nothing.

'Josh told me that Brian gave Adam a lift to and from the village when he was released from prison in 1987. That's when he gave him the guitar. Did Brian talk to you about that?'

'I was pregnant with Alice that year, and then busy coping with a new baby, so I don't remember. I do remember the guitar coming, because for ages I thought Brian had bought it as a particularly stupid present for the baby.'

When Georgia left the farm, she was still mulling over the possibility that Alice's death stemmed from Brian Winters' collection. She longed to be back in Haden Shaw hurling ideas around with Peter. Not quite yet; she still had one more mission.

Picking up the car, she drove down to End Cottage. Inside the undrawn curtains she could see Dana moving around. It looked homely, it was the Gibb home, and it seemed entirely sensible that she should move in here for a few days. Even if Luke *was* attracted to Dana.

Nine

'Georgia,' came a roar as soon as she arrived in Peter's office. 'Luke's here.'

Immediately her stomach churned, partly in pleasure, partly in recollection of how they had parted two days ago, and partly in the knowledge that she had just left Dana. And here was Luke, peacefully sitting in the early-evening sun. She could see him there, still unaware of her return, despite Peter's shout. A rush of love for him grappled with her guilt at her suspicions of his duplicity. Seeing his face in profile, the grey hairs beginning to sprinkle his hair, and the way his long legs were stretched out before him on the lounger, she had a comforting sense of surety that this could go on and on. And what's more, that she *wanted* it to. It was only a small part of her that was mucking things up. She had only to say no more, and the ghosts of the past would vanish, leaving her with Luke. She would do so, she vowed – as soon as Friday Street had ceased to haunt them.

'Lucky for some,' she called out.

Luke looked up from the file he was studying and grinned. 'Mine's a G and T.'

'Tough. Mine's a five-minute cooling-off period.'

He put the file aside and stood up to kiss her. A long kiss that deserved response, within the limits of their situation. Peter's wheelchair was already hurtling down the ramp to join them.

'Well?' he demanded. 'Tell me about this link. All I've had is one text message saying you thought there was a chance.'

'Lo, it is found, and is being examined,' Georgia said triumphantly.

'This does call for a G and T,' Luke murmured plaintively.

'It calls for an explanation *now*,' Peter contradicted him. 'Every detail, please.'

'In that case, I shall make a strategic, if temporary, withdrawal,' Luke announced, 'in the interests of alcohol.'

'Now tell me,' Peter said eagerly, as Luke disappeared inside, and Georgia obliged. It took longer than Luke did to fix the sundowners, and in any case he was back in a surprisingly short time. He seemed to be taking an increasing interest in this case, Georgia thought with pleasure. Then a tiny niggle reminded her that it involved Dana Tucker on its perimeters. The niggle was squashed.

'And there,' she conceded, as she reached the end of her report, 'we're stuck until Jane Winters comes back to me about Alice's collection. If she does.'

'Not stuck,' Peter said. 'We've other lines to explore. Toby Beamish interests me. Why should he be so firmly set against Alice's proposal to include a ghost of Fanny Star?'

'Perhaps,' Luke said, 'because Fanny's ghost hasn't materialized.'

'Or,' Georgia pointed out, with a fairness she was reluctant to concede to Toby, 'because Fanny is part of his real life, and his ghosts are comfortably escapist.'

'Or because he has uncomfortable memories of her death?' Peter suggested.

'No,' Georgia said firmly. 'Jonathan Powell is still the right direction to look. Toby's a creep, but he lives in Friday Street, and Adam Jones believed the murderer did not.'

'Powell wasn't in Friday Street when Alice Winters died,' Peter retorted. 'It's the link or Powell. You can't have both.'

'We can't take the link angle any further until we know what's in Alice's collection.'

'You mean, it might give a clue as to whom she might have arranged to meet in the tower?'

'*If* there was such a meeting. We've only Baines' word

for it. The problem is . . .' Georgia frowned. The gin wasn't doing her concentration any favours. 'The implication is that the meeting was with someone in Friday Street.'

'So what's wrong with that?' Peter shot at her.

'Only that Adam told Brian Winters that Fanny's killer *didn't* live there.' Back to square one. That meant no link.

Peter pounced. '*How* could Adam have known who it was?'

'I don't understand.'

'We're assuming Adam arrived at the crime scene shortly after Fanny was killed. Then he was arrested, and so he wouldn't have had time to gather evidence.'

'Unless,' Georgia whipped back, 'he saw her murderer leave, or saw the murder committed.'

'Then why not tell the police? That,' Peter said crossly, 'is the sticking point.'

A pause while Luke, Georgia noticed, quietly sipped on with a slight smile on his lips. Grand publisher watches authors making prize fools of themselves, she thought. A blackbird having a late supper on Peter's lawn eyed them speculatively, decided they were going round in circles, and continued his worm-tug.

'Of course,' Georgia said carefully, 'we don't know that he didn't tell them.'

'I do,' Peter said. 'Not only was it not in the statement he made to the police at the time, but Mike's been ferreting around. The DI's sergeant only retired a few years back. He disappeared to Spain, but Mike got hold of him. He was quite clear that there was no one else remotely in the frame at the time, either through allegations from Jones or from independent evidence.'

'He could have been protecting someone,' Luke put in.

'He must have loved whoever it was a lot to do fifteen years inside for them. Anyway, Adam was new to Friday Street. He didn't know anyone there to protect.'

Georgia saw the answer. Why on earth hadn't she realized before? It was so obvious. 'He was protecting Jonathan Powell.'

'He *knew* Powell was guilty?' Peter stared at her.

'It's a possibility.' Georgia tried to keep the lid on her imagination, in case this was the G and T talking. It sounded so ludicrous. Adam taking the rap for someone else.

'Why? For the sake of his career?'

Georgia shook her head vigorously. 'Don't be daft, Peter. If he took the rap for murder, his career would go nowhere. He could hardly top the charts from inside.'

Luke coughed politely and she turned to him, startled. She was so used to these rallies with Peter that the outside world disappeared as they locked horns with each other.

'Excuse me,' he said, 'but I think you should look at these pictures.' He picked up the file he had been looking at and brought it over. It was full of photocopies of newspaper articles and pictures. Georgia peered over Peter's shoulder while he was looking at it. 'It's hard to tell from the poor reproduction, but don't you think there's a sporting chance that Powell is gay? I know you were uncertain, Georgia, but look at his body language in this photo when he's standing between Adam and Fanny.'

'Yes,' she said doubtfully, 'but so what? Adam wasn't gay, so far as we know. Most people, including Powell, said he loved Fanny.'

'Suppose Adam was both ways. Wouldn't that produce a nice triangle?' Luke suggested complacently.

Georgia raced this through her mind. He was right. It would. Hadn't Toby written in his statement that Fanny had said, 'This triangle's bloody impossible'? That could apply sexually, as well as to his close involvement as manager. 'Jonathan loves Adam, who loves Fanny, who loves Adam,' she said. 'Jonathan therefore concludes that if he gets rid of Fanny, Adam might turn to him, or indeed *had* already turned to him.'

'No dice on that one,' Peter said promptly. 'He could get rid of Fanny by encouraging her to go solo. Why murder her? Nor, if he did have reason to want her dead, would he choose her home patch, at a very public venue, and then let his beloved Adam take the rap. No, this doesn't fly for me.'

'It does for me.' Of course, *of course*. 'It would give Adam a motivation for keeping quiet in prison, if he knew Jonathan had killed Fanny because of his love for him. Adam might have even returned it, and so could well have felt guilt. Fanny was fed up with the threesome, *and* she was insisting they got rid of Powell as their manager. He overheard that as he arrived. Fanny left and Adam and Jonathan had a battle royal.' She looked expectantly at them. 'It *had* to be that. Powell was so beside himself because she was intent on taking his beloved Adam away that he killed her. Adam knew – and blamed himself.'

She saw no similar realization on her father's face. 'I don't go along with it,' he said after a moment or two. 'Too much hanging on too little. A few words overheard in the garden – and why, if Powell loved Adam, would he sit by and let him take the blame?'

'I don't know, but Adam said,' she repeated as patiently as she could, 'that the murderer didn't live in Friday Street. Who else but Jonathan Powell?'

'Oliver Ludd,' Peter whipped back at her. 'He was in the States by then.'

'How would Adam know that?' Georgia countered. Surely, surely, Peter was being particularly obtuse over this.

'Brian Winters told him while in prison or on the drive.'

'United we don't stand,' Luke observed happily.

Georgia rounded on him. 'Divided we don't fall, Luke. If Peter and I agreed over everything, we'd get nowhere.'

Luke held up his hands in surrender. 'Apologies, apologies. I'll go back to my newspaper files.'

Georgia took the offered opportunity to switch tack, before she blew her top with her father. 'Where did you get this material from, Peter?'

'A lady by the name of Petra Gossington-Harvey.'

'Who,' Georgia breathed slowly, 'is she?'

'Former reporter on the *Musical Recorder*, former reporter

on the *Ashford Courier*, currently freelance journalist and, even more to the point, the webmaster and chair of the Sweet Fanny Adams United Kay fan club. Knows Dana Tucker.'

That woman's name, Georgia thought unfairly, comes up far too often.

'She copied all this stuff,' Peter explained, 'and sent it in return for a donation to her funds. Willingly given. She was there at Downey Hall in the afternoon. She was a junior reporter on the local rag at the time and took some remarkable pictures on her little Kodak. Also, she still has the notes of the interview she had with Fanny that afternoon. Never used, since the newspaper was naturally more concerned with the murder than Fanny's thoughts. The interview was along the lines of what it was like to be back in the dear old place, all old quarrels forgotten, and how the world must learn forgiveness, as she had. She said she felt at peace for the first time for many years. The newspaper made great play with that.'

'And shortly before or afterwards, depending on what time she gave the interview, she was shouting the odds with Adam,' Georgia pointed out.

'Yet forgiveness seems to be the theme. Could you fetch the red file on my desk?'

Georgia flew in to the house to fetch the file and bore it back.

'A photo of Fanny with her parents,' Peter said, opening it at the page. Even in black and white, the eye immediately went to Fanny, she thought. A smiling Fanny had one arm round someone she could just recognize as Doreen Gibb, and the other round – according to the caption – her father. The father she hated, probably the father of her own child. Forgiveness indeed.

Should she spoil a happy evening by mentioning Dana and her arrangement to lodge with her? No. After a session with Suspects Anonymous, they had all dined at the White Horse in the village and Luke requested permission to stay over. It was granted with great pleasure.

'There's a concert in Otford on Thursday that you might like. Care to come over?' he asked.

'Ah.'

'Oh. Friday Street beckons?'

'It demands.' Should she explain about Dana? No, she couldn't bear it. Reason joined hands with emotion. Why couldn't she bear it if there was nothing to worry about? 'I need to prise Oliver Ludd's address out of Josh,' she continued. 'Peter will never go with the Powell theory while Oliver remains a loose string.'

'Good luck.'

She continued, trying to sound casual, 'I'm going to stay a night or two with Dana.' She succeeded only in sounding aggressive.

'Good of her.'

'Yes.'

And on this unsatisfactory note, they went to bed.

Being a resident in Friday Street, albeit a temporary one, gave a different slant to Georgia's thinking. It would put the case in perspective, giving the village an air of normality that it lacked when she visited only for a day. Then her mind was concentrated on the case, but now it would have to be diverted to consider the necessities of life, such as eating, walking, exchanging small talk.

For all her misgivings, Georgia was glad she was lodging with Dana. Not only was she interested in Fanny Star, she was also a pleasant, undemanding companion. Furthermore, she had met Jonathan Powell.

Georgia entered the Montash Arms on Thursday morning with some confidence. She and Josh shared common ground now over Jonathan Powell, and he would surely see the need for her to contact Oliver Ludd.

As so often with him, she was proved wrong. He listened to Georgia's new theory about Powell without undue excitement, and nodded. 'It could fit, but where does that leave Alice?'

'I don't know yet,' she admitted. 'But I need Oliver Ludd's address.'

His face darkened. 'Why?'

'He knew Fanny in London. He might me able to tell me more about Powell and Fanny's relationship. And after all, if those allegations about Fanny having other lovers were true, it might even—' She'd said the wrong thing too quickly.

'No,' Josh said sharply. 'Wrong track, Georgia. Don't go that way.'

Her hackles went up immediately. 'Oliver was in the gang,' she said defensively. 'He was part of Tom. If he met Fanny in London, their relationship could well have developed, for good or bad.'

'There's nothing to it,' he said angrily. 'Will you never give over with your wild ideas?'

'You can't possibly know what life Fanny had in London,' Georgia said gently. 'Tread softly,' as Yeats wrote, she thought, 'for you tread on my dreams.' Frances Gibb was Josh's dream. 'It might explain why she came here that day. Why Henry sent the invitation in the first place. And might even—'

'Give a reason for murder? Careful, Georgia.' Josh's eyes were glittering. 'Oliver's alive and well and married in the US,' he continued. 'If he loved Frances, he wouldn't want to murder the girl, but Adam Jones might. Thought of that?'

'Yes. I also thought of what you told me, Josh. That the murderer didn't live in Friday Street.'

'Brian meant Powell. You said so yourself just now.'

'Do you know that, or are you just assuming it?'

Josh said nothing, his face blank. Then at last he threw at her, 'You want to know about Oliver? I'll give you his address. You can ring him up or go all the way to North Carolina for all I care, and he'll tell you just what I've told you.'

'Hi.' Dana came into the kitchen and dumped her bags on the floor. 'I saw Jane on the way home. She says she's dug out some stuff for you.'

'Great.' That was good news. Only one problem: it would have to wait. She was seeing Jonathan Powell tomorrow in London.

'You look done in,' Dana said curiously. 'Good job it's my turn to cook. Did Josh attack you with a tomahawk?'

'Yes.' Georgia made a face. 'But I wrested Oliver Ludd's address out of him.'

'So he's Public Enemy Number One.'

'No. I'm still . . .' Georgia hesitated, remembering that Dana knew Powell.

'Still what?'

'Going to talk to Jonathan Powell again first,' she amended lamely.

'Josh's favourite candidate,' Dana interpreted correctly. 'He told me. Don't worry. Powell is no particular chum of mine.'

'There would be a possible motive,' Georgia said cautiously. 'There's no link with Alice Winters, though. When you met him in Dorset—'

'Here, actually.'

'In Friday Street?' Georgia stared at her in astonishment.

'Sorry if I didn't make that clear. I was lodging in Faversham at the time, just arrived. I wanted to meet him and he told me he had business there so we arranged to meet in the town. He offered to drive me out to Friday Street next day – I'd no idea it was so near. He knew I was interested in SFA and he fancied seeing Pucken Manor and Downey Hall again. We had lunch in the pub and the barmaid told him about this cottage. It was then I managed to rent it.' She looked troubled. 'I didn't think it was that important.'

'It probably isn't,' Georgia reassured her. 'When was it?'

'It was the day Alice Winters died.'

'Take care,' Peter said. It was the nearest he would ever get to vetoing a trip on safety grounds. They had talked for thirty minutes on the phone early that morning about the implications of Dana's revelation. Had she been telling the truth? Peter had asked. Why hadn't the police heard about this? Georgia was sure there was no reason to doubt Dana. The police had only just begun to look beyond Jake Baines for Alice's murderer and before that Dana wouldn't have known they were seeking any kind of link between the cases. After all, it could still be coincidence.

'So could Wallace's alleged phone call on the night his wife was murdered,' Peter said scathingly.

'Now that,' Georgia said, roused, 'is an entirely different matter.' They had never agreed about this strange murder case from the 1930s.

'Go if you must, but take care,' her father warned her again.

'Even if Powell's a double murderer,' she observed, 'I doubt if he'd try anything on in the Royal Overseas Club.'

'Why did he agree to meet you?'

'I rang to ask if Adam was bisexual.'

Peter blinked. 'Nothing like the direct approach. I'm surprised you kept your enquiry solely to Adam.'

She ignored this. 'If he'd proposed we met in a Soho back street at two a.m. I might have had second thoughts.'

'I'm relieved to hear it.'

Friday Street seemed a million miles away as she walked into the club that afternoon. Jonathan was already waiting for her, and escorted her into the restaurant.

An early photograph of him in the files Peter had been sent revealed a long-haired, earnest young man with flamboyant fashion sense, which seemed to relate very little to his senior version, when she had met him in Dorset. Seeing Jonathan in his former milieu, London, it seemed much more likely. There was what she could only describe as a 'city awareness' about him.

'I gather from your telephone call that your proposed book is still going ahead,' he said, with the pleasantries over and the coffee before them.

She could see a sticky area ahead, but there was no harm

in advancing straight for it. 'Yes, we now have a link between Fanny Star's murder and that of Alice Winters.'

His eyes flickered. 'Really? She was the poor girl murdered earlier this year by her boyfriend.'

'Yes and no. He's been released, which throws the case wide open again.' No need to mention that the police might not take it up again, or that Jake was released for lack of evidence rather than proof of innocence. In theory there was no difference, but in the mind of Alice's mother, there would be an impassable gap.

'Ah.' Jonathan offered her the sugar as courteously as though this were a first date. 'I presume you feel I can tell you more than I did earlier.'

'I do. I realize one doesn't always pour one's heart out to a stranger, especially one who writes for a living.' Especially, she thought, if one has something to hide.

'Precisely. I saw no point in giving you private details since they were irrelevant to the murder. You asked me on the telephone whether Adam was gay. Pointed, Georgia. What you really meant was am I gay, did I love Adam and did he return that love?'

Somewhat stunned, she nodded.

'This conversation would be easier if I were thirty years younger,' he continued. 'I still find it hard to speak so personally, particularly where Adam is concerned.'

'I'm sorry, but it is relevant.' And it must be a no-brainer for him as to why it was. Remember you are probably sitting opposite a murderer, she told herself, but it was hard to believe in these everyday surroundings.

'Adam was of both persuasions. He adored Fanny – and you can imagine how difficult it still is for me to admit this, since Adam was, as the cliché has it, the great love of my life. Had it not been for my introducing him to Fanny, he and I might still have been together. When he was released from prison, I still hoped, but he eluded me. With Fanny present, any feeling he had for me took a back seat. Not easy for me, since at the same time I was responsible for their careers and they for mine.'

'Did he "elude" you because he believed you killed Fanny?'

'I beg your pardon?' His cheeks flushed red.

'According to one source, Adam might have believed you guilty of the crime, and that's why he did not appeal against the verdict. He felt he should carry the blame.'

His face was rigid, either in pure shock, or in preparation for attack. 'Nonsense,' he spat out.

'Perhaps it is, and perhaps not. Unless we have proof, there's no way we would publish this story, of course.'

'I'm most grateful. Though no doubt you have the libel laws in mind rather more than my feelings.'

'We also like to have the truth in mind. What we've been told might be wrong, but if so you will know it yourself. You must have visited him in prison . . .'

'Frequently. He said nothing.'

He's lying, she thought. His hands were betraying him. Previously his left hand had been at ease on the table. Now his forefinger was working its way up and down his left thumb.

'Then I must accept that.' She gave him a friendly smile. 'Is there any way Adam might have got that impression? Did you see him that evening after he returned from the Gibbs' house?'

'No.'

That forefinger was still at work. She'd ease up and switch to more objective ground. 'I know this might be painful for you, but did Fanny sleep with Adam?'

'Yes.' He was obviously anxious to get this over with, as soon as he could. 'I guessed they were lovers, and Adam confirmed it.'

'You believed him? He could have been lying to—'

'Avoid hurting me by rejecting my advances? It's the sort of thing Adam might have done, but he didn't. I'm sure about that.'

'Did Fanny know you loved Adam?'

'Of course. And, before you ask if that provided me with

a motive for murdering her,' he said briskly, regaining his poise now, 'the answer is no, it did not. There was no longer anything illegal about my situation, and Fanny would have been the last person to want to upset me by flaunting Adam's love for her.'

'Really? So the quarrel you walked in on after the afternoon concert wasn't about her wish to sack you as manager because she felt you were coming between herself and Adam.' If she sounded confident enough, she might get the truth.

Jonathan kept himself under control with visible effort. 'Do you have evidence of that?'

'Enough to pursue it.'

'I find that hard to believe. It isn't correct, and after all this time no outsiders' memories could be relied upon. I can only assume you have concocted this fantasy in order to give me a motive for killing dear Fanny, because you have failed to find the true solution. Adam was innocent, but that, Miss Marsh, does not mean I am guilty.'

Jonathan was giving every indication that the meeting was over, but Georgia was determined. She hadn't finished yet. 'Then who do you think did kill Fanny? You must have some idea. She was your golden goose, after all, apart from your love for Adam.'

He sat down again, but gingerly, as though ready to leave at any moment. 'You know Fanny had an abortion before I met her. Do you also know that it was as a result of rape?'

Georgia was shaken. 'You mean by her father?' she asked uncertainly. 'I heard rumours of an incestuous relationship.'

'I certainly never had that impression.' It was Jonathan's turn to look surprised. 'She referred to it as rape, and implied one violent act rather than an ongoing situation. She could have meant Ron Gibb, I suppose. But I think not. She would have had no hesitation using the word incest as well as rape.'

Whichever it was, no wonder Fanny had left Friday Street, Georgia thought, yet something had brought her back again. Something strong enough to overcome the repulsion she must feel. Or was Powell producing this to keep her quiet?

'Then who could it have been?' she asked. 'How did you find out? Did Fanny tell you?' Questions poured out.

'Fanny said nothing to me. Nor Adam. It was Oliver Ludd who told me after Adam's arrest. He and Fanny were close friends in London – very close, I imagine. He was a student doing his Master's at King's College in the mid-1960s. She told him, but not Adam, and he said she would not say who had attacked her.'

'Did you believe him?' It was beginning to sound genuine.

'No. I could not force him to tell me.'

'Are you in touch with Oliver now?'

'No.' He was showing signs of impatience.

'But you visited other members of the gang recently.'

His eyes fixed on her. 'Did I?'

'On the day Alice Winters died.'

He must have been expecting this. His eyes held hers. 'A sad coincidence.'

Georgia chewed the next step over with Peter during the weekend. He'd been relieved to see her back safely.

'I told you Friday Street holds the secrets,' he said. 'That's the answer. You're blinding yourself to the truth.'

'So it was mere coincidence that Powell was in Friday Street that day when Alice died?'

He frowned. 'It happens.'

'You'll at least make Powell a Burglar Bill in the Alice Winters file?' So far Powell hadn't been an entry for this in Suspects Anonymous.

He'd agreed, and she supposed she should feel satisfied with this small victory.

When she next checked in at the Gibb cottage on the Tuesday evening, Dana seemed delighted to see her. 'I'd offer you a sundowner in the garden, but it would freeze in this weather. I've put the central heating on.' So much for early June.

'How was our friend Powell?' Dana continued.

Georgia grimaced. 'He claimed he knew nothing about

165

Alice. I need more on it. Where he went, and why he was here.'

Dana looked concerned. 'I can't help. After we'd had lunch he said he'd pick me up later in the afternoon, and he did.'

'Jonathan also told me Fanny wasn't just pregnant, she'd been raped. Do you think . . .' She broke off, seeing Dana's shocked face.

'Raped?' she repeated.

'It might not be true,' Georgia continued uncertainly. 'I'm undecided whether to press Josh on it, since he was in love with her.'

'Raped by whom?'

'Jonathan doesn't know.' She decided not to enlarge on this. She hadn't told Dana about Ronald Gibb, but it was quite possible that Josh had. 'That makes it even worse,' she continued. 'I'll have to follow it up.'

'Yes,' Dana said briskly, recovered now. 'I see that. I'll prepare the ground with Josh for you.'

No 'would you like me to', Georgia noticed. She could hardly complain. A disinterested outsider such as Dana could help, where this was concerned. 'Thanks. I've brought stuff for dinner,' she added.

'Good,' Dana said warmly. 'I was hoping you might.'

Back to normal, Georgia thought with relief.

It wasn't until Wednesday evening that she went to the Montash Arms, and then with some trepidation. With good reason, because Josh came marching over to her the moment he saw her. 'So you met Fanny's murderer, I heard.' He made it an accusation.

'I met Powell.'

'Been fobbing you off with a load of stuff about Friday Street?'

'Some.'

'How would he know?' No smile now. Josh was in prosecution mode.

'Sit down and I'll tell you,' she suggested. 'I can't talk with you looming over me, and we can't fight standing up.'

Somewhat disconcerted, he did so. He's worried, Georgia thought, as well as upset.

'He told you Frances was raped, did he?' he shot at her. 'Well, it's true. I didn't tell you because it didn't bloody well affect her murder.'

'How can you possibly be sure of that?' Damn the man. He'd *still* been holding out on her.

'Georgia, Frances has been dead nearly four decades, but it still turns me over to think about her. Okay?'

'Yes, I understand that.' She felt ashamed of her anger. 'But the rape might well have something to do with the murder. You can't prove it doesn't.'

'Oh, I can. Look, the girl told me she'd been raped. I was a hothead in those days. I wanted to go out and kill whoever had done it to her. Frances told me not to bother. She was getting the hell out of Friday Street, she said. The rape had happened weeks ago and now she was pregnant. No point asking who did it. Why should I? She said it was a family thing, so no need to look further than Ron Gibb. She was off, she said. The abortion was arranged and she wouldn't be back.'

'Can you be sure Gibb didn't murder Fanny too?'

He glanced at her. 'Yes, Miss Interfering. She was raped seven years earlier than she was murdered, poor kid. Ronald couldn't have killed her. He was with Doreen and Adam Jones, and couldn't have got back in time.'

'Only according to what Adam told Brian Winters,' Georgia reminded him. 'At the trial Gibb said he left Adam at the gate.'

'He would, wouldn't he?' Josh said scornfully. 'Face it, Georgia, you're on a false trail. Friday Street's dirty business is bad enough without resurrecting anything that doesn't have to be dug up.'

Ten

'Missed you last night,' Georgia sang out next morning, as she heard Dana coming downstairs. 'Want some cereal?' She and Peter had their date with Jane Winters this morning, and she'd made an early start.

'Yes, please.' Dana came into the kitchen, still yawning. 'Hope you didn't wait supper. I dined in state at Pucken Manor with Toby Beamish.'

'Really? Any ghosts at the table?'

'Only Cadenza, who for all the notice he takes of her might as well be one. On second thoughts, she'd have a better deal that way. I shouldn't look gift suppers in the mouth, though. It was a decent shepherd's pie and home-grown veg.'

'Is she his regular cook?' Georgia poured her out a cup of coffee, which Dana immediately seized.

'I don't imagine with Toby anything's very regular. When he has need of her, I suspect.'

'Romantically?'

'Between me and Toby, or between him and Cadenza?'

Georgia laughed. 'The latter. I don't see you making a future home in Pucken Manor.'

'Too right. I've had enough of matrimony. Tried it once and didn't like it.'

Georgia was surprised. She had put Dana down as long-term single, perhaps because she seemed so very independent. But then so was Georgia, and she was divorced. She was also ashamed to note her relief that Dana was apparently not hankering for another partner.

'I've a daughter up at Cambridge,' Dana continued, 'and I split up with her father when she was ten. How about you?'

'Only an ex who's roaming the world somewhere.' No, she would not mention Luke.

'They're safer that way,' Dana reflected. 'One can almost remember why one loved him in the first place.'

Oh, yes. No problem about that, Georgia thought, and no problem in disentangling past from present – well, only a little. If Zac marched through the door, she'd run for her life. Or would it be to Luke? No. She had to solve her own problems. And that, she reminded herself, included not fussing about Luke and Dana. She longed to ask Dana why on earth she'd wanted to see Toby, but decided it wouldn't be politic. Either it would emerge or it wouldn't.

'Peter and I are off to Winters' Farm shortly,' she told Dana.

'Give Jane my love. I'd rather be there than selling semis. I shouldn't complain, I suppose. It's a living, and I enjoy it on the whole.' Dana hesitated. 'I suppose I should explain,' she said diffidently, 'that after you told me about Fanny and the rape, I thought I'd try to find out more. Toby seemed a good bet. Michael and Sheila are friendly enough, but I got the impression that Toby is a *watcher*. Do you know what I mean?'

'Yes.' Georgia most certainly did. If one looked carefully, watchers were everywhere, watching and listening, not doing. Nothing wrong about that, for they were one half of life's equation, but if one wanted information, then – if they so chose – they would be the source to go to. 'Did Toby cough up?'

'Toby supports what Josh says, which is that Ron Gibb is in the frame,' Dana continued, 'though he wasn't very communicative about it.' She looked questioningly at Georgia.

'To me, it doesn't add up.' Georgia buttered toast vigorously while she thought this through. Now Dana was in the picture, she could speak more freely. 'I trust Josh, but not his story. Ron Gibb as a child abuser, that's one thing, but Fanny was seventeen when this rape occurred. If she was cowed and meek by nature it might be understandable, but she wasn't. If it was regular abuse, why hadn't she left home earlier? It beggars belief that she just went on taking it – and anyway, would she have used the word "rape" about someone who had been regularly abusing her?'

'I agree, it's odd,' Dana said. 'I asked Toby about the gang, but got nowhere. He maintains it was composed of jolly girls and boys, mutually supportive and tender-hearted.'

'If Josh were lying,' Georgia reflected, 'Toby would be top of my list for rape.'

'I'd second that, but I don't think Josh is lying.'

Peter arrived at nine o'clock precisely and tooted impatiently. The comparatively early hour was Jane Winters' own choice. She would already have been working for some hours and this would be her first break, she had explained. Peter had no problem with early mornings and today drove with great gusto through the village.

'Nothing like North Downs air,' he proclaimed. 'No wonder all the tubercular patients used to come here. It's just like Switzerland.'

'A vivid imagination helps,' Georgia murmured.

Jane Winters ushered them into the large farmhouse kitchen, where the large oak table was loaded with promising-looking piles of papers and files.

'I've laid it out here, as you can see,' Jane said, 'but if you'd like to see where I found it . . .?' She looked at Georgia, who promptly replied, 'Yes, please.' The hiding place might be relevant and, at the very least, seeing Alice's own room might give her an idea about her life.

She followed Jane to a small room tucked away on the first floor. 'This is her den,' Jane explained. 'Her bedroom's next door. We spread ourselves a bit after Bill died, so that we felt less like peas rattling in a pod.'

Georgia looked round the den: a modern hi-fi system and posters mingled with dolls, ornaments, a guitar – Adam Jones'? she wondered.

'Alice liked things straight and orderly,' Jane continued, 'and so I'd have expected to find Bill's collection here in the desk, and I wanted to show you this first. In fact I found it at the back of the wardrobe in the bedroom. You're welcome to look through anything you like. Dana's been helping me clear out the clothes. That's the worst. She said the best thing was to bundle everything up and she'd take it away, but somehow that seemed disloyal to Alice. So we've sorted it, and left it in bags in the bedroom. Silly, I know, but it seemed best to me,' she said hopelessly. 'I don't know which is worst, the clothes hanging in a wardrobe or the empty space. Both remind me – as if I needed it. At least they're in bags so that I can pretend all I need do is whip them out if this all turns out to be a bad dream and Alice comes marching in, demanding to know where her clothes are.'

Georgia hated to ask Jane her next question, but there was no option. The police would have searched everything, but now there would be new lines of enquiry, and other material might be relevant. 'If we find something here, amongst the papers or her possessions, that the police should see,' she said hesitantly, 'should we take it or will you?'

'You. I've had police up to here,' Jane said firmly. 'I know they did what they could, but the thought of starting all over again makes me want to run like hell.'

After Jane had left to return to work, Georgia browsed round the den and the bedroom with the least disturbance she could manage. There was plenty here to record a life, but nothing that she could see, apart from the guitar, to indicate an interest in, let alone an obsession with, Sweet Fanny Adams. That was puzzling, as though Alice had put SFA in a compartment of its own, a subject apart from her everyday life. She discovered nothing more, and it was with relief that she left these all too poignant personal memories to join

Peter at the kitchen table and gratefully share his cafetière of coffee.

'Interesting,' Peter observed, as she sat down beside him. 'There's a lot here, and yet nothing tells a complete story.'

Georgia had a preliminary rummage through the piles of handwritten notes, one or two formal-looking documents, a few loose photos, an album of photos, a pencil drawing of what looked like a cameo pendant or locket, and a file of letters, with computer-generated letterheads giving the Winters' Farm address and a mobile phone number. She scored an immediate bull's-eye as a name leapt out at her from a letter written in early March that year.

> *Dear Mr Powell,*
> *My grandfather was a fan of Sweet Fanny Adams and amongst his papers were some interesting notes about the day of her death that I think you would like to know about. If you wish to hear more, please tele-phone me on my mobile, number as above.*

'What the blazes is this about?' Peter wrinkled his fore-head when she showed it to him. 'It looks like "My first attempt at blackmail, by a young girl".'

Georgia felt torn between an odd relief that the link between Powell and Alice was firmly established at last, and the real-ization that if they were right, Mike Gilroy would almost certainly be following this up. If the case were reopened, so would Jane Winters' wounds. 'Obviously he did ring,' she said reluctantly, 'and they met here in Friday Street. The day she died. Not just coincidence after all.'

'Proof needed,' Peter said briskly. 'If this is new to Mike, Alice's mobile phone records need to be checked, or rather re-checked.'

'Hold your horses,' Georgia said crossly. 'What evidence is there that this letter is for blackmail purposes? She might not even have sent it.'

'Unlikely, but possible.'

'Let's look further.'

He pushed a photograph album over to her, and she turned over the pages with interest. These were the best photos she'd seen yet of Friday Street forty-odd years ago. Josh as an eager young man. Michael looking tall and as weedy as Drew. A young Toby. A picture of Brian and Liz, according to the caption, arms wrapped round each other, and a similar one of Sheila and Michael. A jokey one of Fanny with her head under Josh's arm, pulling a face. Even Hazel with Oliver, a gangly youth looking remarkably like Henry.

'None of Sheila and Fanny together,' she observed, 'though there's one of them taken with Michael, who looks like the cock of the roost.'

'Chance,' Peter said. 'Snaps aren't taken with posterity in mind, only with the opportunity and impulse. The photographers don't consider the poor biographer who comes along years later and wants to pick out the significant from the rubbish. That's what makes albums fascinating and frustrating at the same time.'

'The first in the album is one of Brian and Fanny,' Georgia pointed out. 'Does that tell us anything?'

'That he fancied her? It's more probable that he made up the album after the notoriety of her death, which puts a different perspective on the choice of pictures, if he thought there was a case to answer over Adam Jones.'

Later in the album, she found three or four pages of photos taken on different cameras on the afternoon of Fanny's death, simply captioned 22nd June, 1968.

'Thus confirming,' he said, 'that this is a volume dedicated to the story of Fanny Star.'

'Yes,' she agreed. 'Look at this one. Adam Jones and Jonathan Powell, lounging in deckchairs with drinks in their hands. It's captioned "AJ and JP at four p.m.", and here's one of Fanny and Henry, at the entrance to the house. "F and HL at four fifteen." Looking relaxed and happy.'

'Why the times?' Peter mused. 'Watson, do you think the game's afoot?'

'Not sure.' She looked through the remaining pictures, all, it seemed, in chronological order. Pictures of groups on the terrace, but nothing to explain their inclusion, save perhaps a bad one of Jonathan and Adam at 7.35, neither looking at the camera. Neither did they look happy. There was another one of Jonathan a little later, now on his own, at what looked like an outside bar. She put the album on one side and continued looking through the papers.

'I presume you've seen this, Sherlock?' She studied the formal document. 'It's headed "Statement by Brian Winters, second October 1990, sworn before Commissioner of Oaths, Richard Tanner, solicitor". It's initialled at the foot of each page, BW, but there's no final page or pages with the signed stamp on it.'

'I thought you'd notice that.'

Georgia quickly read it through. Brian had sworn:

'I wish to set on record my memories of the afternoon of twenty-second June, 1968, based on diary notes I took at the time. When I heard the Friday Street music played that night, I decided not to come forward because I had no evidence to offer, nor any theories. I now have some supporting evidence, but the police would laugh it to pieces. I need to speak out somehow, just in case what I saw was important. I passed Fanny Star about twenty to five and said how good the concert was, and she was relaxed and happy. About half an hour later I saw her again. She was in a terrible mood and said she was heading for Owlers' Smoke to get away for a while. She said Adam clearly thought more of Jonathan Powell than he did of her, and I could tell him that she was going to cancel the next concert and walk out. I could see she meant it, so thought I'd look for him. As I approached a walled garden, I could hear two men arguing behind it. I hesitated for a bit because they were talking about Frances, and then it became clear it was Adam Jones and his manager. Adam was saying that Fanny was deter- mined to get rid of Powell, but that he would try to talk her out of it. Fanny felt they needed more time to themselves.

I didn't understand fully at the time, but thinking about it afterwards I realized it was not only work but also their personal lives that were at issue. Jonathan Powell was too emotional for it just to be about work. He told Adam that Fanny was coming between them, and that he'd make sure that never happened. He'd fix her. Adam could count on that. Adam would be better on his own, with him. They were meant for each other, and Fanny was deliberately wrecking their chance of happiness. If only Adam would go solo, all would be well.

'Later when I visited Adam in prison he told me that on his return from Mr and Mrs Gibb's home he had come into the gardens through the garden gate, not the house, intending to go straight to the stage. He could see there wasn't anything happening there, even though music was blaring out over the amplifiers, so he took the woodland path which went by Owlers' Smoke. Frances had shown it to him earlier that day. As he approached, he saw Jonathan Powell heading from the woodland towards the house, as if he had just come from the Smoke. Adam thought that meant Frances might still be there, so he went to see, and found her dead . . .'

'So there we are,' Georgia said. 'The story with a ring of truth.'

'If not embroidered by age,' Peter pointed out.

'You seem determined to clear Powell,' Georgia said crossly. 'Yet you can't deny that everything comes back to him. And,' she quickly read on, 'Brian turns next to what Adam told him when he was giving him the lift, which we know from Josh.'

'So nothing helpful, except for the interesting part about Owlers' Smoke.'

'Isn't that enough?'

'No,' Peter said flatly. 'This statement could be missing quite a bit. Not just the signature, but at least some of the text. Would you agree? For a start, the last page we have ends mid-sentence: "When I heard . . ." We've no idea how much else was in the complete statement, or what it was about. There could be another twelve pages, for all we know. Think of the logic. If Brian Winters was so sure Powell was guilty, why didn't he take it further?'

'Because he had no proof.'

'He would have had enough at least to tell the police or the court that Powell was lying. Why wait until 1990 to write this statement?'

'I don't know,' Georgia muttered savagely.

'Then let me suggest it's because Brian Winters had *conflicting* ideas about what happened that day, and that it took time to mull over. All we have here is part of them. The part, dare I suggest, that Friday Street would prefer we saw.'

'Then where is the rest of it?'

'With these missing photographs, and who knows what else? The locket, perhaps.'

'I searched the bedroom and the office thoroughly, and Jane has too. There's nothing else that refers to SFA and no sign of any locket like that in this drawing.'

'Then Alice must have hidden it even more successfully.'

'Your logic isn't adding up any more than mine.' Georgia had been thinking furiously. 'There's a flaw in your soup. Alice writes her pathetic blackmail letter to Jonathan Powell and we have at least *some* evidence that looks black for him. If, as you proclaim, she actually has a secret cache with more damning stuff about somebody else, then why try to blackmail Powell? Or do you think she handed the proof of Powell's guilt over to him?' she asked hopefully.

'I don't, and I think, dear child, we are getting ahead of ourselves,' Peter said after a pause. 'Just as a hypothesis, perhaps Alice wished to explore every avenue until the real truth emerged, and she had the glory of solving the case. She wrote to several people and waited for the right response. A dangerous game. And one that led to her death.'

*   *   *

Peter departed, after lunch in the pub, straight back to Haden Shaw and Suspects Anonymous. The atmosphere had once again been strained. Michael and Sheila had been there, and Toby, with Cadenza in his wake, had emerged as they arrived. Tim and Drew popped in for lunch but there was no sign of Josh or Hazel. Instead their son Bob's formidable presence loomed over them. Perhaps he saw himself as defender of his father's privacy, but once again Georgia felt a pariah. The quicker she got Alice's evidence to Mike, the better. Peter had rung him on the mobile and it was agreed Georgia would drive it over this afternoon.

She realized she was beginning to long for her own home again now, not to mention missing Luke. Being so near made the separation worse. If she were in Haden Shaw, there would be no problem, but staying a mere ten miles away was frustrating. She missed the familiar interchanges between herself and Peter in his office. They had a concentration that was hard to achieve here. It was time that her jumble of thoughts and evidence gelled into one, and that could only happen in Haden Shaw. Thank heavens she could leave tomorrow for the weekend, go home and regroup. She'd be away from this feeling of a hundred eyes upon her, and she might be able to see things more clearly. Dana had asked her to stay for the village fete on Saturday afternoon, and the Ludds had promised her a starring role serving teas if she wished. She had declined with thanks.

She walked back to the cottage, carrying the holdall containing the collection, glad that at least this marked a step forward in the Alice Winters investigation. Fifteen minutes later she left, relieved to be driving out of Friday Street towards the A2. She still couldn't budge Jonathan Powell from her mind. It was pointless assuming there *was* missing evidence in the collection. There might only be the end of that sentence and the signature on the missing page. She was pondering on Brian Winters as she turned the wheel for an unexpectedly sharp bend. She'd be glad to get home; even the car felt odd today.

She had only a second to register this before it was out of her control. The trees in the field on her right were rushing towards her as the car veered across the verge, then through the fence. Then everything went black.

Luke was up there looking down at her. What on earth was she doing in bed? Luke and Peter, too. Her head hurt and she felt sick. Nevertheless she registered that they looked awfully worried.

'Georgia!' she heard Luke say with great thankfulness, and Peter seemed to be crying. 'You're all right, don't worry.'

'Of course I am,' she said uncertainly. She tried to look round but it hurt. 'What . . .?'

'You're in A and E,' Luke told her briskly. 'Concussion only, with luck. Don't move,' he said, as she began to struggle. 'Stay right there. They might let you go home later if you're good.'

They didn't. She was whisked into a ward. Overnight only, they said, as if she might clamour to stay in for a fortnight. 'Just to be sure.'

She slept for some hours and woke up to find Luke still at her side. Her head was clearer now. She remembered the car; she remembered where she had been going.

'The Winters material,' she said with alarm. 'I was taking it to Mike Gilroy. Was it still there in the car?

'Taken care of. The police have it. The car was on its side, a local farmer found you, called the ambulance and police who, finding a bag in the back of the car marked DI Mike Gilroy, cunningly jumped to the right conclusion. The car's still there. I'll deal with it.'

'What happened?' she asked.

'That's what we want to know. Not like you to be drunk at the wheel.' Luke might be joking but his face was flatteringly strained.

'I wasn't,' she said flatly. 'It was the car.'

'Peter rang Mike about it, and he checked it out. A wheel came off, but whether that happened after the crash or caused

178

it isn't clear. All the signs are that it did cause it. You were unlucky in coming round that bend at the time it decided to come loose.' His voice sounded soothingly matter-of-fact, as though this happened all the time.

'That's crazy. The car's just had its MOT and I refuse to believe that Sid Cooper' (the Haden Shaw garage owner) 'left the wheel nuts loose.'

'You don't think,' Luke said politely, 'that Friday Street might be making a point?'

'I'm not giving in,' Georgia said firmly, established in an armchair the next day in End Cottage after Luke had brought her back from hospital. 'I'll go back to Haden Shaw late tomorrow. If Friday Street has a point to make, they can make it direct to me. They'll find me at the fete.'

'Then I'm coming with you,' Luke informed her.

'Village fetes aren't your thing.' Nevertheless she felt a great sense of peace. It was nice to be looked after – once in a while. She could rejoin battle with the world later.

'Dana's told me I can sleep over,' Luke retorted. 'I don't intend to have any villains climbing through the window to bang you over the head again. This threat wasn't meant to kill you; the next one might.'

'So you think I should give up?' she asked baldly, contemplating the thought of Dana, herself and Luke here together. She felt so wobbly she realized she didn't care, even when halfway through dinner she was forced to abandon them at the table in favour of bed. Some time later she was aware of Luke crawling in by her side. She reached out to him, and was rewarded with a kiss on the palm of her hand, then one on her cheek, and then a whispered, 'Georgia, I love you. Don't frighten me like this again.'

She thought of Luke's first wife killing herself in a stupid, unnecessary car accident, and of what thoughts must have rushed through his head this afternoon. I'll make it up to you, she vowed silently. I will.

The next morning Luke ordered her to stay in the garden at End Cottage and not to answer the door to strangers, while he and Dana went to help set up stalls at the fete. At first she insisted on going with them, but on consideration the best plan seemed to be to do as she was told. Peter had told her Mike was coming over later in the morning and that was good enough reason to do nothing for a while.

He turned up at eleven, as composed as ever. 'Trying to get yourself killed, are you, Georgia?' he said, sitting down next to her at the garden table.

'That hadn't been my plan.'

'If you'd been *really* unlucky, that's what would have happened. Highly inefficient way of doing things.'

'I suppose there's no doubt that the wheel nuts were deliberately loosened?'

'We've got fingerprints, DNA and signed confession and photo stuck to the wheel,' Mike assured her without a glimmer of a smile. 'I've looked through the bag of sweeties you were bringing me. Interesting, but no—'

'Solid evidence for the DCI,' she finished for him. 'Would my dead body help?'

He looked at her reproachfully. 'Cheap shot, Georgia.'

He was right. 'Sorry, Mike. It's getting frustrating, sensing that Friday Street is sitting on a heaving volcano, and keeping the lid on far too tightly.'

'Volcanoes don't have lids. Be careful, Georgia. Don't want you buried in a Friday Street Pompeii.'

After Mike's departure, Dana's neighbour called in to see if she was all right – Dana's instructions, she said. Georgia assured her she was, and she had scarcely left before Sheila Ludd appeared, box in hand and immaculate as ever. No jeans and shirt for Sheila. 'How's the invalid?'

'Recovered, thanks.'

'I thought you and Dana might not feel like cooking this evening, so Michael's sent one of his specials for you.'

'That's very kind.'

'His *coq au vin* pie,' Sheila said with pride, displaying the contents of the box.

'I didn't think of Michael as a pie-maker,' Georgia said, amused.

'It's a joint effort. He does the *coq au vin*; I do the pastry. I must rush and do my bit at the fete. Don't bother about the teas,' she said graciously to Georgia, who had no intention of bothering. 'Henry's opening the fete and I have to be ready for the hordes by then.'

She watched Sheila depart in her elegant linen two-piece and wondered how it was that ladies of the manor went on from generation to generation with exactly the same stamp. The pie looked good and she stowed it in the fridge with a note telling Dana to enjoy it, since she'd be going home with Luke after the fete. She ate the salad that Luke had left for her, and then left for the festivities.

A village fete should be a gentle affair, and it was a reasonably good day for it, considering the unseasonable June weather so far. She enjoyed walking alone to Priory Field. No need for an armed guard. As she approached she could see roundabouts and the top of a bouncy castle, and could hear children's cries. Everything seemed normal. When she arrived, the scene was like every other village fete she'd been to her in her life. Perhaps the inhabitants of Friday Street were acting out the play that this was a normal village, where people ate cakes and played childish games. Or perhaps this was the real Friday Street, and it was simply taking time off from its darker side to see what it could do if it tried. It was hard to imagine there had been two murders here, to her knowledge, and perhaps a third attempted one. Perhaps this fete was an indication that the waters were gently closing over the whirlpool of the horrors of the last few months? No, Georgia disciplined herself. She mustn't think like that. Someone had deliberately tampered with her car. She couldn't deal with that this afternoon, though. Today was a day off.

She had hoped to see Toby Beamish running a haunted

house, with ghastly spectres leaping out at unexpected places, but she was disappointed. The nearest to a ghostly residence was a 'Krazy Kottage', a magnificent structure of crooked beams, bulging corners and windows at odd angles. There were other obviously touring attractions, a hook-a-duck stall, the bouncy castle and roundabouts, a candy floss and popcorn stall. Toby was contenting himself with an old-fashioned coconut shy. Dear me, Grandmama, what powerful arms you have, she thought hazily as she watched Toby, sleeves rolled up, encouraging the punters. No doubt Cadenza longed to be encased within them, but she would settle for Luke. Where was he? she wondered. With Dana, obviously, but she felt too tired to care very much.

There was a central area where, according to the programme she had bought, the primary-school children would be giving a display. Tim Perry was running a win-the-pig competition. Tempting, that. She'd like to return home with a grunting piglet under one arm. Then she saw that the said pig was a pink fluffy replica and lost interest. Josh was running a plant stall and nodded awkwardly when she approached.

'I heard what happened,' was all he said. 'Glad it was no worse.'

She had half expected another lecture on getting out of Friday Street, but none came. Hazel, he told her, was in the tea tent, selling her beloved cakes. Georgia had gathered that there was some rivalry as to whose cakes on the stall went first: Cadenza's creamy Black Forest gâteau, Hazel's iced carrot cake, Sheila's amaretto cheesecake, and the chocolate cakes made by Bob's wife, Mary Perry. Nearly all the plants on Josh's stall had already been sold, and those remaining looked like wallflowers at the first real dance of summer. It was so hot today that it was hard to tell whether it was the heat or the accident making her head feel muzzy.

Such village fetes were timeless, and she wondered how many Fanny had attended. Had the gang come in force? Had they sneered at such humble village pleasures? Georgia almost felt part of Friday Street now. She began to feel she understood it, even though its darkest secrets hadn't yet been penetrated. Perhaps there were none. Then she thought again of yesterday, and felt sick once again.

'Come on,' Luke said, miraculously materializing at her side and steering her towards the tent. 'You look in need of tea and cake.'

She let herself be led, for her head felt as if it was filled with candy floss. She could see everyone without even using her eyes. She just knew they were *there*. Henry chatting with the vicar; Sheila, Dana, Cadenza and Hazel at the tea stall, performing an intricate dance with the plates, teacups and money. Cadenza spotted her first.

'My dear Georgia.' She was full of concern. 'Sit down and I'll bring you some tea. You must try my cake.'

'Try Sheila's cheesecake. It's delicious,' Dana said.

Cakes seemed to swim before Georgia's face and she pleaded sickness. All she wanted was tea.

Cadenza brought it to her and then sat down at her side while she drank it. Squashed between her and Luke, Georgia felt like Alice at the Mad Hatter's tea party. 'I used to come here as a child,' Cadenza confided.

'To the tea tent?' Georgia was confused.

Cadenza laughed merrily. 'To this field. The old priory, which we used to call Solomon's Temple. I feel I can commune with the true murderer of Lady Rosamund here. It was from here the wicked knight must have set out to murder her.'

'You could appeal to his better nature to come forward,' Georgia said idiotically. Why couldn't she think straight? Cadenza would think she was mocking her, but she had no such intention.

'Yes, yes, you do understand. If he confessed, if we could speak to his ghost, then I feel Friday Street might be much easier in its mind. I feel he cast a blight over this whole village by blaming my poor ancestor, Piers. If only he would come forward. Meanwhile,' she laid her hand over Georgia's, 'you are facing great danger. Do please take very special care.'

Eleven

Sunday, the perfect antidote to Friday Street. Georgia lay back on the lounger in her garden, dozing, aware that somewhere far away was the sound of Luke in the kitchen preparing lunch. Next door she heard a door to the conservatory being flung open and her father's routine wrangle with Margaret. This was usually good fun to overhear, since Margaret always won, but today she was content to let it drift past her. Her head no longer ached, but felt sufficiently heavy to excuse her remaining here, absolving her from duties for at least another day. Tomorrow would come the reckoning: who in Friday Street had wanted her dead? That, however, was apparently disputable.

'Daft way to try to kill someone,' Mike had pointed out. 'It was only that corner did for you. If it had come off somewhere else, you probably wouldn't even have lost control. He couldn't bank on it.'

'It felt pretty final to me,' she'd muttered.

'I'd say you were being warned off. We'll station a community officer in Friday Street for a while.'

The offer had not inspired confidence. What could one person do if a whole village was united against her?

Mike had rung Peter yesterday evening, however, with the news that the Alice Winters case was officially being reopened. He'd added, so Peter had told her, that that meant Marsh & Daughter could continue looking into (or, to use Mike's words, messing around with) the Fanny Star murder. 'Which means,' Peter had cynically suggested, 'that we can do their donkey work for them – on the off chance that we're right and there's a firm link between the two.'

Today, from her lounger perspective, that link seemed far more likely than Mike would still credit. Nevertheless she wasn't going to worry about it today. This was an official day off. She could even ignore the weeds growing in her garden. She'd done her major weeding for the year months ago, so any that grew now could have a free rein until autumn. Even lawn mowing was—

Her pleasant train of thought was interrupted by the intercom ringing inside her house. This was odd, for Peter had said he wouldn't disturb her. Moreover it was tacitly acknowledged that the intercom was only for work purposes. If it was a paternal call, he'd use the landline. There was no rhyme or reason to this; it was just one of those habits that had grown up over the years. So why ring now? She heard the murmur of Luke's voice, and sank back thankfully. For once she could wait and let the problem come to her.

It did. Luke came out into the garden after a few minutes, bearing two cups of instant coffee and a very worried look. 'Anything wrong with Peter?' she asked tentatively.

'No. It's Dana. Josh rang Peter.'

'What's wrong?' Crazy scenarios whizzed through her mind.

'It seems she ate something that disagreed with her. She's in hospital.'

Bad, but not the worst, and why should Josh . . . Then she realized the answer to her question. 'You mean *really* disagreed?'

'Yes. She's in a coma, and it doesn't look good. She was just able to dial nine-nine-nine late last evening but was in a bad way when the ambulance got there. Her neighbour alerted Josh this morning.'

'Why?' Her brain didn't seem to be working. 'Why is he involved?'

'The police arrived to search the cottage early this morning, and the grapevine swung into action. Obviously the police need to check what Dana had been eating. Peter's rung Mike, who wasn't best pleased on a Sunday morning, and he's sorting it out with uniform. It was a large dose of something unpleasant, not yet identified. Any ideas?'

Salmonella, ancient cold meats, fish, chicken, all the usual suspects flashed through her mind. When she'd last opened Dana's fridge yesterday it had looked fairly empty. Perhaps she had brought something home for supper. The answer then struck her with terrible force.

'The pie!' she said, aghast. 'Sheila Ludd brought a *coq au vin* pie yesterday.'

'There's no such thing.'

'It seems to have been a Ludd speciality. She,' Georgia swallowed, 'brought it round for us both, and since we were coming back to Haden Shaw, I left it with a note for Dana.'

Luke went very white. 'You mean it was intended for *you*?'

Georgia grappled with the implications. 'I don't know. I think so. No, for both of us . . .' She stopped rambling. 'Yes,' she added quietly, 'Sheila said for both of us.' She couldn't get her head round the idea that it was Sheila and Michael Ludd who had baked it. 'Does it have to be the pie?' she asked, aware that she sounded pathetic.

'No.'

Luke the comforter, Luke the strong. Georgia pulled herself together. 'Which hospital is she in? I should go.'

'The William Harvey at Ashford. And *we* should go.'

Of course, she thought dully. This was Dana, and Luke too must be suffering greatly. Dana held at least a part of Luke's heart. She must acknowledge it, and be generous.

Lunch was a hurried affair with the sunshine gone from the day. All Georgia could think of was Dana, as she was convinced that she, Georgia, had been the real target if the pie proved to contain poison. Accidental poisoning to such a severe extent seemed unlikely, she and Luke had agreed, and yet the alternative was too much to take in all at once.

The hospital was a maze of endless bright sterile corridors

of anonymity, intensifying her fear of what they might find at the other end. They found Dana, still in a coma, in a room by herself. Looking down at her sleeping, peaceful face, the dark hair tumbled around her and the mass of tubes sticking everywhere, Georgia felt perilously near crying. Come back, she willed her, come *back*. We'll start again. A second chance at a friendship that she'd in her heart of hearts resisted. But there was no movement. Nothing.

She and Luke remained for an hour, talking to her, trying to break through to her, but to no noticeable avail, and finally decided they should leave. 'If you can hear us, Dana, we'll be back. Both of us,' she promised.

Another visitor arrived as they went into the corridor. Henry Ludd of all people. So Friday Street had a heart, Georgia thought. One member of the family showed sympathy while two more apparently conspired to kill both Dana and herself. The pie loomed large in her still woolly head, and she found it hard to be natural, even though she was condemning without evidence.

'Is there any news?' Henry asked. He looked much older than when she had last seen him at the fete. The effort of coming here must be quite considerable, and though he had no need of a wheelchair he leaned heavily on his stick.

'No change, I'm afraid.'

He nodded. 'I'll sit with her for a while. It can do no harm, can it?'

They left him at Dana's side, and Georgia glanced back as they walked along the corridor. 'I may be slightly cuckoo today, but what's Henry Ludd doing here?'

'You think he's here to finish the job?' Luke stopped and looked at her kindly. 'Georgia, *if* that pie was poisoned, and *if* it was meant for you, then there's no more harm coming Dana's way. If it was meant for both of you, including Dana, which seems very unlikely, then the idea of a twosome conspiracy of Ludds is hard enough to envisage, let alone the whole family mucking in with attempted murder. My love, you've been watching too many TV thrillers, and reading too many Agatha Christies. Comfort yourself that there was some cunning plan to get Dana out of the house for the evening, which failed, and that the pie was meant solely for you.'

She managed to laugh at that. Nevertheless, Friday Street was getting to her at last, and that was the barrier she could not overcome.

Luke returned to South Malling, with a promise to visit Dana on the Monday evening and come over for dinner afterwards.

'Which leaves me as your guardian angel, Georgia,' Peter said. 'That'll be a change. I can be your food taster.'

'Not funny,' Georgia replied.

'Very well. I'll be serious, and you'll like that even less. One, possibly two attempts to stop you, and therefore us, from investigating the Friday Street murders. The first could have been a warning shot, but not the second. What does that suggest?'

'Incompetence' was the frivolous word that came to her mind, but she could hardly voice it. 'It means we must be getting near the truth.'

'Quite.'

'But logically that doesn't make sense, since I've been shouting aloud in the Montash Arms that it's Jonathan Powell I'm interested in. The idea that the Ludds were involved never seriously arose.'

'Consider whether you have not been mistaken, Georgia,' Peter said gravely. 'I've always been convinced that the answer lies in Friday Street, and might well be in Downey Hall. Didn't you tell me that Dana went to dinner at Pucken Manor very shortly before this attack?'

'Yes, but how does that affect the issue?'

'It could depend on what was said during that dinner. For all this feud between the two families, which I'm sure is real enough, there is a close coterie between the Ludds and Toby Beamish. It's held together not so much by cordiality as by something that I can only define, in the absence of knowledge, as "the past". Until we reach into that, we don't see the true picture. I do believe we're getting closer, however, which brings—'

The telephone rang, and Peter broke off to answer it.

'She's here, Mike,' he said after a moment. A pause while he listened, then 'Hold on', and he turned to her. 'Mike says the pie has been cleared of suspicion. Half of it was left, and there's no trace of anything but well-cooked chicken, red-wine sauce, and the usual ingredients. Short of a poisoned mushroom having been popped into one half in the hope that it would be the half to be eaten, the pie is innocent. And the symptoms of amanitin and phalloidin, the mushroom poisons, don't tie in with Dana's. Any idea what else Dana could have been eating that day? The reaction time could have been some hours.'

'Pub lunch, if any, and the tea tent,' she remembered. 'The cake!' she exclaimed. She could hear Dana's voice. 'Sheila's cheesecake. Delicious.' Her head began to spin, wondering if she was fantasizing. No. No chance of that. It was too vivid a memory.

'You're sure?'

'Certain.' With sickening clarity.

Peter spoke quickly to the police on the phone, then turned to Georgia: 'They'll check out the rubbish from the fete and the pub.'

'Even if the cake was poisoned,' Georgia said, 'anybody on the tea counter could have added something to it – Cadenza, Hazel, who knows?' It was weak, and she knew it. Georgia had no particular liking for Sheila Ludd, but nothing against her either, and the idea of her poisoning something deliberately seemed unbelievable. 'It's Friday Street,' she added wearily. 'There's just something about it.'

'Villages are made up of people, Georgia. A rose is only a delightful word because the flower is. If the flower were ugly, the word "rose" would be too. Friday Street's ugliness comes from what went on there. The fingerprints of time are blacker than usual, that's all.'

The next day Peter forbade her even to think of driving to Friday Street. Better by far, he told her, to spend the day quietly with notes and computer. When, in defiance of orders, she reached the office late in the afternoon, Peter had news. 'Mike's sergeant has rung. They've identified the poison as hyoscine. Highly toxic.'

'But that's a plant poison, isn't it? *Datura*? The thorn apple?'

'Correct. Can be found here in the south, in Kent, but mostly in hot countries. Every part of it can be lethal.'

'Grown at Downey Hall, do you think?'

'Immaterial. He had more results too. The cake as well as the pie is blameless, judging by the remaining crumbs and a leftover slice. And if someone decided to add it to Dana's own slice, it would be difficult to do so on the spur of the moment. The odd green leaf tucked into a cheesecake might be noticed.'

'So we're back to square one. Why did someone try to kill me? And who?'

'The why is interesting,' Peter said, not very tactfully. 'Over Fanny Star or Alice Winters? Neither adds up. If someone thought you were getting too close to the Fanny Star solution, why should they be worried? After all, we're not likely to have sufficient evidence at this stage for the CPS to prosecute. We couldn't publish specific names because of the libel laws, so why risk everything by trying to kill you? All we could do is try to clear Adam Jones' name. The real killer could just laugh in our faces.'

'Unless, of course,' Georgia gently reminded him, 'the same person also killed Alice Winters.'

'In which case the police are on to it, so again why try to kill you?'

'I think my next step—'

'Georgia,' Peter interrupted, 'Luke and I have been talking.'

'So?' She glared at him suspiciously.

'We feel it's time you had a holiday.'

'I don't want one. I'm working.'

191

'Not at Friday Street, you're not. It's time to let the dust settle.'

'You mean *my* dust settle, and you'll go right on with Alice Winters?'

'Something like that,' Peter agreed. 'Mike and I—'

'Conspiracy!'

'Your work lies overseas. Luke feels he could take a week off. Not long, I know, and tiring, but distance helps perspective.'

'What on earth are you talking about?' Georgia said wearily. She didn't want to go anywhere.

'It's time we talked to Oliver Ludd.'

'First concussion, now jet lag,' Georgia grumbled.

'Nothing but complaints, even though I got us an upgrade to Club Class,' Luke retorted amiably.

'I am very grateful.' She had been; she could stretch out and snooze to her heart's content, but that still didn't help the jet lag.

Rather than fly to Charlotte, which was the nearest airport to where Oliver and Liz Ludd lived, they'd elected to fly to Atlanta and hire a car so that they could drive through Georgia – her eponymous state, she pointed out. The Ludds lived just over the border in North Carolina. Despite an overnight stop at a motel outside Atlanta, she still felt dizzy and was glad they had a day to recover before meeting the Ludds. The heat alone was hard to deal with. Stepping from their air-conditioned Ford into the summer heat was like a plunge into a steam bath. So far they had dashed from air-conditioning to air-conditioning systems while being presented with huge platefuls of food and surrounded by smiling, upbeat American faces whenever they stopped. All very different from England, and it seemed to her like driving through a stage set. Even Luke, who looked (blast him) cool and relaxed in the six-dollar casual shirt he'd bought when they stopped overnight, began to look more like a film star on set than her publisher-cum-lover here on a working mission.

'You only want a Texan ten-gallon hat to complete the picture.'

'Next stop, honey,' he drawled.

Dana remained in a coma and the hospital was making no promises. She might or might not come out of it. Georgia felt badly about having come away, especially with Luke. Had he really wanted to come with her, or had Peter nagged him into it? Would he have preferred to stay with Dana? *Shouldn't* he have stayed with her? She couldn't work it out, but how grateful she was that he was here, and not in Friday Street. She felt almost herself again now, jet lag excluded, but the tiny gap remaining between herself and normality was profoundly thankful for Luke's presence.

Oliver Ludd had sounded reasonably friendly on the telephone, once Josh had paved the way. Josh appeared very anxious to help now. She suspected he had been shaken by the sabotage of her car, and even more by the attack on Dana. When she'd rung him, there was a distinct air of 'this has to be stopped' about his voice, and he had raised no obstacles to putting her in touch with Oliver.

The landscape changed little. Endless flat fields, broken by the occasional mountain range, were dotted sporadically with small townships as the road swept onwards. Every so often they'd stop for a cup of coffee at a wooden country shack that seemingly sprang up in the middle of nowhere as they approached. Their presence must indicate a local market for it somewhere, but to her eye there was no human habitation for miles around. Each had its own balcony to give shelter from the sun, and slow-moving owners serving petrol or coffee or a thousand and one other daily needs as required.

Taking the drive easily, they reached the border at Hiawassee. 'According to the map,' Luke said, 'on the other side of this lake is North Carolina, and Oliver and Liz's house on Route 64 overlooks the water.'

'Nice.'

It was. The Ford wound gradually up a hillside, with houses so discreetly sheltered from the road that, from all angles,

the hillside looked entirely forested. Each of these little para-
dise homes overlooked the lake. Brightly coloured blue jays
darted everywhere and oleanders blossomed. Haden Shaw
seemed a million miles away.

'It *is* a film set, isn't it?' Georgia said. 'I'm waiting for
Sheriff JohnWayne to come riding along.'

The Ludd home was almost at the crest of the hill, a huge
wooden bungalow in essence, but with a basement half below
ground and the obligatory balcony; below in the garden a
few roses struggled for survival in the heat.

It wasn't John Wayne who greeted them, but Oliver Ludd
could have made a passable James Stewart – tall, grey-haired
and rather distinguished-looking, despite his casual cotton
clothes. He resembled Henry much more than Michael, with
the same calm grey eyes.

'Liz,' Oliver called as they shook hands, and an answering
shout indicated she'd be joining them. Georgia waited, agog,
intrigued to find out what the former wife of Toby Beamish
looked like.

Liz, when she finally appeared with a tray of cold drinks,
proved to be entirely unlike anyone Georgia could have envis-
aged in connection with Toby. She was tall, elegant, with
grey hair twisted up on to her head, rather like a younger
Katherine Hepburn and just as intelligent, Georgia guessed.
Clad in sundress and sandals, she looked casual, cool, interesting – and tough. More so perhaps than Oliver, who had
something of Henry's mildness about him. Perhaps he also,
she thought, had Henry's inner steel.

'Welcome, Brits,' she smiled.

'Aren't you Brits any more?' Georgia laughed.

'We're both. We get the nostalgia of still being English
but we don't have the queues at immigration. Not that we
rush in and out too much.' Liz spoke with a slight Georgia
accent, although Oliver seemed to have retained more of his
English intonation.

'Oliver says you're here to grill us about Friday Street,'
she continued. 'It must be mighty important to come all this

way, not to mention Josh Perry stirring himself to make a transatlantic call. How is the old place, and how's my dearly beloved ex-husband, by the way? Still playing ghosts?'

'Yes. I took the tour,' Georgia replied.

'And survived that infantile performance? My dear girl, well done.'

'Did you ever trip over any of these ghosts yourself?' Luke asked.

'Nary a one. And yet,' Liz added, 'that was some spooky house, I can tell you. Now it spooks me even to think about it. Of course, the family had its other interests too.'

'The deodands?'

'Yes.' Liz grimaced. 'What kind of family gets into murder weapons?'

What kind of family uses them? was Georgia's reaction, but all she asked was: 'So you didn't live at the Manor?'

'No. Toby's parents were alive when we married. He was in the army then, and we were moving around. Toby only moved in to the glory hole after I left.'

'So there might be ghosts there after all,' Luke pointed out cheerfully.

'There might,' Liz agreed without enthusiasm. 'What do you think, Olly?'

'I saw a spook there once,' he said surprisingly.

'A real one?' Georgia asked incredulously, then she laughed at her own absurdity. She was still struggling with the image of Toby as a soldier.

'A presence,' Oliver said. 'I used to go over as a kid with Michael. We were welcome there even though my parents weren't.'

'Whose ghost?'

'Heaven knows. I was hiding in a cupboard in a game and felt this, well, presence at the back of my neck seizing my hair. I couldn't move. I shouted out and suddenly I was free. I got out of there like a bat out of hell.' A pause. 'I probably got caught in a clothes hanger. That what you wanted to ask me about? Ghosts? I thought it was Fanny Star.'

'Yes. Josh told me you were friendly with her. My father and I are working on the theory that Adam Jones was innocent. Do you think so? You knew him?'

Oliver chuckled. 'Is that a polite way of asking if I knew Fanny well?'

Georgia grinned, deciding she liked Oliver Ludd. 'Yes.'

'And of hinting that Liz might wish to leave the room. No way. We've no secrets. We both knew Fanny. She was a great girl. As for Liz—'

'I fancied Brian Winters,' she picked up cheerfully. 'Oliver was just another Ludd to me then. One of the high and mighties.'

'I was never that,' he protested.

'Unlike brother Michael,' Liz retorted.

'You're very like your father,' Georgia said to Oliver diplomatically.

Oliver sighed. 'He says he's too old to come over now, but I miss the old fellow. Perhaps I'll go back for a visit.' He glanced at Liz.

'I gather that you knew Fanny in London.'

'Sure did,' Oliver replied promptly. 'We were good friends – I heard her singing in a sleazy pub. I thought, "I know that voice", looked closer, and recognized her. We got together.'

'Did your family know about that?'

'No. She didn't want anything to do with Friday Street except for me.'

Georgia hesitated in view of Liz's presence, but there was no choice. 'Jonathan Powell – you remember him, Oliver? – says it was you who told him about Fanny's rape and abortion.'

'*After* her death.' Oliver looked livid. No longer the genial American host. 'That bastard. I don't like Powell. I never did. He created their careers, but ruined their lives. He's responsible.'

'For Fanny's death?'

'I'd like to believe it. He had every reason. You know he's gay, and was in love with Adam?'

'Yes.'

'He didn't know whether to follow his pocket, which needed Fanny in his life, or his love for Adam, which wanted her out, away, expunged, deleted. That's why he suggested she went solo. What he meant was, Adam should go solo and he would manage him. He wanted Adam all to himself, pulled him two ways and made him into an emotional mess. Fanny loathed him by that time; he was a good manager but they could do without him. As for the rape,' he continued awkwardly, 'she told me about it when she got the invitation to sing at Downey Hall. I'd asked Dad to send it, and Fanny went berserk. She told me she'd never go back. And then she told me why.'

'What made her change her mind?'

'Because I told her she should face the past,' he said bitterly. 'It was the biggest trauma of her life and she had obviously never got Friday Street out of her mind. I thought if she came back, saw her mother, saw everyone, she could put it behind her. You have these cracked ideas when you're young. Only when you're our age do you know it's better to walk away.'

'We did,' Liz said drily.

'Fanny agreed. Time for forgiveness, she said,' Oliver continued, 'and Adam was keen for her to go. So we all went, and I didn't even look after her. And what happens? She gets murdered. Well done, Oliver. A great day's work. I tell you, I heard the music played that night, and I cried my eyes out. Fanny was a wonder; funny, quick, adorable, the best friend I ever had, except for Liz here, and that's what I did for her.'

Georgia let a moment or two go by, since he was clearly upset. 'Is there anything you remember about the day of her death that might help?'

'Not about Powell. Wish I did. I had a girlfriend there, so I spent time with her after the concert. We had tea, then my father came looking for me to have a chat. That would be about an hour or so before the drinks began.'

That wasn't in his witness statement, Georgia thought, but then why should it be? It had nothing to do with Fanny. Then a niggle in her mind told her that everything that happened might be relevant. 'A chat about Fanny?' she asked.

Bull's-eye. He hadn't expected his casual remark to be taken up.

'I guess it was.' He glanced at Liz, who nodded vigorously. 'Dad was kind of hurt when Fanny left the village. They'd got on well, so he wanted to know why she'd walked out without a word to him. Well, she told him, and that's why he came raring after me. To find out more. Fanny . . .' He cleared his throat, and Liz took over briskly.

'Fanny told Olly's father she'd forgiven the guy who did it.'

'Doesn't that imply she at least met the man who raped her? Josh is convinced it was Ron Gibb.'

'Old Ron?' Oliver looked surprised – no, relieved, she realized uneasily. 'He was a nasty piece of work, but if he'd attacked Fanny, or even lusted after her, she'd have told me when we talked about her parents coming to the show.'

'If not Ron, who was it?' Georgia persisted. 'Toby?' Too late she remembered Liz had been married to him. She need not have worried about being tactless, however.

Liz snorted. 'Rape? No way. He's a voyeur, not a doer. I should know.'

'Brian?' Georgia hazarded.

'Of course not,' Liz snapped.

They were all looking at her strangely – even Luke. Why? And then she knew the answer. 'It was Michael. *That's* why Fanny was reluctant to tell you, Oliver, and so reluctant to return to Downey Hall.' Michael Ludd, she thought. Always just out of the frame, and now firmly in it. Oliver's silence confirmed it. 'Did Henry know?'

'Sheila did,' Liz answered. 'Fanny told her. Sheila was crazy over Michael, even in 1961, so she was all for Fanny getting out of town. She kidded herself that if there was any rape involved then Frances had provoked Michael into it.'

'And did she, do you think?'

'No. I had a lot of time for Frances. She exuded sex but not purposely. A real sweetie.'

She was giving Oliver time, Georgia realized, and Luke obviously agreed, for he indicated it was now time to push.

'And Henry, did he know?' she asked again.

'Yes,' Oliver shot back at her. 'I told him, because Fanny wouldn't. I'm not proud of it, but I still think it was right. With the proviso that—'

'It could have led to her death?'

'I don't know,' he said wearily. 'And out here I didn't have to think about it, until the mighty Josh put the word out. He cared for Fanny, so I listened and you're the result. I told Dad on the day Fanny died. He went straight to have it out with Michael. That would be just before drinks began. Fanny found out what I'd done as soon as Michael rejoined the group after his tongue-lashing from Henry. Fanny was not pleased with me, I can tell you. I tried to find her after dinner to make up, but there was no sign of her.'

'And Michael? How did he take it?'

'Michael believes in keeping on the right side of Dad. When I opened my big mouth that day he had some deal he was hoping Dad would finance, but my father was naturally sticky about it in the circumstances. Wouldn't make his mind up, though he did agree eventually. He's a funny old bird, very correct, believes in family and all that, but still hasn't made the house over to Michael and Sheila. He holds the purse strings tightly. Last time I saw him he joked about their wanting power of attorney and the house in their name, because Mike's pension from the company has gone up the creek, like so many others. It would be in his interests, they blithely assured Dad, to avoid inheritance tax. He said he'd rather give the house to Toby Beamish.'

Georgia blinked. Black humour indeed. 'He's a fair age, so I suppose Michael and Sheila have a point, however crass it seems.'

'I'm quite sure he has his will tucked away, and won't be

telling anyone what's in it until he's tucked away himself, which I hope won't be for a long time yet. Michael and Sheila can stew in their own juice till kingdom come, as far as I'm concerned. All Michael was worried about that day when I put him in the spotlight was the threat to his business deal. I tackled him later about the rape but he shrugged it off. Tried to slag Fanny off even when she was dead. He took the same line as he probably fed to Sheila. Fanny provoked him into it, he said, and she enjoyed it as much as he did. I never forgave him for that.'

'You never got near the point of loving Fanny yourself?'

He and Liz exchanged glances. 'No.'

'Yet you were so close to her.'

'Are you trying to stitch me up for murder?' he demanded.

'Trying to eliminate you.'

He sighed. 'I tell you about Michael and you suspect *me*?' Why should I be involved?'

'You were part of Tom.'

'What the hell's that?'

'Toby, Oliver, Michael,' she reminded him. 'Tom. She was scared of all three of you, so Josh said.'

Oliver groaned. 'Do you know, I'd completely forgotten. But you've got it wrong, Georgia. Toby, yes, he was after her, so was Michael. But I was her O in the middle; I protected her. I might only have been fifteen, but I packed a hefty punch. I was the one between, she said. *That's* why she called us Tom. A great protector I turned out to be. My own brother rapes her. I idolized Frances as a kid, and as an adult. It was great when we met again, but we just slipped back into friendly ways. She loved Adam, she really did.'

'Powell said at first their relationship wasn't sexual, then changed his mind.'

'Wishful thinking. It was.'

Georgia was still puzzled. 'It seems an odd quartet,' she said. 'Jonathan Powell loved Adam, who loved Fanny, who loved him in return – with you on the outside. Are you sure, whatever your feelings for her, that she didn't love you?'

'Absolutely sure.' He looked at Liz. 'Shall I tell her?'

'Go ahead,' Liz replied. 'Friday Street has to be straightened out one way or another. We might as well fire the starting pistol.'

'Okay. Yes, Georgia, I know Fanny only loved me as a friend.'

'How can you be so sure?'

'Because she was my half-sister.'

Twelve

Henry welcomed them in almost like old friends. 'I had wondered how long it would take,' he greeted them genially.

It had taken Georgia three clear days after returning early in the week to digest where the Fanny Star case now stood, and Suspects Anonymous had taken on a new look.

'News travels quickly,' she said wryly. Save for Josh (of course), she had not told anyone, and so had been surprised to find when she telephoned Henry last night that he already knew of her visit to the US. Josh had obviously spread the news, although she didn't count him as one who passed on gossip for gossip's sake. Which would suggest that he had felt Oliver Ludd was a special case. And that would suggest that Josh too knew about Fanny's parentage. Something else he didn't consider relevant?

Peter had announced he was coming with her to see Henry. He had also added casually that at last he had the autopsy report but that it would keep. Good, because there was quite enough to think about where Henry was concerned, without details of last meals and so forth. There was some difficulty in manoeuvring the wheelchair through Henry's hall, but between herself, Henry and Henry's cleaning lady, they managed, with Peter delivering a non-stop commentary on the eighteenth- and nineteenth-century cartoons which adorned the walls.

Luke had had to return to South Malling and Frost Publications, complaining bitterly about the hard life of publishers who were excluded from really interesting matters by such necessities as marketing and budget discussions. Having sat in on several of these laid-back affairs in the past, Georgia was not inclined to feel too sorry for him, though she promised him a verbatim report this evening as compensation.

There had been some good news to return to. There were cautious signs for optimism over Dana, Peter told her, although she was still in a coma, and there were major question marks over what might transpire if and when she returned to consciousness.

Georgia had thought it right to explain to Henry on the telephone what Oliver had told them. He had greeted the news with a resigned, 'Ah.'

'I take it,' she now said, as they manoeuvred the wheelchair through his living-room door, 'that the fact that you are Fanny's father is not generally known here.'

'Only on a need-to-know basis,' Henry replied, as he ushered her towards the sofa, while himself selecting an upright chair. Good business tactics, she thought, amused. He intended to remain in charge. 'Over the years my immediate family has been told; the Winters know, and the Perrys. I suspect our chum Toby Beamish is also in the picture, if only because his nose twitches at anything to do with the Ludds. It's quite flattering.'

'When did Fanny herself find out?' Peter asked. This was a crucial question, she and her father had agreed. Her statement to Josh, that the rape had been a 'family thing' now appeared in a new perspective, and Oliver's belief that it was Michael looked all too probable. Did Michael know about the relationship between himself and Fanny when he raped her? That was a terrifying thought.

'When she was about fourteen,' Henry replied promptly. 'Ronald Gibb knew about my . . .' He paused. 'I hate the word "affair". It doesn't describe the situation at all. My *love* for Doreen Gibb. Not unnaturally, although he seems to have been infertile himself, he resented Frances, and of course myself. He took his fury out on both Doreen and Frances, despite the fact that faithfulness had hardly been one of his virtues as a husband in their early married days. I believe in later years his relationship improved slightly, so far as Doreen was concerned, but hardly to the point where she could be said to lead a contented life.

'You will want to know what Frances's feelings were about it,' Henry continued. 'I can tell you that very simply: relief. She hated – no, too strong a word – heartily disliked Ronald Gibb, who made no attempt to act as a father towards her. I like to think that, limited though our association was, she valued it, though I doubt if as much as I did.'

He must be wrong there, Georgia thought. Fanny *had* come back, and to see Henry and perhaps her mother must have been the reason.

'Was it known in your family at the time, or only after-wards?' Peter asked, to her relief. She had been dithering about asking the question.

'My late wife Joan knew about Doreen and myself during the war, and about Frances. She did her best not to blame Frances, and Joan and I had long since sorted out our private differences. And as for Michael and Oliver – they knew *after* Frances had left the village, but before the day of her death. In any case, her parentage is hardly relevant to that.'

Georgia strongly disagreed. It seemed to her that 22nd June, 1968 could have been the boiling point for emotions on both sides. Fanny's predicament must have been terrifying. She had known she was being raped by her half-brother, even if Michael wasn't aware of the relationship. It didn't lessen the crime, but most certainly must have increased the anguish for Fanny, particularly when she discovered she was pregnant. No wonder she wanted a quick abortion. The comment she had made to Josh now had even more relevance. Had he realized the significance of 'the family thing'? Had he just assumed that she meant Ronald Gibb, because he didn't yet know about the other family connection in the form of Michael? Or had he been deliberately misleading her in the hope it would deflect her from the affairs of Friday Street? There was only one way to find out.

'When did Josh discover your relationship to Fanny, Henry?'

'Not, I believe, until much later, when Adam Jones called here. Frances had told Adam the truth, and that is why he came to see me.' Henry answered obligingly enough, but she still sensed he was keeping his distance. It must be hard for him to talk about such matters, and distancing them, in answering by the book, might be one way of dealing with them.

The silence that followed made Georgia fear that Henry was going to clam up, but he seemed to have come to a decision, because he continued, 'I told you Adam came to play me a song, "The Banks of Allan Water". It was a particular favourite of Frances's and of course became the basis of one of their great successes.

'Adam explained to me that Frances believed that through their music they could lead the world to peace. Her wildness was her rage against the forces of the world that prevented it. She sought peace through the LSD drug and that had failed. She sought it through her love for Adam, and he told me that hadn't worked because someone had come between them. Music was her pathway. The folk songs she and Adam adapted, such as "The Banks of Allan Water", represented the past; she sought a future that the past had failed to attain.

'What Adam played and sang to me, however, was the original folk song. You know it?' He began to sing with cracked and uneven voice:

'But the miller's lovely daughter,
'Both from cold and care was free,
'On the banks of Allan Water . . .

'That was Frances's pet name for me, The Miller, owing to my family firm.'

Free from cold and care. Georgia remembered. 'The words on the memorial stone,' she said. 'Didn't the verse continue,

205

"There a corpse lay she"?' She shivered. No wonder Adam chose that song. It was a message to Henry not to forget. As if he could.

'Indeed,' Henry replied. 'What happened here was so devastatingly terrible, both the murder itself and in what it did to me, that I felt I had to mark it. Where else should it be than where she died, in Owlers' Smoke? When I told Josh, he insisted the former gang should contribute. They were all involved, he said. Free from cold and care. My lovely Frances.' Henry's eyes were moist, but he continued briskly, 'When in the 1980s Josh began to realize that Adam might have been innocent, he tried to convince himself Powell was guilty. I'm not sure he succeeded. How, after all, would Powell know about the place? He was an outsider.'

'Fanny might have told him,' Georgia said. Chillingly, Friday Street was beginning to exert its power again now. Even she was beginning to see Powell as an all too convenient solution.

'I would prefer to think that,' Henry said quietly.

The name Michael was shouting itself in her mind, but she forced it to remain there. She could not expect the truth from his father, and how could she hurt a man of his age by even mentioning the possibility that the rape had anything to do with Fanny's murder?

'You know that Fanny was raped before she left Friday Street?' Peter said matter-of-factly. The ground where Georgia had feared to tread was now open territory.

Henry's face did not change. 'I feared we would come to this. I could lie to you, but I have a duty to my dead daughter. Nevertheless, without proof it would be defamatory, and I cannot see how that proof would be obtainable today.'

He was challenging them, but they had no answer, and so he continued: 'I learned about the pregnancy and the rape only on the day that Frances died. I asked Frances why she had left the village without a word to me and disappeared from my life. She told me about the pregnancy then, but would not name the father. She had come in a spirit of forgiveness, she told me. Peace was all that mattered. Perhaps she was right, but I did not see it as such then. I contained myself, but I was in a rage. I demanded the truth of Oliver, knowing they were close friends. I hardly expected his answer that it was Michael, but Michael confirmed it himself. He claimed Frances had led him on, and at the time he had no idea that he was her half-brother. Frances had forgiven him, I told him, and I would show the same attitude. Then we went to join the company for pre-dinner drinks. Three hours later my lovely Frances was dead.'

'Thank you,' Peter said gravely. 'I appreciate it can't have been easy for you to talk to us about this.'

Henry looked at him uncertainly as if expecting further questions, but none came. Georgia was too well schooled in Peter's ways to take over at such a point. If he fell silent, there was a reason. It left the pressure on Henry to speak again, and he did.

'No account could be the whole truth, in my view, for that is known only to God. Fortunately I cannot see that a rape seven years earlier could have anything to do with my daughter's death. Frances was presenting no threat, and I had told Michael so. At the time Adam Jones' guilt appeared both to us and the police incontrovertible. You will have read our statements to them about our movements in that context. The period during which Frances could have been killed, I recall, is between approximately a quarter to eight and an hour later, if we assume that Adam is innocent. During that period my son was either with me or with other guests until Jonathan Powell came to say he could not find Frances.'

'At a party, of course . . .' Peter murmured. He had a knack of making strong implications acceptably. How could Henry be certain that Michael was busy circulating? He would have been doing the same.

'That is true.' Henry took the point immediately. 'I kept an eye on him, however, because he was in a high state of excitement when we talked briefly after the dinner. Not only was it his engagement party, but he was planning to buy a new business, a printing company, over which I had decided to help him financially to a crucial extent. I admit I had been dragging my heels over the previous weeks, largely because I was aware that I would shortly be seeing Frances again. I told myself I had two other children to consider besides Michael. Oliver was determined to stand alone, but Frances was more fragile. She had plenty of money at that time, thanks to her singing, but it was a volatile calling, and that might easily change. When we talked before the dinner, I had been in two minds about going forward in assisting Michael, in view of his admission of the rape. However, seeing Frances in an inebriated state, clearly doing her best to upset the party despite what she had said, I decided to have no more hesitation over Michael. He asked to talk to me again, and we duly had a brief talk, I suppose about eight fifteen, for a few minutes before we rejoined the party.'

Henry's objectivity about his son was remarkable, Georgia thought, but if he spoke the truth it did away with any motive Michael might have for murder. 'Did you discuss money with Fanny?' she asked.

'No. I merely longed to see her again. When I did, I saw the dear child I had known, even in that one brief talk with her. I wanted to tell her more about her mother's life and about why she and I had come together. When Frances left the village, she was still a child; now she was mature. I hoped she would understand, and if she had not already done so, forgive. She listened, but I could tell she regretted coming back at all, because we had invited both Ronald and Doreen. It wasn't possible for her to see Doreen without facing Ronald, and she blamed him – not me, you notice – for much that had gone wrong in her life.'

'Did he abuse her sexually?'

Henry looked genuinely startled. 'Dear me, this is an unpleasant world where such things should even be talked about, let alone take place. The answer is no, not to my knowledge.'

'Sheila told me he did.'

'That is strange. I wonder if she got the wrong end of the stick? Frances, as I told you, was a kind girl. Sheila was always very keen on Michael, but unfortunately as a youth he seemed to prefer Frances. I watched carefully, but I saw no signs of her showing him anything other than the mutual friendliness of gang members.'

Henry changed the subject, clearly eager to do so. 'I'd like to tell you about Doreen. Let me show you this.' He reached inside his trouser pocket and extracted a locket which he opened and passed to her. Immediately she saw it, she remembered the sketch in Brian Winters' collection.

'Adam Jones brought me this the day he came here in 1987,' Henry told them. 'It's a locket I once gave Doreen. If I needed any proof of his innocence, this was it. He was given it by Doreen when he went to their home the night of the murder, and Doreen confirmed this. She asked him to go all the way back to the cottage because she had something to give him to pass on to Frances. She had been deeply affected by seeing our daughter again. That's why Adam, despite what Ronald Gibb testified at the trial, could not have returned in time to find, quarrel with and then kill Frances. Unfortunately, so he told me, when he returned to Downey Hall he went in search of her immediately to give her this locket, especially as it was getting near the time of the concert. The true murderer could not have counted on this stroke of good fortune.'

'Why did Ronald Gibb lie?' Georgia was puzzled. 'He must have known it would help get Adam convicted.'

'I believe he saw it as his chance to get back at Doreen and Frances, even though she was dead. He resented the fact that Doreen gave Adam the locket, for it brought back bitter memories. Adam had kept the locket, knowing it would have meaning for me, and brought it here. He naturally had no desire to meet Ronald Gibb again. Let me show you what it contains.'

He leaned forward, took it from her, and opened it. Inside were two small photos, one of Doreen, much like the one

Dana had shown her, and one of Henry as a young air force officer. Then he opened the other side, revealing a small lock of fading ginger hair.

'Frances's hair, of course,' he said quietly. 'We could never work out where the colour came from, Doreen so blonde and I was – well, mousy, once upon a time, and now . . .'

'Distinguished white,' Georgia said stoutly.

'You're kind. When I look at this, I see no such distinction. I see a raw RAF airman, unhappily married, posted away, and falling in love for the first and only time in his life. In 1941, when an injury put paid to active flying, I was posted to Downey Hall, then an RAF HQ. There was an advanced landing airfield nearby then. Doreen was working at the Hall. She'd married Ronald just before the war, as I had Joan. Ronald was then in the Navy, and Michael a toddler. I hardly saw him, or even Joan, who was still living near Biggin Hill where she had been in what was then called the Women's Emergency Service, and I had been stationed with Thirty-two Squadron in 1938. I was regular RAF, you understand, not hostilities only. We married quickly – too quickly perhaps – and Michael came quickly too.

'My love for Doreen began as an innocent friendship between young people, and ended with deep love. We were very different. She was outgoing, with a golden heart to match her hair; I was diffident and far from outgoing. I was intent on moving here after the war, and my wife raised no objection. My affair – that word again – with Doreen finished not long after the war, when Oliver was born, but of course we remained in love, and often met just to talk or to play with Frances. It was easy enough if we had the children with us, or the dogs.' He stopped and looked very tired, asking with obvious effort, 'Have you met Doreen?'

'Yes,' Georgia answered, 'I went to the nursing home.'

'Can you imagine what she was once like? *Is* like, if only one could penetrate the haze.'

'I think so. Do you still visit her?'

'Of course. And does she recognize me?' Henry smiled.

'In a way. When Ronald died I thought we might have a sort of life together, but illness has taken her away from me more effectively than death. At least it is not dementia; she is the same gentle person that I first knew.'

Georgia thought of the blowsy, giggling, hapless Doreen, and realized how differently he saw her.

'If Frances wasn't killed by Adam Jones, it's at least probable that someone here in Friday Street either murdered her or knew who did. Yet still the village prefers to keep its secrets,' Peter said, bluntly changing the subject. 'We're having to bludgeon them out, and there seems no reason why that should be so.'

Henry regarded him thoughtfully. 'Perhaps we all cling to a tiny piece of knowledge, or even guilt, which we presume to be irrelevant. No one fits the story together, not even Josh. Perhaps we are too afraid. Perhaps we no longer have the strength.'

'Someone does,' Georgia said sharply. 'Someone killed Alice Winters.' She had touched a very sore nerve, judging by his stiff reaction.

'You are of course correct, if you assume one death is linked to the other. Josh tells me this is so.'

'Alice inherited the results of her father's and grandfather's researches into the case. That seems a good enough reason to look into any possible links,' Peter said.

Henry bowed his head. 'I accept that. And as Brian Winters was a member of the gang, I must talk about that.' He reflected for a moment. 'Frances had the unconscious gift, or rather curse, of attracting male attention and desire, although without provocation on her part. Her mother had the same curse. They both only sought the love of one man, but attracted far more. This was so in the gang, from what Oliver has since told me. They were all young, but Frances never showed sexual interest in any of them – apart, perhaps, from Josh, for whom she had genuine affection, which might have flowered had it had the chance.'

'Did the other girls in the gang resent this?'

'It annoyed them. Jealous? I gather not. They might have been had they thought their own interests threatened, but I don't think they did.'

'Sheila, for example, or Liz, or Hazel?'

'Sheila was very close to Frances and knew Michael was attracted to her, but also that Frances was no danger to her interests.'

Henry spoke with great detachment. Did extreme age achieve that? Georgia wondered. Could it distance one from one's own family as well as friends?

'Hazel,' Henry continued. 'No. She was a sensible girl and only married Josh some years later. Liz? Now, Liz is temperamental. It is a nice thought that chum Toby Beamish was the object of passionate desire not only to Liz but also to Frances. Alas, I cannot see it, although it is true that Master Beamish has taken a great interest in Frances since. He often asks me questions, I suspect merely to upset me.' A pause. 'When Mr Powell returned to the village – I believe on the day of Alice's murder – he brought Dana Tucker to see me about the cottage. I recall he told me he was going to Pucken Manor. He thought he might take the ghost tour.'

'And so we come back to the gang again, with Jonathan Powell in the middle like a maypole,' Georgia said crossly. Having had the weekend to mull the case over, she'd hoped things might make more sense, but at the moment she felt as though she was dancing round to the Friday Street tune herself. Monday morning had not brought enlightenment.

'If Powell took the tour, he couldn't have murdered Alice. Did you believe what Henry told us? Are you sure it's Powell and not Henry Ludd who's playing maypole?' Peter asked.

'With reservations, but Henry surely can't be guilty of either murder.'

'The strings are in the dancers' hands,' Peter pointed out. 'Henry said some strange things. Don't you find it odd his wife knew about his affair but didn't mind living in the same village? And he was quite happy to set Michael up in business even though he'd just discovered Michael had raped his half-sister. It seems to me Henry's like one of those contraptions for cats; they press the right button and a measured dose of water arrives in the tray. He's releasing information on a need-to-know basis.'

'We can't be sure of that.'

'The possibility is there. Now, about the autopsy report . . .'

Georgia was still thinking about Henry. 'Powell taking the ghost tour – that *is* odd, isn't it?'

Peter sighed. 'Very well. Have it your way. He wanted, so Dana said, to see Downey Hall – that's understandable, given the circumstances – and Pucken Manor. Why the latter?'

'To talk to Toby.'

'About what?'

'Toby was in the gang.'

'So was Josh.'

'He could already have talked to Josh. He'd been in the pub earlier. Alice was there that day, he talked to her – in answer to her letter. That's why he was there.' Coulds, woulds, whys . . . Georgia could have cried with frustration. 'I want something *positive*,' she stormed. 'When, oh when, will it come?'

'Right now, if you'd only be quiet and listen to me for a moment,' Peter said plaintively.

She stopped instantly. 'What about?'

'The *autopsy* report.'

'And?'

'Fanny Star had had at least one baby at the time of her death.'

Georgia tried to assimilate this. 'You mean there was no abortion? She *kept* the child?'

'Possibly. Or else she went on to have another.'

'Let's assume the first. Search for both certificates?' she asked eagerly.

'Of course,' Peter said speculatively, 'there's been no hint of a child since.'

'It could have died.'

'That's one possibility. Or . . .' He fiddled with a pen on the desk, looking very smug. 'Perhaps it was adopted.'

Her brain snapped into first gear. 'Is it possible—'

'Likely—'

'A chance anyway.'

'That it was a girl.'

'In her early forties. In whom Powell and Henry Ludd seem to have taken great interest. The Gibb cottage, incidentally, is owned by Henry Ludd.'

'Dana,' Georgia breathed with conviction. 'It would explain so much.'

'Leaping to conclusions.'

'We're not acting on them – yet.'

'We're entitled to leap.'

'Not too high.'

They looked at each other. 'The poisoning,' she said eventually, then remembered. 'No, the pie was for both of us.'

Peter sighed in exasperation. 'The pie was blameless. So was the cake.'

'*My* car was sabotaged.'

'A false scent. It didn't kill you.'

'But it could have done.' Didn't anyone care?

'Would that have mattered – to our murderer?' Peter added hastily. 'One or two murders to his name already.' He reached for the phone.

'What's that for?' she asked.

'I think I'll suggest to Mike he might like to keep a guard on Dana now she's showing signs of recovery.'

Georgia shivered, trying to sort the rational out of fantasy land. 'No one's going to creep in with a dagger.'

'No. Any visitor could poison the tea though, once she's off drips.'

A jolt ran through her. 'The *tea*,' she said. 'The poison could have been in the tea at the fete, not the cake. Why didn't I think of that earlier? Anyone could have added it,' she finished uncertainly.

Peter eyed her. 'Who was in charge of the tea?'
'Cadenza Broome.'

The office was beginning to hum, and so was the new
Suspects Anonymous file on Dana, peopled with Burglar
Bettys this time. They still called them that, but now they
had lost any thought of it being a game. Every time they
moved the magnifying-glass cursor, it brought home the
growing nightmare of Friday Street.

'Tell me again, Georgia,' Mike commanded. He had been
on his way to Friday Street, and had called in after Peter's
phone call.

Georgia closed her eyes, and visualized that tent again,
step by step. Her own haziness, the people moving slowly
like stickmen as they moved around. Henry, over there, Toby
coming in for a word with Cadenza, cups of tea, slices of
cake, Dana saying, 'Try Sheila's cheesecake, it's delicious.'
It was also innocent of poison. Did she see Dana drinking
tea? Did she see a teacup near her? She couldn't swear it.
Teacups were arriving and leaving all the time and she had
been feeling dizzy anyway.

'Sheila was in overall charge,' she said. 'Cadenza was
handing out teacups, mostly, though Hazel I think did some
too.'

'But it was Cadenza's job?'

'I didn't check the hierarchy. I just remember seeing her
do it, but Dana had – *if* she had any tea – already finished
hers when I arrived. Cadenza offered some to me, though.
Hazel was cutting the cakes. But you know what those stalls
are like . . .'

'Never served on one, Georgia.'

The idea of Mike's large figure whizzing around at a garden
fete amused her. 'Everyone mucks in and does whatever's
necessary. If someone's held up on cakes, the person taking
the money will help out, and vice versa. I can only tell you
what happened to me.'

'This plant, thorn apple. You say you've seen it at Downey

Hall, but it could be anywhere in the village. I can't search every garden. The juice is most poisonous, I gather, and it wouldn't take much to extract it, pour into a small bottle and, bingo, into a cup. This Cadenza. What do you make of her?'

'Devoted to Toby, rather than to ghosts, though she does a fair job of pretending to be. Old-fashioned sort of woman. You must have her statement from the Alice Winters enquiry.'

'Sure. We've got that, and Powell's recent one, and Beamish's. Powell swears that he talked briefly to Alice Winters in the pub about some detail on the day of the Star murder. He went on the tour, had a private talk with Toby for ten minutes in the middle of it, during which Cadenza took over the festivities. Miss Broome claimed she stayed at her desk for the entire tour. Toby Beamish says that his talk with Powell lasted forty minutes, while Cadenza took over. At which Cadenza remembered she *had* taken over the tour, but can't remember for how long. Over to you, Georgia. Ferret out any links to the Star case.'

Asked to do something to help. Now that was something.

'Henry Ludd's granddaughter, as Henry must know full well,' Peter remarked to Josh. They had arrived at the beginning of visiting time together. Georgia stared at the unconscious Dana. Where was she inside? Fighting to get out, or in a peaceful world of her own? The police had found sufficient evidence in birth and adoption certificates amongst Dana's papers to confirm she was indeed Fanny's daughter. And therefore Michael's, Georgia thought sadly. A tough legacy for Dana.

'Why would anyone want to kill her, Josh?' she asked wearily.

'Like I told you, Georgia. Could be the sins of the fathers, coming home to roost.'

'I can't think of Henry sinning.'

'Nor me,' Josh replied quietly.

Then whose? Georgia wondered. Michael's sin? Brian

Winters' sin? Ronald Gibb's or Josh's himself? Or was it Henry's, who by his affair with Doreen had innocently set all this in train?

'Killing *her* just because she's Fanny's daughter seems an odd motive,' Peter said.

'Is it? Henry still hasn't made the house over to Michael and Sheila.'

'Unlikely,' Peter said dismissively.

Georgia was stung. 'Dana was here the day of Alice Winters' death. Perhaps she saw something that could be important. Something she told Toby Beamish the night before she was poisoned. Something that explained why and how he could have killed both Fanny and Alice.'

'Powell wasn't here to make the attack on Dana, even if he did chat to Toby the day Alice died.'

The two-pronged carver snapped. At last she was willing to put the Powell prong to one side. Peter could be right. The answer lay in Friday Street now.

Thirteen

'Who begins?' Peter demanded, logging on to Suspects Anonymous.

Did she want to be challenger or challenged? Georgia considered. They had one suspect, Michael, who had no motive and no opportunity (if Henry was to be believed), and another, Toby, with no apparent motive and plenty of opportunity. No contest. Toby was on the screen. Time to activate him.

'You,' she decided. Normally she was more confident as to where they were heading. Usually when they held such reconstructions there was an obvious line to challenge, but this one would be more like a puzzle maze. In there somewhere was the centre, and they were growing closer to it all the time, but still the tantalizing solution had no straight path to it. Perhaps there wasn't one, she thought gloomily. Perhaps the Fanny Star and Alice Winters link was a false alley and they had come bang up against a hedge instead of the maze's centre. At least if Peter took the lead, she would have something firm to strike out against.

Peter began in suitably formal tone. 'What is your impression of Beamish?'

'He's a creep.' If all the questions were as easy as this one, she'd have no problems.

'Always a creep? When he was an eighteen-year-old boy, for instance?'

'Yes.'

'Evidence?'

'Remember Tom? It begins with a T; T for Toby.'

'Accepted. Liz married him though. What did you think of Liz?'

'Iron fist, soft heart.'

'A mania for rescuing the weak?'

'Perhaps.' She hadn't thought of that. There were indeed women who consciously or unconsciously saw it as their mission to save people from themselves.

'Would Liz have wanted to rescue Toby if he had murdered Fanny?'

Georgia snorted. 'She'd have run screaming in the opposite direction.'

'It's happened. Look at briefs who marry their clients in prison.'

Georgia considered this. 'Accepted.'

'Let us therefore attack Mr Beamish with gusto . . . where did that word come from, I wonder?'

'From Latin, and no sidetracks please,' she commanded. 'Why would Toby want to murder Fanny Star?'

'I have a theory,' Peter said helpfully. 'What about you?'

Georgia hesitated. 'Because he slept with her seven years earlier or something else happened between them and he was afraid the story would come out. He was married to Liz by that time.'

'Weak. In fact, as wobbly as a jelly in a heatwave.'

'I withdraw it – no, I don't.'

Peter looked at her expectantly.

'Remember that song Toby wanted played during the Lady Rosamund re-enactment?' she asked. 'It was "The Banks of Allan Water" again.'

'What of it?'

Georgia ran through the words in her mind. 'Henry might be the miller in the song,' she said, 'but Toby could have been the soldier. He was in the army, or was about to be.'

'Explain.'

'The lyrics run, "For his bride a soldier sought her, And a winning tongue had he . . .". And later: "For the summer grief had brought her, And the soldier false was he".'

Peter looked at her. 'You want my opinion, Georgia?' He didn't wait for the answer. 'Neat, but hardly proof.'

'Even though the same song was quoted on the memorial stone,' she said obstinately, 'to which they all subscribed?'

'Coincidence. Though you might have hit on something by chance.'

'Thank you,' she murmured.

'From all our excursions to Friday Street I have concluded that we still haven't penetrated that inner core, and that's Tom. Something still links Toby, Oliver and Michael.'

'And Josh?'

'He might be suspect, but he's on the perimeter, not inside. I put Josh on the side of the angels.'

'Is that wise?'

'I think so. The cabal of Tom would be too strong otherwise. Any villainy by Josh would have been made public long ago. No, our secret lies within Tom. Suppose—'

'That word is *supposed* to be banned in reconstructions.'

'I can't help that,' Peter said impatiently. 'Rules can be broken in the interests of the end. Let's look at the rape from the point of view of Tom. We have a cabal that for some reason scares Fanny, even with Oliver as the middle O. Henry Ludd is already very fond of Fanny, and that, even if Michael didn't know of their closer relationship, might have given him and even Oliver every reason to dislike Fanny. Suppose "Tom" drew lots to teach her a lesson?'

'Are you implying a gang rape?' Georgia was aghast. She couldn't get her mind round the possibility. The past didn't always remain tucked away and objective. Sometimes it came up and shook you by the shoulders, throwing you right back there with it, away from the comfort of the present day. Yesterday's problems were today's problems, only distanced by time. If Peter was right, no wonder there was unfinished business in Friday Street; no wonder the fingerprints of time had left their mark on Downey Hall.

'I'm merely setting up a thesis for examination,' Peter said patiently.

Instinct told her it was wrong, but she at least would play by the rules.

'Suppose Fanny had the dagger with her,' Peter began.

That was a googly, and it stopped her in her tracks. 'Why on earth would she?'

Peter looked complacent. 'I thought that would shake you. Think about this. Fanny is a lady who has scores to settle with Tom, for whatever reason, and what happened during the day made her decide it was time for action either against Michael or Toby. We'll leave Oliver out of it for the moment. She's drunk, grabs the dagger and, knowing she will shortly be with her enemy, is ready to take revenge. Only Toby's too strong for her.'

Georgia had a vision of those powerful hands chopping trees in the grounds. A soldier's hands. 'Hang on,' she said slowly. 'That could apply to Michael, if we disregard Henry's statements, not just Toby. You've no proof about either of them, apart from the fact that they scared her. For heavens' sake, Toby would scare me if I met him in the twilight in the middle of a remote copse of bushes. Moreover, the rape,' she added, 'was a *family* thing – Michael, in other words. Or are you suggesting she deliberately didn't mention Toby was involved too? If so, why?'

'I return to where I began. As yet we haven't reached Tom's heart.'

'In that case, my lord, I request an acquittal for the suspect.'

'Alice Winters didn't.'

Once more she'd been caught asleep at the switch. If Peter's outrageous thesis was correct, only the evidence in Alice's hands could still implicate Tom.

'Alice decides to make money out of the evidence Brian had collected,' she said. 'At eighteen it might have seemed halfway between a bit of a giggle and a bold, bad adventure. She talks to Powell, who duly turns up in Friday Street, and she also— *Oh!*'

'Yes, *oh*,' Peter said tartly. 'I believe it was agreed I was in the hot seat, not you. You have neatly jumped into the heffalump pit with great aplomb. *Whom* does she arrange to talk to? We have to assume Brian had *some* evidence against Toby and/or Michael, just possibly Josh, and that one of them arranges to meet Alice in the tower. The most likely is obviously Toby. There are discrepancies between what he told the police and what Powell did. So let's sort him out.'

'He would know Jake could arrive at any moment,' Georgia objected.

'Please let me continue.' Peter was in lofty mood.

The great brain at work, she thought crossly. This was the disadvantage of being the challenger. One had to wait for one's opportunity and at this stage she didn't want to wait.

'Toby had to take time out of the tour,' Peter continued, 'and there is a gap of half an hour in his movements, time to walk to the tower and more if he took the car.'

'Cadenza would hear the engine.'

'Cadenza was taking the tour, and whatever Toby did, I think she would be disinclined to query it,' Peter whipped back smartly. 'He had the opportunity to kill Alice, whereas Michael Ludd has an alibi. He was with Henry when Alice was killed.'

'Where did that come from?' Georgia asked incredulously.

'Henry. I rang him before you arrived.'

'And Josh?'

'In Canterbury, shopping with Hazel.'

That answered that. The chances of Oliver nipping over unseen from North Carolina were slim. It was a clear field for Toby as suspect number one if these alibis stood up. The missing piece was a motive for his killing Fanny. 'So Toby goes down to the tower, kills Alice, returns to pick up the tourists and arrives to find the body – with Jake now helpfully present. Toby would have to be a pretty strong guy, emotionally as well as physically,' Georgia pointed out.

'My impression of creeps, or watchers if you prefer the politer word, is that, far from being weak, they have the self-determination and self-interest of the very strong.'

'What had he to lose if Alice spoke out?' Georgia challenged him. 'There'd be no *proof* even if he did murder Fanny.'

'It depends on Brian Winters' evidence.'

'And what about Cadenza? She'd know he was in a position to kill Alice.'

'Cadenza is entrapped in a fairytale of her own, where every step of the path towards her prince means hardship and denial. The question is, can life be a fairytale?'

'Reasoning please.'

'She took over the tour that afternoon for Toby. She saw Powell, but thought nothing of it. She wouldn't know who he was, and had probably taken the tour for Toby before for perfectly innocent reasons. When Jake Baines was arrested, again she would have no reason to think of Toby, even when the dagger was identified. Toby would have pretended to complain about the missing dagger when he officially came to leave for the tower at four o'clock, but any knife would have served for that. Cadenza would find out soon enough where the missing dagger was.'

'That night the music is played,' Georgia said, working the thesis through, 'to indicate Jake Baines is innocent. Cadenza would have done some hard thinking, but the thought of dear Toby being involved would never have entered her head. Even if her parents had gossiped about the Fanny Star murder years earlier, Toby's name wouldn't have come into it. But then *we* come along, proclaiming that Adam Jones might be innocent. Cadenza is mildly interested, and perhaps after my visit becomes uneasy. She questions Toby . . .'

'And then Dana comes to dinner, and tells them,' Peter supplied when Georgia broke off, realizing what lay ahead.

'Tells them what?' she asked flatly. Reconstructions were apt to arrive at an unbridgeable gulf, which then had to be covered over with a warning sign until further notice. And in this case the possible source of that further information was in hospital, still in a coma. Thanks to Cadenza? 'Let me try,' she suggested.

'Proceed with caution, Georgia. We're treading water here.'

'Something Dana says makes them see her as a danger. And don't,' she said firmly, 'tell me she'd gone to tell Toby he was her father.'

'It's a possibility—'

'No!' she exploded. 'If she had, he would hug her, not try to kill her.'

'I agree. Toby wouldn't harm her, but Cadenza might, with or without his knowledge. She was in the tea tent. She has a garden, she has the knowledge, she had the opportunity. Short of the poison vehicle being Mr Mulworthy's sausages, the tea is still the obvious suspect.'

'I don't buy it. We're missing something—'

She was interrupted by the phone. Peter, his eyes on Georgia, picked it up. 'Mike,' he mouthed to her, and listened for a few minutes. 'I'll be a while,' he then said to her. 'Mike wants us to know he's bringing in Toby and Cadenza Broome for questioning, ostensibly because of the discrepancies in their statements.'

Perhaps Mike would manage to winkle out what Marsh & Daughter were failing to achieve.

Once back home, Georgia found herself prowling restlessly round her empty house. Luke wasn't here – visiting Dana perhaps. She felt too tired to care. Normally she felt uplifted near the end of a case – and that's what this looked like, didn't it? All they needed was a motive for Toby to have killed Fanny, and it would be over to the police. So what was wrong? She couldn't work out the answer, but something was amiss. Something didn't fit. Something that had been mentioned today. Oh well, it would come to her. Or, if it didn't, it couldn't have been important.

Everyone, it seemed, was coming to see Dana. Even Jonathan Powell. She had telephoned him on the spur of the moment. Even though she'd reluctantly excluded him from their thinking as Fanny's killer, he if anyone might be able to explain her disquiet over Toby Beamish. It still remained with her, for all her attempts to put it to one side.

'The police have been to see me, Georgia. You know that, of course,' he had said.

'Yes.'

'I gather they wish to speak to me again. I propose to visit Kent to see them, to visit Dana and, if you wish, I will certainly talk to you. Perhaps we could meet at the hospital? That would be convenient.'

Would it? Was it strange or natural that he chose to meet where Fanny's daughter was fighting for her own life. *Was* Dana fighting, or was she gently slipping away from them? There had been no more progress. Georgia frequently met Dana's adoptive parents at the hospital. They had travelled from the north of England to keep a constant vigil. Watching their distress was as agonizing as waiting by the bedside herself. She had also met Dana's daughter, Sarah. A nice girl. Georgia desperately wanted Dana to recover, for everyone's sake. Even Luke's.

She met Jonathan in the hospital café before going to visit Dana. He had already seen her, he told her.

'Any change?' she asked.

He shook his head. 'You find it strange that I came here?' he asked, as if reading her mind.

'No.' She knew the answer to her own question now. It was not odd at all. Fanny and Adam had been at the centre of his life, and it was natural that Dana should now represent them.

'I thought I should tell you what I told the police earlier today.'

'About your talk with Alice Winters? Or about your visit to Owlers' Smoke just before Adam arrived?'

'Both.' He didn't seem fazed by her attack 'The subject arose at the police station, I'm sure, thanks to you. Don't think I blame you, however.'

'Thank you,' she said drily.

'I am not capable of murder, whatever I might have said during that quarrel – which was much along the lines you suspected. I didn't care greatly about Fanny's career or about mine, or about anything save Adam, both for himself and for his career. I genuinely believed that he was in Fanny's musical shadow and that he had gifts of his own that might be developed. If only she had not been there. If wishes were horses, beggars might ride, as they say.'

'It was her choice to go,' she pointed out. Was this a plea by Jonathan for her understanding? Perhaps, and perhaps she had wrongly withheld it earlier.

'I agree. I admit I was incensed that evening. I was greatly upset by the quarrel with Adam. He refused to give me an answer as to whether I was still their manager – whether in fact he had chosen Fanny in preference to myself. I decided I had to find Fanny and talk to her. *Talk*, Georgia – this was before dinner. I could not find her, and asked Brian Winters if he had seen her. He hadn't but suggested I tried Owlers' Smoke since many of the gang used to retreat there to sulk – and Fanny often did. I did try it, and did find her there. She told me to get out, that I'd ruined her career, her private life and now her return home. I replied with some similar compliments and left with her still hurling abuse at me. At dinner consequently, as everyone observed, she was not in a good mood. Despite the reason, I was appalled by Fanny's behaviour at dinner, and the lack of objectivity that a good meal, wine and even the presence of the evening itself can produce drove me to behave abnormally. Just like Fanny, in fact. In the evening one sees, as Shakespeare pointed out, bears where there are only bushes. I didn't let well alone.

'While the others were having coffee and liqueurs on the terrace, I buttonholed Adam privately and asked him what he and Fanny had decided. I was none the wiser. Was there still an SFA and was I still its manager? He told me yes, but to watch my Ps and Qs. I was profoundly upset that he had chosen Fanny and not myself, even if he had saved my job for me. Adam said stiffly that he had to take Mr and Mrs Gibb home, and I went for a walk in the gardens, unable to face the other guests. Then I forced myself to my professional duty and went to check that all was well, as I told you, and to make sure Fanny was fit enough for the gig. I couldn't find her in the house or outside, so I went over to see the sound chaps were doing their job, and asked if they'd seen Fanny. I began to get worried because there was no sign of her there either, or Adam. I thought about Owlers' Smoke and set off there, but changed my mind. I gather now that Adam saw me leave, and received the wrong impression.

'He had every reason to believe I had just left her, but my fingerprints naturally were not on the dagger, only Adam's. I had no blood on my clothes, nothing. Adam had. I couldn't believe that Adam had killed Fanny; he had no reason to do so, and almost no time. I longed to give evidence, but he would not permit it, thinking I would incriminate myself. He felt guilty because he knew of my love for him, which to some extent he shared. He felt he must have driven me to it. It broke my heart – and I have one, Georgia – when you told me he still believed me guilty. It explained why he was so reluctant for me to visit him in prison. I misled you there.

'Now,' he continued briskly, 'as regards Alice Winters. When I received her pathetic attempt at blackmail, I decided to meet her in the Montash Arms, a public place so that she had no fear of me. She was known there, and she would feel safe with me. I intended to warn her about the dangers she might face.'

'And what happened?'

'I asked permission from the publican, Bob I believe, for five minutes of her time. She began by telling me about her grandfather's statement, but I told her gently she was on a false trail, and there was no evidence against me otherwise. She didn't seem surprised, and informed me that she had, as she put it grandly, other lines of enquiry. I begged her to go to the police. She said she'd consider it but she had her future to think of.

'I pointed out that if she had evidence of murder, then she might not have a future. She laughed, and said she could take care of herself. She had the evidence tucked away so safely that no one would find it, and therefore no one would risk killing her. She was wrong, alas.'

'I take it she gave you no idea who this person was?'

'No. She said it would all be settled by the end of the day. It was, poor girl. The police wanted to know my movements that afternoon, but fortunately I was picking up Dana from Henry Ludd's home at the time of the murder. She is, as I'm sure you now know, his granddaughter, and I feel a special concern for her. Shall we visit her together and call it a truce?'

When Georgia returned to Haden Shaw she wanted only two things: to forget about Friday Street, and to see Luke. She wasn't allowed either. Peter called as soon as she had kicked off her shoes. 'Can you spare a moment?'

'Of course,' she muttered. 'Nothing I'd like more.' She found Peter in the conservatory, a half finished ice-cream sundae before him – one of his passions, in which Margaret indulged him. Unfortunately today it had obviously not done the trick. The last peach and some melted ice-cream proclaimed its failure.

'Time for another reconstruction,' he said grimly. 'They've released Toby Beamish without charge.'

This was disappointing. 'Waiting for more evidence?'

'I presume so.'

'And Cadenza?'

'The same.'

'Which may never come. There's only one thing can advance this case now. The rest of Brian Winters' statement and evidence.'

'Where is it?' Peter groaned. 'This damn thing,' he said savagely, slapping the side of his wheelchair, 'means it's up to you.'

Georgia tossed and turned that night, half awake, half dreaming. She was an eighteen-year-old girl, full of her own importance, off to university in the autumn and seeking money to do so. She worked hard, but that didn't bring in enough dosh. She'd try blackmail. But it wasn't really blackmail, she reasoned, for Toby Beamish was a murderer, and so it was justified. After all, when she'd got the money she could go to the police at any time. True, she would no longer have the evidence, but nevertheless she could spin an interesting tale. She might even keep some of the evidence back. Take it to the police later. She'd arrange a meeting in a place where she knew that lots of people would shortly be arriving, and anyway she wasn't afraid of him. He was just old Toby.

Just a minute. Georgia jolted herself full awake. If she, Georgia, thought Toby Beamish was a creep, then Alice would too. She *would* be scared of him – or perhaps she would think she knew him well enough, because she worked for him. He would never dare harm her, she'd assume.

So far, so good. Now Alice had to hide that evidence, and it must be close at hand to give to Toby when he had handed over the money.

Or would Alice keep it somewhere far away, for safety's sake? No, she wouldn't get the money then, and she wanted it safely in the bank. Where did she hide it?

Back to the beginning. Georgia was an eighteen-year-old girl. Good grief. The same girl who had gone up to university herself, fallen for a conman and married him a few years later. Who was she to talk about girls being sensible? On the other hand, she did have one fleeting memory of her eighteen-year-old self. She'd had a confidant, her roommate Jennie, who had strenuously tried to warn her off Zac.

Who would Alice have as a confidant? Drew Ludd? Tim Perry? No, she might flirt with them, but she wouldn't confide in them. Dear, reliable, Jake Baines? That's whom she'd confide in, not that he would necessarily know all about it, or think it important. But it was worth a try.

'What you want now? Harassing me again, you are. It's the police, innit?'

'Not so far as I know,' Georgia said truthfully. 'Have you got a job yet?'

'Winters' Farm again. She's taking me back.' Jake's face lost its suspicion, and momentarily glowed. Good for Jane, Georgia thought. She'd decided to take the chance.

'We're looking for something that Alice might have hidden near the tower and I thought you might have an idea.'

He looked blank. 'Nah. What sort of stuff?'

'Letters, papers. Did you write to each other? No private postbox for you both?' She had plucked the idea from a past which it was clear was more romantic than Jake could grapple with.

He stared at her in amazement. 'You've got to be joking. We texted, didn't we?'

'She had something she might have wanted to hand to someone else, and keep safe in the meantime. In the barn probably.'

'Nah. The tower maybe. She was there a lot. We both were.'

'Did Toby allow that? Surely it must be dangerous.'

'Didn't know, did he?'

'There was only one key, he said.'

'Yeah, well. There's a spare too. By the stone near the fence.'

'When you went into the tower, what did you do? Where did you go?'

He looked awkward. 'Her joke it was. She used to dash up them steps to the top and yell down at me when she heard the bike in the lane. "Oh, Piers, Piers, bring up your pipe and fuck me, do. Tis Lady Rosamund summons you."'

'And did you?' she asked out of interest, imagining young love on top of the tower.

He blushed. 'Yeah. Every time.'

The tower. It all came back to that tower. Georgia decided to park her car in the church car park, which was less open to view than the one at the Montash Arms or the public one.

She didn't want to shout her mission aloud to the village and she'd seen Toby as she drove through the village, just going into the pub. Parking here would cause less attention.

Some hopes. As she parked, Cadenza walked by and greeted her. She didn't seem to blame Georgia for her ordeal at the police station, thank goodness, and Georgia hoped she wouldn't be interrogated. Fortunately Cadenza was in a hurry.

'Tea and cakes in the church just starting,' she announced. 'Do come in. We'll all be here.'

Georgia had planned to take the footpath to the tower, but that would be to invite curiosity as Cadenza was lingering, assuming she'd come with her. She would be harder to throw off than the Duchess hanging on Alice in Wonderland's arm. Georgia made an excuse about needing something from the shop and dived back for the main road. She'd walk along through the village and down the lane instead, trying not to let Toby see her.

As she walked down the lane, the July sun was warm and comforting, but even so it was all too easy to remember this was the lane to the gallows. It was the original Friday Street, along which Piers Brome had walked to his death, pausing to pay his respects to the late Lady Rosamund, done to death by dagger, by one of the local lords attached to the Hospitallers. Piers had been playing his tune, the tune that had later proclaimed his innocence, and this was a lane of memories. Behind her to the left she could see the church tower. The church where they'd all – whoever *all* were – be guzzling tea and gorgeous cakes. Without hyoscine in them. The church . . . A thought passed through her mind so fleetingly she could not grasp it. No matter.

It was hard to recreate the legend here now, even though in her imagination there was a sense of loneliness and loss about this lane. She was glad when the trees came into sight, anxious to get her mission over. She had decided the top of that tower was the most likely place for Alice to have hidden the material. Even though Toby would have had ample time to return and hunt for it, it was still worth looking on the off chance. Nobody else would know about that key, she reasoned.

In the stillness the squeak of the hinges grated on her, setting her nerves on edge. She walked through the gate, feeling a thousand eyes upon her. But when she looked up, half fearful of seeing Toby Beamish, there was no one, save a curious cow in search of company. She found the key easily enough, opened the padlock, and went in to the tower. She looked upward at the roof. It seemed very high, and, never good at heights, she quailed at the thought of the climb ahead. Did the steps really lead all the way up there? She could see crumbling masonry even from here. She took a deep breath and went over to the steps. She'd take them one by one. After the first turn, she was greeted by the smell of decay and trapped air, but she forced herself on. Some steps had almost crumbled away, and there was no grip at the side. She told herself that if Alice had done it, then she could too – even though she was only relying on Jake's word, she remembered uneasily. Suppose – no, that word was banned. She wasn't heavy for her height, which was just as well, she thought.

At one point she glanced down to see the ground beneath where the side masonry had entirely gone and her head swam. Ahead was another turn, and she forced herself to look upwards. Now she could see the remains of the entrance to the roof. To her horror there was a gap of about two feet where there were almost no footholds and nothing to cling to, save the roof of the tower above her to her left. If she fell she would fall right to the ground inside the tower. No, upwards. She must think *upwards*.

Half hauling herself, half sprawling, she managed it, wriggling on to the roof itself and breathing the fresh air. Here it would be safer, and she could hunt for Alice's treasure trove. Only then would she think about the descent.

The top of the tower was about ten feet square, larger than it looked from below, with nothing, not even a wall on one side, and just crumbling crenellations on the others. Look, she told herself, *look*. She inched round what had once been the walls, and quickly found it, to her relief. A loose stone behind which was a cavity – and Alice's bag. A waterproof holdall, containing papers. She didn't stop to look at them, she tucked it under her arm and prepared to descend.

There was a sound below. No, it was her imagination. It must have been in the lane. But it wasn't. There *was* somebody below.

'Jake?' she called out, her voice cracking with fear.

There was no reply, for Toby – who else? – must be mounting the steps; she could hear the slight sounds. She could sense his presence coming nearer. It might be the cow, she tried to joke to herself, but imagination squashed it. This was danger coming, no friendly face. She could sense the threat in the air.

She was trapped here. Any moment now he would reach the gap, and then she would see his owlish face, the face of a murderer. Even if he couldn't cover the gap himself, he had her trapped. She couldn't stay here for ever. She clutched the bag in her arms, wondering whether to yell, but there was no one to hear but the rooks in the trees, and the empty road. Any moment he would be at the last turn, and then she would see him. She sensed it near . . . and then the face appeared.

To her relief it wasn't Toby Beamish.

It was Sheila Ludd.

'Oh, thank goodness—' She was cut short.

'You've found it then,' Sheila said pleasantly. 'I thought if I followed you, you would. It's a small village, I'm afraid. Word travels quickly when Jake has his lunch in the pub. Suppose you just give me the bag. I'll see it reaches the police.' She sounded perfectly normal. Was she here on Michael's behalf? Henry's? Toby's? Idiotic thoughts rushed through Georgia's mind.

But then she knew.

'It was you all the time.' Georgia sounded calm, which was odd for she was frozen with terror.

233

'Just give the bag to me, then we can go home *safe and sound.*'

What to do? Nothing. She began to back towards the corner, no plan in mind. Sheila still had to cover the gap and get on to the roof. If Georgia hit her, she would fall to the ground. If she didn't, Georgia knew she might die herself. Why should Sheila stop now? Reasonable force? Would that be reasonable if Georgia hit her first? Mind stopped body, frozen with fear.

Too late. Sheila was on the roof. 'Let me have it,' she said, not even hurrying. 'Come now.'

No more murders. There would be a tragic accident as Georgia was pushed over the tower to the ground beneath. There was only one thing she could do to save herself.

Sheila was on her feet now and moving.

'I'll throw it over,' Georgia shouted, using all her remaining strength and waving the bag. She had to count on surprise to stop Sheila realizing that this would achieve her nothing. With luck Sheila might rush downstairs to pick it up.

She didn't. Sheila made a pounce for the bag, the rush taking her off balance – and off the tower, over the crumbling masonry, to the ground beneath.

The inevitable scream, the inevitable crash.

Georgia's breath came in short gasps, as she reached for the mobile phone in her pocket. The sound of those gasps in the still air would remain with her for ever.

Fourteen

'Are you ready, do you think?'

Peter was looking at her doubtfully, but Georgia had made up her mind. Nearly a month had passed since it had all happened, and her father had taken on the main burden of the work since then, sitting in on her interviews with Mike, then taking over from there. Phone calls, post, emails, updating Suspects Anonymous, all had wafted by her. Now she was sloughing off that protective chrysalis to test the feel of normal life once more. She needed to know what had happened, how they could have been so wrong. After Sheila Ludd's death it had been clear, even through the little that Peter had told her, that Michael Ludd had co-operated fully with the police and had made a complete statement, not only for them, but for Marsh & Daughter, which was brave of him. Georgia hadn't enquired further, although even in her semi-stupor she thought of the shock waves that must be flooding Friday Street.

'Very well,' Peter began. 'First, we don't blame ourselves for what happened. We were on the right track, but we got off at the wrong station. Okay?'

Georgia grimaced. 'It's hard to think even now of Toby Beamish being squeaky clean. As I walked along that lane, I nearly got it, but the thought went. It's come back now. The church flower rota. Hazel was in Canterbury the afternoon that Alice died, but on the rota I had seen in the church Saturday was *her* day, not Sheila's. But I was so stuck on Toby, I paid no attention. Even though,' she remembered, 'the Friday street tune was running through my head. Power of association, do you think? Or the effect of hindsight?'

'Just Friday Street, Georgia.'

'Of course,' she said gratefully. 'In Friday Street one always sees through the glass darkly.'

'Especially in the Montash Arms.'

She managed a laugh. 'I don't think I can blame Josh. I suspect the glass was as murky for him. He only did what we're all tempted to do. Dismiss suspicion as just that, and not follow it through.'

Peter cleared his throat. 'This is based on Michael's statement and Brian Winters' evidence. Here goes: Fanny told Sheila the truth about the rape, not realizing how keen she was on Michael and how jealous she therefore was that he seemed to prefer Fanny. Michael claims he was goaded by Fanny beyond endurance, egged on by Toby, and that he had no idea about the coming child. Sheila urged Fanny to have an abortion, and leave the village. Fanny didn't need much persuading apparently. Why Sheila was so determined to marry Michael, knowing or even suspecting him of rape, is mystifying. Probably she did indeed persuade herself that Fanny had asked for it.'

'Or,' Georgia suggested, 'that Fanny was lying and that Josh or Ron was the father of the child. Then that became truth in her mind as the years went on.'

'We'll never know. The afternoon went pretty much as we already know except that Henry tells Michael he is not as forgiving as Fanny and he's still in two minds about handing over the cash. Fanny, furious with Oliver and Powell, is in a foul mood at dinner, and when Sheila rushes after her, vents her spleen on her, saying that there are still a few secrets Henry doesn't know. She means that Dana is alive and kicking, not aborted. Perhaps Sheila tells Michael this, who sees his chances blown sky-high if the result of an incestuous relationship could walk in at any moment, particularly since Henry is so fond of Fanny.

'Financially, Michael's situation was far from rosy, as we

236

know, and matters were at a delicate stage. Fanny could have ditched them with a few words. Sheila hopes Michael can scare her into silence. Michael says Sheila (although it might have been him, of course) seized the dagger merely to scare Fanny, and went in search of her. Fanny has vanished, however, and it's at that point that Brian Winters spots Sheila. Sheila tracks Fanny down to Owlers' Smoke, they have a row, and Fanny is killed. Sheila returns via the side entrance in order to change her clothes in case any blood is on them, despite the mac, and returns to the party to await developments.

'Michael believed, so he claims, that Adam had killed her, since Sheila told him that she had left Fanny after ten minutes or so and come looking for him – by that time he was chatting to Henry at his request. The music played that night troubled Michael, but he believed if it wasn't Adam then it was Toby who killed her. He had no evidence to offer, so didn't come forward.

'Enter Alice Winters, who was off to university and realized she needed a source of money. She'd worked out the significance of the evidence she had. Now we know what that evidence was. When Brian saw Sheila setting off across the grounds, she was wearing the plastic mac and evening gloves. He noticed the gloves because they looked incongruous with the mac, as they were pink silk ones. They were the same ones found on Fanny's body, and the blood on them was put down on the autopsy report as having come from Fanny's attempts to defend herself. Sheila couldn't afford to meet anyone and blood be noticed, so she left the mac and gloves with the body. When Brian did his ferrying around for the Gibbs, these must have been amongst her effects returned after the trial, and he kept them, assuming they wouldn't want such a grisly record. Then he began to think about them, and how they had come to be on Fanny's hands.

'Only when Jake was released did Michael begin to realize Sheila must have been involved in both murders. She swapped her day of flower duty in the church with Hazel and went to the Manor to pick up the key from Cadenza. Then she nipped in to pick up the dagger on the way out. Why the dagger? She knew it was there – and, to be blunt, that it worked. Then she went to the church, performed her duties there, and walked across the footpath to her meeting with Alice to finish this matter for good. She wasn't so concerned about the actual evidence linking her with Fanny's murder, which after all this time could well be thrown out by the court. But if the slightest rumour reached Henry that Fanny's death was at her hands then their old age would be seriously prejudiced. When we began to sniff around though, the problems mounted.'

'You mean it was her who fixed my car?' Georgia asked incredulously.

'Of course. That was easy, and done merely so that attention wasn't drawn to Dana. You had enemies in the village. She didn't. Sheila had discovered who Dana was, but didn't know whether Henry was in the picture or not. It couldn't be long before he was, she reasoned, and the truth of his learning at his age that he had a new granddaughter and great-granddaughter, as a result of rape by his son, would have been fatal to her hopes, and probably to Henry too. Though I doubt if she worried much about that.'

'I'm beginning to think that Henry's in *every* picture,' Georgia said. '*How* did Sheila know who Dana was?' Then she realized there was only one answer. 'Don't tell me. It was Toby Beamish who told her.'

'Poor Dana.'

'Poor you.' Luke made a grand entrance into the garden. He'd been coming over daily, bless him. 'You could have died if you'd been unlucky, and it wouldn't have been much comfort that you weren't her ultimate target.'

'And then you come waltzing into the church car park,' Peter picked up the story again, 'and word flies through the pub, courtesy of Jake, that you're interested in hiding places in the tower. Sheila is in the church, and hears about your arrival from Cadenza, and bingo. She follows you to see if you have any more luck than she does. After all, she wanted that evidence, and even a sad accident for you might have been avoided and the whole matter wound up. If you'd only gone up the tower, found the stuff and come down again, she could have pinched it from you, destroyed it, and left you shouting "Foul" in vain. We couldn't publish anything damaging without firm evidence.'

Georgia began to feel tired. She still wasn't entirely convinced, but it was all too easy not to pursue it. There was something, logic told her, that was weak, and instinct (Suspects Anonymous couldn't do everything) added that it *still* had something to do with Tom.

Georgia marched up the drive to Pucken Manor, pleasantly relieved that Friday Street now seemed to have an entirely different feel about it. In the pub Josh had been friendly and sympathetic over her ordeal at the tower. No one had said anything about the Ludds. It was, she realized, just an ordinary village after all. Or had the fingerprints of time vanished with Sheila's death, both from the village itself and from her?

Only Toby remained to be vanquished. Her sense of humour showed signs of returning. What would the ghosts of his ancestors feel about being joined by these new ones? She contemplated her former opinion of him: Toby the lech, Toby the watcher, Toby the creep, Toby the ghost hunter, Toby the possible rapist and murderer. Could that Toby ever be banished?

'Come in, come in.' It looked hopeful. Toby seemed the same, but Cadenza no longer looked like the witch of Endor; she was merely a middle-aged woman with a penchant for floaty summer dresses. Georgia was ushered into the living room, and Beamish ancestors looked down on her benignly. It was a dark, comforting room, not spooky at all.

'I suppose I have you and your father to thank for our interrogation at the police station,' Toby began jovially.

'Thank Friday Street,' Georgia said gently, but extremely firmly.

Toby actually laughed. 'Point taken. Too much past history, eh?'

'And some still to be explained.'

'Ah, Cadenza,' Toby turned to her innocently, 'I wonder if our friend might like some coffee. A few private family matters to discuss.'

'Oh.' Cadenza put her finger to her lips and tripped out of the room.

Toby sighed. 'A dear lady. I suppose I'll have to marry her one of these days.'

'Excellent,' Georgia said heartily, by no means sure that it was. '*Tom*,' she began firmly. 'I've read Michael's statement. Something lacking, I feel.'

'Do you?' Toby beamed as though this was praise indeed.

'The Ludds and Beamishes didn't get on, yet Tom was a cabal of three: Michael, Oliver and yourself.'

'I don't recall a cabal.' He pushed his spectacles further up his nose.

Frontal assault necessary. 'You knew that Michael raped Fanny; why didn't you make a fuss about it?'

Toby regarded her thoughtfully. 'None of my business, Georgia.'

'Come on, Toby. You can do better than that. Were you blackmailing him?'

He went pink in the face. 'Certainly not,' he spluttered. His indignation sounded genuine.

'Then why keep silent?'

He looked trapped as though he might fly to the safety of Cadenza's arms at any moment. 'It was a family affair,' he muttered.

'*What*?' She thought she had misheard.

'A family affair,' he repeated more loudly, and distinctly red in the face.

'Can you explain that?'

'Yes. You might find this foolish, but there was a bond between myself and Michael that has never been broken. I felt, shall we say, some loyalty towards him.'

'And the bond is?'

He hesitated, then: 'In view of what you have been through, and since Michael intends to leave the village – not entirely to my regret – and on the presumption that this would not be revealed without Henry's consent . . .'

Henry again! Her mind whirled. Where on earth was this leading? Would Toby never get to the point?

'In short, Michael is my half-brother.' He looked at her quickly, as if wondering whether she was about to faint. Her head certainly swam. He *must* be joking. Or was he?

'You see,' Toby said, emboldened, 'that I therefore had a tug of loyalty. Firstly to Frances, of whom I was very fond indeed. I can never hear that tune, "Allan Water", without a little weep. To have it played during my drama on Lady Rosamund was a private tribute, although I could never countenance a reconstruction of Frances's story as dear Alice had so innocently suggested.'

He looked genuinely distressed, Georgia thought. 'I also had loyalty to Michael, however,' Toby continued. 'I have seen his statement to you, and there are one or two little things he does not mention. Unfortunately Fanny told Sheila in the bathroom that night in 1968 that there were still a few secrets Henry did not know. Michael must have leapt to the conclusion that it was his own parentage that Fanny was referring to, not Dana's. In fact, Fanny did not know of our little secret. With his pride in family Henry would never have countenanced Michael's illegitimacy after the revelations of the afternoon that Michael had raped Fanny. He is *so* proud of his family, is dear Henry. Oliver or Frances would most certainly have been his heir.'

'You mean Henry still doesn't know?' Georgia asked, appalled.

'He knows now. It rather popped out at Sheila's funeral.' He caught her look. 'Michael told him. Rather brave, I felt. Michael's hopes for his business ventures would have vanished. It was I who discovered it and rather too eagerly told Michael in our youth. I regret to say I rather enjoyed doing so, and then when I showed him the – er – letters to convince him, he was eager that Henry should not know.

'As I understand the story, Joan was pregnant by my father, who was already married. Joan was not then married, and speedily married Henry as a result. They were all serving at the same RAF station. When Henry wished to move here, Joan was all too eager. My mother, as I told you, was not, although my father was, shall I say, ambivalent. In 1968 Michael was terrified, believing Fanny knew his parentage by that one simple remark, and he was convinced she would tell Henry about his and Joan's bastard son. Rather self-centred, is Michael,' Toby reflected. 'I assured him I would tell no one, but I doubt if he believed me. Poor Frances and then poor Alice lost their lives probably as a result of that.'

'What about Dana?' Georgia asked weakly, wondering where this family saga might end.

'Michael was upset at being obliged to me,' Toby said complacently. 'When he discovered – again I'm afraid from me – that Dana was Henry's granddaughter and therefore his own daughter, he was even more terrified. Another little financial crisis was brewing. Once again Sheila became his Lady Macbeth, to rid him of his woes. No paternal feelings for Dana, I'm afraid. Or many for his son. Philip lives in Australia, as far away as he can get. I admit Michael's relationship with Drew is good. Or was,' Toby added. 'Michael still believed I would go hotfoot to Henry with this information, when Dana told me. I was rather annoyed at that. How could I sneak on my half-brother? Not done in the best of English families. The ghost of my father would rise up indignantly.'

Georgia began to laugh, obviously to Toby's surprise, at the idea that with all the moral issues surrounding Fanny's death, gentlemanly behaviour should seem a major one. 'I'm sorry we even suspected you. We saw nothing here clearly.'

Toby sighed. 'Friday Street is like that, I fear. Or should I say *was*. You seem to have successfully cleaned the Augean Stables.'

*   *   *

To Georgia's pleasure, Dana was sitting up in bed when she and Luke walked in. Very thin, very pale, but alive and even eating, she told them proudly.

'No more pies for you,' Georgia said firmly.

'Actually it was delicious, from what I remember, though I gather from Josh that you and I only received it as a decoy from the poisoned tea. I must say poisoned tea at the village fete seems rather a cliché.' She grimaced. 'What a mess. I'm sorry I caused you all so much trouble. If I'd declared who I was from the beginning I'd have saved a lot of this. I was trying to be tactful until I'd got to know my grandfather. Do you know, he'd been hunting for me for the best part of twenty years, ever since he knew I existed? Adam Jones told him. Humbling, isn't it? That's what I came here for the day Alice was killed. He wanted to meet me.'

'What happens now?' Georgia asked.

'I'm moving into the house he's living in now,' Dana said happily. 'Michael's moving out of the Hall, Henry's moving back in, Drew's staying with him, and I'll be on hand for jolly chats. Sarah, my daughter, can meet her new great-grandfather, and my parents – sorry, can't think of Michael that way – are moving to Faversham, which is nice. So I'll be a sort of neighbour of yours,' she finished.

Was that good? Georgia had mixed feelings. With Dana's recovery, worms of suspicion were rising again.

'You're very silent,' Luke complained when they reached home.

'Contemplating my new neighbour,' she said truthfully.

'You might have two.'

She froze. Was he breaking bad news to her? He seemed very casual about it if so. 'You mean you and Dana are an item?' She could hardly get the words out.

Luke looked at her as though she had taken leave of her senses, and pray God that she had. 'Is that what's been wrong with you all this time? You thought I was slowly ditching you for Dana? Are you crazy, Georgia?'

'Sometimes I think I am. Why did you keep meeting her, Luke?' She tried to keep the panic out of her voice.

'I didn't. Only twice. She's an estate agent, for heaven's sake. She had a house she thought I'd be interested in.'

'In South Malling?' Was this still a cover-up?

'Here, you chump,' he said affectionately. 'Near Haden Shaw. My mountain decided it would be a good idea if it rolled along nearer to your Mahommet. I couldn't expect Peter, and therefore you, to uproot – and oh, Georgia, I'm so damned sick of commuting. And of a weekend arrangement only for my bed.'

She found herself locked in his arms. No, he was locked in hers. It was she who had moved. So what did that mean?

'You know I want to marry you,' he continued matter-of-factly. 'Okay, you don't want to, but if I'm on the doorstep it's going to get more difficult to keep refusing me.'

'Did you buy the house?'

'No.'

She began to laugh. 'Big talker, eh?'

'But there is another one. And there's always tomorrow, thank God.'

Just one more duty to Friday Street and Fanny Star. A visit to Doreen Gibb from herself and Peter. All this trouble and it hadn't touched Doreen at all, she reflected, as Peter steered himself towards her.

'Hello, dear,' Doreen greeted her in delight, and to Peter, 'You're new here, aren't you? Settled in, have you? Don't die on us, will you?'

Peter took it on the chin. 'Not for thirty years or so.'

A slight worry crossed her face. 'What are you here for, dear?' she asked Georgia.

'To show you these photos of Frances.' Georgia had dug them out of their files on purpose.

'Oh yes. Very nice.' Doreen glanced at them, but then up again to the door beyond them. She let out a squeal of delight at seeing a new visitor.

Henry Ludd was strolling across the floor to greet her. He bent down to kiss her, handed her a bunch of flowers, took it away again to hand to a nurse and put a bottle of whisky at her side. It was obviously a well-worn routine, for Doreen watched each step keenly.

'I'm glad to see you,' he said courteously to them.

'And we're delighted about Dana,' Georgia told him.

'Shall we talk?' he asked.

'Please.' Georgia went to move but he stopped her.

'Doreen likes to listen. It means nothing. It's all right.' Of course it was. Doreen wasn't in this world. Stupid of her.

Henry said gently. 'Thank you for what you did for dear Frances, despite all the pain it has brought.'

'Did you know about Michael's . . .?' she started to ask, but could not complete the question.

He answered anyway. 'Michael told me. However, I had known for a long time. My late wife had told me about Michael's parentage very early on; it was one of the reasons I needed Doreen's love. I was unaware that Michael had discovered it, and it saddens me greatly. For that, I find it hard to forgive Toby Beamish, especially as I fear it did play a part in Frances's death. Quite unnecessarily. "The sins of the fathers", dear Josh says. Charles Beamish, Henry Ludd. It is true I have a belief in family, but how does one define that word? Growing together, living together, affection – these can count as much as genes. When Frances was killed, I suspected Michael might have done it. He was rather too anxious to have a little chat with me to provide an alibi. I continued to do so until I learned of Sheila's involvement after her death. I had no evidence, and regardless of his genes he was my son. I have a grandson I love, and now, thanks to Adam – whom I failed – I have a granddaughter, and great-granddaughter. I spent a considerable time in hunting for Dana, and now, thank heavens, she is with me. She is a dear girl, like Frances returned to me.'

'You said you had no evidence,' Peter said. 'So you took your own steps. Am I right?'

Henry smiled. 'You are. I played the music that night.'

'Did it achieve anything?'

'No. Josh was right. Everyone believed Adam guilty. Michael was my son; how could I speak to the police without proof in such a case? And when Alice died, Michael was definitely with me. It seemed to me there could therefore be no link between the two cases, even when Jake was released. I heard the music then, but had nothing to offer the player.'

'It was Tim Perry?'

'I believe so. I heard it, and thought of Frances. The music had done no good then, and I doubted if it could now. No one came forward.' He added gently, 'Except you, of course. The music brought you.'

'We'll leave you with Doreen,' Georgia said. 'I'm sorry . . . Does she recognize you?'

'Let's try.' He leaned forward, and took her hands. 'Do you know who I am, Doreen?'

She laughed in excitement. 'Of course I do, you silly man. You're my Solomon, and I'm the Queen of Sheba.'